Other titles by Aaron T. Brownell

Reflection

Contention; a Sara Grey Tale

The Long Path

Progression; a Sara Grey Tale

Shadow of the Fall

THE SONS OF SAVA

A Kristin Hughes Operation

AARON T. BROWNELL

THE SONS OF SAVA
A KRISTIN HUGHES OPERATION

iUniverse books may be ordered through booksellers or by contacting:

iUniverse
1663 Liberty Drive
Bloomington, IN 47403
www.iuniverse.com
844-349-9409

Because of the dynamic nature of the Internet, any web addresses or links contained in this book may have changed since publication and may no longer be valid. The views expressed in this work are solely those of the author and do not necessarily reflect the views of the publisher, and the publisher hereby disclaims any responsibility for them.

Any people depicted in stock imagery provided by Getty Images are models, and such images are being used for illustrative purposes only.
Certain stock imagery © Getty Images.

ISBN: 978-1-6632-3376-9 (sc)
ISBN: 978-1-6632-3377-6 (e)

Library of Congress Control Number: 2021925454

Print information available on the last page.

iUniverse rev. date: 01/13/2022

Thank you:

As usual, I have to thank my good friend Jeffrey for suffering through the editing of this story. He makes my awful punctuation and grammar look adequately acceptable. I owe him beers, at some point.

CHAPTER ONE

KRISTIN HUGHES SAT in front of the main display consoles for the assistant's station and twisted a strand of hair around her finger. It was a reflexive gesture that would normally signal boredom. Currently, she wasn't as much bored as emotionally displaced.

Everything scrolling down the display monitors in front of her appeared to be in good order. The tritium levels were inside normal tolerances for a shielded nuclear source, and the neutron counter wasn't as much as twitching. Yes, everything inside the containment area seemed to be just fine. The only problem was she wasn't a nuclear emissions specialist. To be honest, she wasn't even a nuclear scientist anymore. She was a nuclear bomb technician.

Kristin had been the lead field technician for the Department of Energy's Nuclear Emergency Search Team almost since the day her college doctorate was finished. At 29 years old, holding a PhD from Princeton University in nuclear physics and master's degrees in nuclear physics and mathematics, with years of real-world field operations and loan-outs to various United States government bureaus and foreign countries on her resume, she was now quietly recognized as the best nuclear bomb technician in the world.

It was safe to say that what she was currently doing was not her job. If forced to be honest, she'd admit she really didn't know much about storing or maintaining nuclear weapons. She was the girl who made them not go off.

"Everything in the primary inspection bay, as well as the assembly and maintenance hangar, appears to be just fine, Doctor Kumar."

The head of the Indian Tata Institute of Fundamental Research smiled broadly at his young American guest.

"That is very good, Doctor Hughes. We strive to keep all of our nuclear material in a peaceful state."

Kristin looked around the control room as he spoke. It was as state-of-the-art as anything else she had seen in this part of the world. The Indian government had spared no expense when they constructed the nuclear maintenance facility housed at Ambala Air Force Base. As one of the three primary locations for the storage of nuclear weapons held by the country, Ambala Airbase was located on the southern edge of the disputed Kashmir region. This made it the closest launch point to India's sometimes problematic neighbor, Pakistan.

"Your facility is quite impressive. Your munitions program is obviously closely monitored."

"Yes. We have several layers of electronic and human oversight on the nuclear material. All weapons systems inspections and alterations are conducted with maximum safeguards. We don't want any of the weapons going off until it's time for them to be going off."

They both laughed. It was an old joke. Kristin scrolled through several more screens of data as a team of technicians inspected a medium-yield nuclear bomb of the unguided, free-fall type. This particular device had been designed for use on the SEPECAT Jaguar fighter jet. The technicians and the facility they utilized for inspection of the devices were both models of efficiency.

Kristin pointed to something on the video display screen for the technician's station with a quizzical expression. Doctor Kumar mentioned that it was a secondary core shield. They were sometimes used on the older weapons at the facility.

Kristin smiled as she continued observing and thinking. She was well-acquainted with Doctor Kumar and genuinely liked him. The two had met some years back, when Kristin had secured an invitation from the Indian government to attend one of its underground nuclear tests. There had been great debate by the college deans at the time as to whether she should be allowed to attend the event. The United States and other nuclear countries had been imposing sanctions on India for its nuclear testing, and her university didn't want to be entangled by PR issues. She had met

Doctor Kumar at the introductory luncheon for that series of tests. He had been charged with welcoming the guests and explaining the timing of upcoming events.

Kristin had stayed in contact with Doctor Kumar throughout the years. The doctor was always kind, polite, and happy, though he seemed to possess that faintly lecherous look that some say all Indian men seem to acquire at puberty. Nonetheless, he was at the top of India's nuclear program and as able as any in the world at heading a nuclear research facility.

Kristin adjusted the sari draped over her shoulder. She wasn't used to wearing the traditional Indian garment and it seemed to be constantly moving about her body. She had been vacationing in the southern part of the country when the call for a visit to the facility had come from her bosses. Living out of a backpack, as is her style, required her to do some quick shopping to make a presentable professional appearance for a formal scientific meeting. The fashion store she visited had few options of which most American women would allow themselves to be seen in. But she wasn't like most American women, so she opted for something in the local flavor. From the wolfish looks on the men's faces when she arrived, she assumed that she had made the right choice.

Taking a quick look around, she pulled a pair of thick-framed black plastic geek glasses from one of the folds of the sari and slid them onto her face. The glasses gave contrast to her appearance and accented her smooth, sun-kissed features. They also made her Greek nose stand out somewhat, which she didn't find overly flattering. The glasses really weren't about style, they were a necessary accessory to see the tiny script migrating across the bottom of her computer terminal screen. If she had been in the states, she would have just adjusted the resolution on the display. Seeing how she didn't read whatever dialect of Indian she was looking at, she opted for the glasses.

Contrary to the beliefs of many people with whom she interacted; the glasses were real – not a prop. She was slightly nearsighted. Her optometrist had made the assumption that the degeneration was brought about by her all-but-constant need to squint at phone-sized screenshot schematics during her workdays. It didn't seem logical to her, but he was the eye doctor. Why she had chosen the thick black plastic frames, as opposed to something more stylish, didn't seem logical to him. The glasses just seemed to compliment her nerdy and comical sensibilities. Her boss, DOE NEST Operations Chief and ex-SEAL Lou Stenson openly hated them. This, if nothing else, meant that she was never getting rid of them.

Once clear to read, she saw the numbering on the proton counter in the second assembly lab had moved off its baseline. Kristin turned to address Doctor Kumar, who was having some amount of trouble putting her glasses together with her outfit.

"It seems the proton counter is registering activity. Is that normal for your facility? We normally don't see proton activity, unless there is a shielding inconsistency."

Doctor Kumar nodded at the questions. The glasses still causing his brain some logic abnormalities.

"Yes, on some of the older models. The early versions, especially the air-drop variety, weren't built with as many layers of core shielding as current designs are constructed. There is some proton seepage, along with an increased alpha count that occurs over time. That is why we utilize the secondary core shielding, for safety purposes. We have also been utilizing the older core packages for tests, when they are approved. This removes them from inventory."

Kristin nodded as her fellow scientist talked about the material handling. The facility was obviously taking every step to safeguard its people.

"Would you like to look at the inspection area, Doctor Hughes? I know that hands-on operations are more your specialty."

Kristin smiled a broad smile.

"If that isn't going to be a problem for your personnel or safety protocols, that would be great. But I don't want to cause you any tension with your people."

The relations between India and the United States had been one of flux since India developed its first nuclear weapon. India had been one of the countries that refused to sign the Comprehensive Nuclear Test Ban Treaty, but was an active member of the International Atomic Energy Agency. The fact that they still test-fired live nuclear weapons had led to sanctions from the United States in years past. Kristin knew all of this history quite well and didn't want to be the trigger for yet another political disaster.

"No. It should be fine," Doctor Kumar said with slight hesitation.

Kristin was about to respond when a quiet chirping sound came from under one of the layers of her sari and she paused to retrieve her phone. Viewing the screen, she saw a familiar Monkey Head emoji with "Boss" scrolled over its top. The image always made her smile. She toggled the phone in her hand toward her host.

"Do you have somewhere quiet that I might take a call. Sadly, it's work."

Doctor Kumar was well-schooled regarding Kristin's primary line of work and understood the potential of an international emergency brewing when she needed to take a call. He showed her to an unused office off to one side of the control room, closing the door behind her as she entered.

Kristin pressed the green button, which was now on its second call's worth of blinking. *Lou must really want something*, she thought as she pressed the button. After accepting the call, she paused as the iPhone 10XGS engaged its built-in encryption. The specially modified phone came with a host of features useful to a globe-trotting field girl, secure communication being just one of them.

"Hey boss, what's up?"

"How's India?"

"Kind of boring, actually."

"What? I've been to Goa. The beaches and nightlife are pretty much every backpacker's dream."

"I'm not in Goa. I was in Goa until Pat Sommers called. *Apparently*, the Indian government also heard that I was in Goa. There was a Chinese telephone game that went something like prime minister to president to Secret Service to me – and then me to an airplane. I'm currently on Ambala Air Force Base, south edge of Kashmir, looking at their nuclear weapons maintenance facility with Doctor Kumar of the Tata Institute."

Lou Stenson, being a well-seasoned recipient of Kristin's angst, gave her a moment to exhale.

"I knew that. Pat called me before he called you. He didn't want another Croatia incident. I was just having a bit of fun at your expense."

At 6-1 and carrying the 10 extra pounds on his 210-pound frame that every ex-operator seems to develop, with greying hair at the temples and enough scar tissue to make his 38 years look a decade older, Lou Stenson was not what immediately came to mind when one thought of a jokester. With 12 years on the SEAL Teams and two at the State Department before joining the DOE, he was actually well-versed in military-level humor. Kristin's own military brat upbringing had bonded her to him almost instantly.

"So, you okayed my lack of a vacation? That means that I can get my expenses reimbursed? Oh, that is good."

"More important question is, do you have your go-bag with you?"

"Yes."

"Good. There will be a nondescript private jet on the tarmac at Ambala in approximately 50 minutes. Get on it."

Kristin normally wasn't personal jet worthy, which meant that something bad was happening somewhere. And since Lou wasn't utilizing the CONUS NEST team, that probably meant it was an international problem. If it was a nondescript private jet, then it was most-likely owned by the CIA. It could be an Air Force jet that was okayed for use by NEST, but considering she was on the other side of the planet, she was betting that it was CIA. She had been chauffeured around by the CIA, the FBI, and the NSA on numerous occasions. Normally, when out of the country, these types of trips also came with her very own CIA assassin/bodyguard.

"Tail numbers?"

"You'll recognize it when you see it."

"Uncle Gene's sending me a ride. Well, this can't be good."

Eugene Taggart, the DCI for the Central Intelligence Agency, and possibly the only true spy left in America, was in a small group of individuals that utilized Kristin's unique skillset. In the years after 911, the president of the United States found that the creation of the Director of National Intelligence position only made the myriad U.S. intelligence services that much more untrusting and territorial. Seeing a problem with no good political solution, the president took a move from the old Cold War playbook and went around the whole affair, establishing a small group of in-the-know-individuals from the major intelligence and national asset agencies to work together independent of all the red tape. The group consisting of a key senior-level member and necessary field operative from the CIA, FBI, NSA, NRO, DOE, Secret Service, and Justice Department became known as *The Group*, and were known only to the president.

Initially, the independent spirits of the group were untrusting of each other, but as success after success came from their interaction, they became a well-bonded unit inside the slumbering U.S. intelligence machine. Lou Stenson and Kristin Hughes were the DOE players for the group.

"You could say that there might be some assistance being granted."

"Where might I be headed?"

"Germany. There is a situation unfolding there that is best served by your direct involvement. You'll get a briefing enroute."

Kristin rolled the whole thing around her brain once. She knew enough to know she should be on the move even without knowing what problem she was on her way to solve.

"Roger that, boss. On the tarmac in 46 minutes, give or take."

"Sorry about your vacation. The fact that you're becoming recognizable worries me. You may need to stop traveling on your own passport."

"Fear not. I blend in quite well."

"Yeah, I heard. Send me a selfie of you in the Indian wrappy dress. I need something to throw darts at."

"Not funny."

"Just make the plane. The problems are immediate."

"Roger that."

Lou Stenson ended the call. Kristin knew there were a few garrisons of military personnel left scattered about Germany, but the nuclear might of the United States military had been moved out long ago. She couldn't think of any reason that there would be her kind of problem brewing in Germany. It must be a Germany problem? The briefing enroute should prove to be interesting. One thing was for sure, she needed to grab her bag and find a plane.

CHAPTER TWO

"WHAT DO YOU think, Zoran?"

Zoran Savic, leader of one of the few remaining resistance fragments fighting the long-dead Bosnian-Croatian conflict sparked from the ashes of the fall of Yugoslavia, removed his eye from the spotting scope and looked at his cousin, Emil. Emil Savic was considered the secondary leader and was definitely known as the hotter-tempered of the two men. The two Bosnian Serbs were a decision-making team for a six-person cell. A cell still doing its best to take the fight to the Croatians.

The cell had been engaged in a multi-year skirmish with a Croatian cell of similar size. The group of Bosnian Croatians had a stronghold just outside the small town of Pakrac, Croatia. All of the local townspeople were in collaboration with the group, and Zoran Savic's success at making inroads in the area had been few. The lack of success and the desperation which had been slowly growing within the cell had led them to their current point.

At first, the idea had seemed ludicrous. It was an idea that had been thrown out to shut up a conversation. But the more that Zoran let the idea roll around in his head, the more it began to make a crazy kind of sense.

The Serb cell had bombed the Pakrac area several times. Car bombs, trashcan bombs and the like were all used. But none had ever been effective enough to do any real damage to the Croatian stronghold. The Croat cell had always been tipped off by sympathizing townspeople, giving them time to shift things around and making the placing of the bombs ineffective. The Bosnian cell had been able to inflict a great deal of collateral damage, but with no real impact.

That was the problem with conventional weapons. They needed to be precisely placed to be effective. But a nuclear weapon didn't require precision. It just needed to be close to the intended target. Close was definitely good enough. It had been a crazy idea, but a small nuclear bomb might be just what they were looking for.

The main problem with the nuclear bomb idea was one of size. It would need to be small. Not standard delivery size small, but Cold War spy era small. The Serbs didn't want to be blowing themselves up as well as the Croats, so they needed a tiny bomb.

Zoran knew regular bombs and warheads would definitely not work. Your standard nuclear warhead these days would be on the order of 475 kilotons. Zoran needed a device a little closer to 1 kiloton. He needed a "suitcase nuke" – the kind you see in spy films. The problem with this plan was they no longer existed. All of the portable nuclear weapons that had been built were on display in museums at this point. There were none left operational, none to be had.

The reason that it had to be small was mostly one of proximity. Zoran needed a device with a minimal fallout radius. That way, the blast radius wouldn't make it south to Bosnia. In essence, what he wanted to accomplish was something along the lines of Chernobyl. The Chernobyl nuclear reactor disaster was just the level of damage he was looking for. The only problem with the Chernobyl idea was that Pakrac didn't have a nuclear reactor. There weren't even any old soviet nuclear reactors in the whole region.

Even though the nuclear option was a crazy idea, it would still solve a lot of logistical problems which had plagued them in the past. But it wasn't actually doable? It really was just a silly idea, right?

That was the thought process some two months back. The problem was that Zoran Savic just couldn't seem to let the idea go. He was, by every account, a ruthless bastard. The things that he had done during the Bosnian war, in the nineties, were deplorable, but in his opinion necessary to send their message. He had done so many things most would think unspeakable to forward the cause: killing and bombing without regard for the civilian population being among them. His men raped and murdered their way across the lands of Croatia, with Zoran leading the way. Whole towns had been removed from the map. He was a focused genocidal monster. A nuclear explosion certainly wouldn't be outside his comfort zone. He had done all his previous deeds with a fixed sense of purpose, and Zoran had now turned that same sense of purpose to the nuclear weapon idea.

Zoran had started his search by reaching out to all of his old sources for help in finding a weapon to suit his needs. They all said the same thing. All of the Soviet Union-era suitcase-sized nuclear weapons were dismantled long ago. None of a useable condition existed anymore. They were all in museum collections. But even the museum displays weren't real bombs which had been disassembled for display. They were mockups of older devices made to look like the real thing. His old supply chain would be of no use to him.

This lack of soviet weapons at least narrowed the scope of his new search. Of all the nuclear nations, only two were known to have manufactured man-portable nuclear weapons. They were Russia and the United States. It was now time for the cell leader to reach out to some more unusual information providers. It was time to see what the Americans had to offer.

Zoran knew that America had been removing its nuclear arsenal from Europe for decades. It was a well-documented fact. It was also a source of concern for the new NATO Eastern European countries. The former Soviet Bloc states all wanted the United States' nuclear weapons to stay. They kept Russia in check. The countries of Western Europe had differing ideas. They all wanted America to move on. They thought that they could handle Russia on their own. All the Eastern European states knew that this wasn't true. Without America to keep Russia standing off, Europe was simply no match for a reassembled Soviet Bloc. But, as always, time changes the landscape of politics, so America began sending its arsenal home.

Current conventional thinking stated that America's remaining nuclear arsenal was stored at Büchel Air Base, Büchel, Germany. The United States Air Force operated a group out of the Luftwaffe base to maintain and help deploy the remaining B-61 nuclear bombs that comprised the inventory. A multi-platform weapon, the bomb was currently being carried by German planes. That was all that was left in Europe, or so said the current convention.

It had taken lots of money and many weeks of digging for Zoran to learn the truth of the situation. As was common with all superpowers, it turned out that America had been giving Europe two different diplomatic faces. It had moved out the vast majority of the European nuclear arsenal, but they hadn't moved all of it. The different European governments all knew about the deterrent weapons stockpile at Büchel Air Base, but none of them knew anything about the *extra* stockpile that was also housed there.

A very private mob-run information system that Zoran finally tapped into gave an inventory that was much more to the cell leader's liking. Supposedly, contained in a bunker hidden at the base well behind a major security presence, the Americans had stockpiled a half dozen W-88 thermonuclear warheads. The warheads had been changed from their multiple reentry design and rigged to fit conventional German short-range missiles. There were a dozen W-76 warheads for the Mark IV reentry vehicle mounted to Trident II sub-launched ballistic missiles. They were there in case the United States needed to reload a sub in the middle of a conflict. The last item on the ghost inventory was exactly the item that Zoran Savic had been looking for. The United States had kept one MK-54 SADM and Its H-912 Transport Container. For some unexplainable reason, the U.S. had kept a man-portable nuclear weapon in Europe.

The MK-54 SADM, or Special Atomic Demolition Munition, was the lightest nuclear weapon to be acknowledged as being manufactured in the west. The warhead had originally been manufactured to be utilized by the 120mm recoilless rifle. Later it had been fitted with an external timer detonator and placed in the H-912 backpack. Weighing a minimum of fifty-one pounds, the nuclear warhead was man-portable in either the backpack or a footlocker-sized container. Where the common yield for the W-54 warhead produced for the 120mm rifles was up to six kilotons, the common yield of the backpack devices was much lower. The MK-54 (as it was designated) on inventory was listed as having a yield of 2.1 kilotons.

The SADM information had made Zoran Savic very happy. It was the perfect solution to his problem with the Croatians. The only real problem was getting his hands on the thing. If it did exist, it was located in a protected bunker on a well-guarded air base. He could also be sure that the bunker didn't appear on any maps or paperwork available for the facility. Still, a Luftwaffe base raid seemed possible. It was brash, but still doable. His cell had broken into military bases in the past. Granted, none of them were in Germany. But to Zoran none of this had seemed an insurmountable problem.

"Zoran, what do you think?"

Zoran Savic looked over at his cousin, Emil, and thought that he looked annoyed.

"I don't know, Emil. It all looks quiet enough, for a military base."

"So, do we go?"

Yes, Emil was definitely annoyed about something. Maybe he just wanted to get things going? He didn't like German food and had been kind of miserable ever since the group had arrived. His behavior wasn't that odd. He was known to be moody at times.

Zoran put his eye back to the spotting scope and took a good, hard, second look at the fence line. Everything between them and the interior of the base was just as it had been for some time as the men watched. All was quiet. He pulled his eye from the scope and checked his watch. The roving patrol had been coming and going in a predictably regular nineteen-minute cycle. The patrol would be returning in approximately five minutes.

"Let's wait until the guard makes the next pass. We will give them about eight or nine minutes to get as far away as possible. Then, we'll make our move."

"That makes good sense."

Emil pulled up a small portable radio and communicated the plan to the other members of the cell. Two different acknowledgements came back in hushed tones. Zoran kept his eye to the spotting scope and watched. Right on time, the roving patrol with his large German shepherd patrol dog came into view and proceeded along the same path as it had done the previous two times. Upon reaching Zoran Savic's chosen section of perimeter fencing, the large German shepherd pulled to an abrupt stop. Everyone laying in the crop fields outside the military base fence line drew a collective breath. The patrol guard turned on a flashlight and waved it about the area. Then, as if sensing something, shined it down on the patrol dog. The heavy-coated dog squatted and commenced to deposit a massive excrement into the grass. Everyone laying out in the crop fields exhaled their collectively held breath.

Zoran could just barely hear the sounds of the guard talking to the patrol dog as the two moved off on their continued patrol. The tone that had been carried on the still night air sounded mocking in nature. Zoran Savic checked his watch as the two disappeared along the fence line.

"Everyone get ready to go."

There was a small bit of ruffling about at the Eastern European terrorist's own position. Zoran retrieved a pair of night vision goggles from his pack and pulled them onto his face. The small GS series goggles were affixed to a harness that Zoran pulled over his head and snapped into place. The goggles lowered down over his eyes with a pivot on the harness. Zoran disliked the chinstrap on the device, but he didn't have any better outlets to technology in this foreign country. The goggles only allowed for a forty-degree field of view. He would need to swing his head from side to side to get a full field of view. He hit the switch and the defused green image glow began.

Zoran checked his watch. It was time to go. He keyed the microphone on his radio to speak: "Everyone go. You know your jobs. Stay sharp and watch for trouble."

Six bodies stood to a low crouch and began to move toward the military base's fence line. The base was shaped like a dumbbell, with a long runway down its middle and a circular ring of hangars and bunkers on each end. In essence, it was a large dog bone-shaped affair.

The fence line, for the most part, cut through the surrounding countryside. The facility seemed to be surrounded on all sides by farmland. Zoran had assumed that it all had to do with the noise created by the base, as he had seen this type of boundary area before. It was situated where few nearby townspeople would be impacted by its operations. The town of Büchel was off to the northeast of the base some distance. The small town of Gevenich lie to the southeast, about the same distance away. All of the remaining ground was given over to cultivated farmland.

Zoran and his men made their way silently to the fence line and paused. The double chain-link fence setup was a standard NATO design. As one of his team went to work disabling the security wire that ran through the outer fence's lower section, Zoran was happy that it had been updated since the fence designs during the Cold War.

The image of men with dogs roving between fences, overlapping paths, with floodlights crisscrossing each other was a very Hollywood creation. The reality of Cold War perimeter security was much more creative. NATO facilities, especially American facilities, were quite famous for using large flocks of geese as security barriers. The wings of the geese were clipped to keep them from flying away, and they were released to live in-between the fences. The geese were ever vigilant and extremely sensitive to change. Also, the noise they produced upon being bothered was almost completely unbearable. Zoran had to admit that it was a clever solution to the security problem and was happy he didn't have to deal with it now.

Alek Lukic, the youngest member of the cell at a mere 28 years of age, nodded to Zoran as he began to pull back a section of fence. He slid the fence fabric free until a complete eight-foot section of the fence line was breached. Alek moved into the gap between fence lines and went to work on the second security sensor. Some alligator clips, a multi-meter, ground clamp, and some wire cutters later, and they were security sensor free. Zoran's young nephew was as skilled at breaking and entering as any person he had seen. It was a hobby for the automotive mechanic, but definitely a useful one.

Aleksander, or Alek to the cell members, pulled a silver canister from his bag and began to spray paint the fence with it. The liquid nitrogen in the canister hit the metal links of chain and basically ate through it. Alek put the frost-covered can back in his bag and pulled free the second section of fence fabric. Once opened, Alek stepped through the void he created with the remainder of the cell hard on his heels. Zoran checked his watch. They had about five minutes remaining before the roving guard returned.

Sporadic trees covered the interval between the inside of the fence and the outer ring of hangars and bunkers outside of the ring road. The cell members moved into the area with little resistance and covered the ground to the bunkers in just under a minute. Zoran located the bunker number and checked it against the numbers on a hand-drawn map he carried. He motioned to the south and the group moved out with purpose. The six-person cell made its way over the top of a grass-covered ammunition bunker and onward to a small concrete building. A secondary building sat perpendicular to it and framed a small concrete parking area.

Zoran knew he had the right building. Even in the din of his green light-enhanced world, he could see the heavy reinforced concrete apron that extended from the building's two overhead doors. The heavy apron also comprised the parking lot and the lead out to the runway access. He checked the building number, just to be sure. It matched the one on his drawing.

Emil Savic stepped to the reinforced steel man door and set to work on the building's security system while the others formed a perimeter around him. Zoran Savic checked his watch. They had less than a minute before the guard would be returning. He pulled a well-worn Tokarev pistol out of his jacket pocket and took up a shooter's stance. It took approximately forty-five seconds of waiting for the shadowy outline of the guard to appear in his vision. He pulled level on the shadowy image and calmly expelled three rounds from the handgun. Only the cycle of the slide could be discerned as the suppressor all but completely absorbed the handgun's noise. A whimper could be heard as the German shepherd collapsed to the ground without resistance. The dispatched K9 went to ground next to its already deceased handler.

"Emil, hurry up. We're really on the clock now." Zoran was calm as he holstered the weapon under his black jacket.

"Done," Emil stated some twenty seconds later.

Zoran looked over at the fully dismantled keypad and retina scanner and saw a slightly ajar metal security door. He smiled at Emil and waved his hand toward the door.

Four cell members filed inside the building, leaving two members outside to provide cover. Zoran made his way straight to the back wall of the servicing building. He looked hard at a second security door, and then motioned to Emil. His cousin set to work on the keypad and retina scanner assembly without comment. It took a good minute-and-a-half before the electronic security was bypassed, but the heavy metal security door gave way just as the first one had.

Pushing through the metal man door into the empty space behind, the group found a full-size reinforced bunker blast door staring at them. Zoran took in the blast door's size, not bothering to mask his surprise. He turned and looked at the shop wall behind them. From the back it was obvious that the wall they had passed through was also actually an outer overhead door. The shop tables and other items stationed against the false wall were all a ruse. And a very good one.

Zoran Savic shook his head in appreciation, and then turned around and pointed toward the massive locking mechanism on the blast door. He checked his watch. They were gunshots plus two minutes and forty-five seconds. It was borrowed time.

Jasna Pavlovic, a 36-year-old school teacher from Central Sarajevo, stepped up to the door and began to place a breaching charge that would disable the locking mechanism. A quiet woman by nature, she was a complete natural with explosives. She had learned her trade during the conflict in Sarajevo, fighting the many different battles that destroyed her once-beautiful city.

Jasna gave several hand motions and the other members of the cell moved to covering positions. She squeezed the trigger on the commercial detonator and the massive blast door rocked from the explosion. Fortunately for the intruders, the thick concrete building absorbed the majority of the explosion's sound.

All four in the dust-filled room grabbed the breached doors and pulled one of them open. Each of them retrieved a large flashlight from their individual bags and turned them on. The four torches did their best to illuminate the utterly black void before them.

In truth, the whole inner bunker they were in was also a ruse. The entire area around the small maintenance building was artificially shaped and graded to hide the outline of the bunker all but completely. The bunker had been built with a descending floor to make the internal volume of bunker sink into the ground and further mask its existence. In reality, the camouflaged bunker was larger than the building that it was hooked to.

All four members of the cell gasped as they took in the enormity of the space. A fully assembled Trident II sub-launch missile could be seen in the flashlight beams, sitting quietly in its custom cradle. A fine layer of dust covering the missile attested to the bunker's lack of visitors.

"Let's get moving. And don't get sidetracked. We came for the suitcase." Zoran moved off toward the heavy metal shelves to the right of the bunker's entrance without waiting for a response. The remainder moved off in other directions. The search lasted for exactly two minutes. Jasna broke the silence in the black void.

"I have it."

Three of her comrades moved to her location. The device they came to find sat unassumingly in a crate marked MK-54. A storage container on the next shelf was stenciled with the marking "H-912 Transport Container".

Zoran and Alek quickly packaged the nuclear weapon for travel and Alek hoisted the backpack carrier onto his back. He adjusted the pack for carrying and turned for the door before the radio broke silence.

"Zoran, we're hearing chatter from the guard's radio. They have called several times now, without a response." Adam Pavlovic, Jasna's cousin, sounded calm but serious.

Zoran keyed his radio mic to talk.

"We are on our way out now."

The four members of the cell backed out of the massive storage bunker the way that they had come and closed ranks with their perimeter security. All six moved silently to the entrance point in the fence line and out into the crop fields. Zoran could hear the sounds of approaching vehicles to the bunker area behind them. The team kept moving without looking back.

Zoran, Emil and Alek climbed into a black Ford Sierra and started the engine. Adam and his wife, Dunja Pavlovic, climbed into a dark brown Opel with Jasna. Adam looked out the rear window as the car began to move. Floodlights were just blazing on as the two nondescript German cars pulled from the fields, onto the L16, and headed south toward the small town of Weiler.

CHAPTER THREE

WHERE THE INFILTRATION and theft at the Luftwaffe base went off as planned, the get away with the stolen nuclear bomb most certainly did not. The two carloads of Bosnian terrorists had barely made Frankfurt-Mainz before signs of the German response started to become evident. They managed to escape Wurzburg just ahead of the roadblocks going up along all routes, narrowly passing by the stern eye of the German polizei.

"We have to stop. We are never going to make our way out of Germany like this." Emil didn't exactly sound worried, but his voice did have an edge to it.

"I've been thinking the same thing. The Germans aren't nearly as slow off the mark as I hoped they would be." Zoran looked at the signs along the side of Autoroute 8 as they passed by them at just over regulation speed.

Alek sat quietly in the back seat alongside the nuke. He knew better than to get between the two Savic cousins when things were getting tense.

Zoran scratched at his chin and looked at the road signs again. Emil waited for him to formulate a plan. Behind them some two hundred meters, the group in the worn brown Opel followed. They all wondered what was going on in the lead car and if they were going to make it to the border. Back up front, Zoran drew a breath and expelled some expletives in his native tongue.

"We are definitely not going to make it through Schweinfurt at this rate, not to mention crossing the border. We'll pull up in this town coming up, Kitzigen, and find a place to lay low while we figure out the best route on secondary roads."

The other two men in the lead car nodded but did not respond. Emil withdrew his pistol and racked the slide part way back to check the chamber. Seeing the brass end of a round, he let the slide go and replaced the pistol in its holster. Zoran watched Emil out of the corner of his eye and really hoped that they would get through the next bit without causing a gun battle.

The black Ford Sierra, followed closely by the worn-looking brown Opel, pulled into a McDonald's restaurant just off of Route 8 on the west side of the small town of Kitzigen, Germany, and pulled to the far end of the parking area. Zoran picked a space as far from the parking area's security cameras as possible and killed the engine. The Opel pulled in tight to the passenger side of the Ford Sierra and Jasna Pavlovic rolled down her driver's side window. Emil hit the button on his door's armrest and lowered his window as well. Everyone waited silently as Zoran scrolled through page after page on his phone's mapping app. He used his fingers to expand the image size and moved the map around the town.

"It seems as if there is an industrial area on the opposite side of the river Main, to the north. We'll head that way. There has to be an abandoned building or service station where we can hide the autos. We can figure out the rest of the route and new transportation once we are there."

Everyone in the group responded positively, and the car windows went back up. Zoran pulled the Ford back out into traffic, followed at a casual distance by Jasna in the Opel. The two cars headed east toward the river Main, followed every foot of the way by the town's closed-circuit TV surveillance cameras stationed along all of its streets.

To the west of the fleeing terrorist group and its stolen nuclear weapon, just clearing the outer boundary of Frankfurt, an NH-90 medium duty transport helicopter streaked east across the sky. Commander Eric Garver, field leader of the Grenzschutzgruppe 9 der Bundespolizei assault squad assembled in the helicopter, tapped the receiver of his Heckler and Koch MP5 assault rifle with his ring finger and stared out the windscreen.

The GSG-9, as they were known to the outside world, were considered one of the preeminent hostage rescue and counterterrorism teams in the world. A branch of the German Federal Police, the GSG-9 was legendary in the world of Special Operations for its professionalism and exacting tactical precision.

The 10-man team assembled in the helicopter with Commander Garver were all considered the best that the GSG-9 had to offer. His group had been the quiet hand behind several terrorist captures, kidnap retrievals, and the taking back of several embassies being held by various criminal agencies. The affair that his group had conducted at the Baghdad Embassy had almost landed Garver and his team on the international news. They had needed to exfil the country in a deliberate fashion after conducting that operation to continue unidentified.

As an organization, the GSG-9 had been formed out of the ashes of Black September's Munich Olympics hostage-kidnapping and standoff in the summer of 1972. The Palestinian terrorists had found a German police force which was ill-equipped or trained to handle international hostage situations. The end result of the situation had been an international disaster for the German government. Where the Israeli Mossad cleaned up the mess later, Germany quickly realized that they needed to develop an appropriate response to such threats in the future. Out of the ashes came the GSG-9.

On this specific night, it had taken the GSG-9 and the German Federal Police just over one and a half hours to scan a country's worth of CCTV footage and review data from several NATO spy satellites that were hovering over Europe. Two midsized cars had been captured by a spy satellite exiting a nearby farmer's field just after the air base breach. Reconnaissance had followed the two vehicles across Germany, through both Frankfurt and Wurzburg and on to the small town of Kitzigen. They were currently in Kitzigen, heading east across the river Main. The heavily sensor-laden spy satellites had not picked up any residual radiation from the vehicles, but that was of no surprise to Garver. If they had stolen what he was told that they had stolen, there most likely would be no residual radiation signature.

Eric Garver made a hand gesture to his men assembled in the cargo/transport section of the helicopter, and each made a hand gesture in return. The commando keyed the mike on his helmet.

"How long until we get to Kitzigen?"

"Just over twenty minutes at this rate of speed." The pilot looked down at his instruments as if to verify what he had just said.

"Can you put on more speed?"

The pilot nodded to the commando and twisted the grip on the helicopter's control stick as the machine picked up speed. Garver went back to tapping the receiver of his assault rifle.

Zoran Savić saw a semi-darkened area off to the east, on a street called IM Gartenland, and turned. Moving quietly down one and then another dead-end street he found a small warehouse that looked to be the right sort. It was minimally sized, had its own parking area that stretched around behind it, and was completely darkened out.

Zoran pulled the Sierra into the parking area and picked a location where the car was blocked from sight from the roadway by a pair of large trash dumpsters. He pulled his pistol from its holster and checked the suppressor for tightness.

"Emil, see if you can loosen the locks on this place. I'm sure it has an alarm, so be careful. If there's a guard, kill him."

"I'll only be a minute."

Emil pulled out his own pistol and grabbed a small bag off the car's floor.

"Alek, once we're comfortable, sneak out and find us new transportation. We have used these long enough. If anyone has had time to look at cameras, they may know what we're driving."

"I'll find something for us that is good and dependable."

The group from the Opel had disembarked and formed a loose perimeter around Emil as he worked his magic on the building's cheap lockset. The door came open, followed by a questioning voice. Two retorts could be heard from Emil's suppressed 9mm Makarov pistol as he dispatched the lone security guard.

The terrorists made their way inside the building and wordlessly began taking up defensive positions to watch the perimeter of the small warehouse. Zoran sat down in the dead guard's chair and began to scan the internet on his phone.

Alek sat the nuclear backpack on the guard's desk and then made his way back through the building's rear door. To his delight, he didn't need to search far before finding what he was looking for. Stationed along the far end of the building's rear wall was a group of delivery vans. They were uniform white Mercedes cargo vans with a splashy courier logo painted on the side. All of them, save one. The van on the end of the row was white like the others but lacked the distinctive logos of the others. From the look of the vehicle, Alek assumed that it had been purchased recently. He made his way to the van and gave it a visual inspection. It looked clean and in very good shape.

Alek tried the van's driver's door. It turned out to be locked. He thought for a moment and then turned and headed back toward the building. Looking around inside the warehouse for a minute or two, he locked eyes on a key box bolted to the wall. The unlocked key box contained six sets of vehicle keys, each designated by a number tag. He hadn't remembered seeing any numbering on the vans, so he considered that maybe the keys were identified by the vehicle plate numbers. He grabbed all six sets of keys and returned to the parking area. Walking down the row, he looked at the license plate numbers on the first five vehicles and then separated out the set of keys that didn't match. Sure enough, it unlocked the doors and started the engine of the one he wanted. He tossed the unneeded keys onto the floorboard of the van and moved it up next to the open man door of the building. Ready, he climbed out of the van and returned inside to retrieve the nuke. Zoran gave him a hooded gaze as he hoisted up the nuclear bomb and turned for the door.

"Success?"

"Yes, sir. We're ready to go whenever you want to leave."

Zoran smiled at the young auto mechanic as he headed out through the door. Maybe, just maybe, it would all turn out to be okay.

The twin engines on the NH-90 flared as the pilot arrested the helicopter's forward velocity and began to drop it down onto a makeshift rooftop landing area some three blocks away from the warehouse. A local polizei officer waved chemical stick lights over his head to guide the pilot down the remaining 10 feet or so to the gravel- coated rooftop. Six black clad commandos jumped from the open side door of the helicopter when it was still some two feet off the roof. The helicopter's landing wheels no more than scuffed the gravel rooftop and the delivery bird was airborne once again.

The pilot of the GSG-9's transport made a wide arc back toward the east side of town, staying no more than a handful of meters above the rooftops. Upon reaching the Main, the pilot dropped the helicopter down into a manmade cavern produced by buildings around a small square and brought the machine to a hover.

Commander Garver checked the stopwatch he had started when the ground team dropped. Four more minutes and they should be in place. Garver gave a hand signal to the men remaining in the helicopter. Each of the men responded in kind.

The countdown showed thirty seconds to zero time, and Garver gave the helicopter pilot a thumbs up. The pilot lifted the machine out of its hiding place and pointed it directly toward the target warehouse.

The first of the GSG-9 commandos was getting ready to radio that the team was ready to go when gunfire erupted out of the warehouse's upper window. The commando returned fire but was hit by the second barrage from the upper observation point. The other two commandos on his side of the building began to return fire but weren't able to effectively cover their fallen comrade due to suppressive fire from adjacent points in the building.

Alek came to life at the sound of the gunfire on the opposite side of the building and ran to a better covering fire spot in the shadows of a roll-off dumpster. He racked the bolt on his AK-47 rifle and waited for the commandos to appear. He didn't have to wait long.

To the downfall of the commando team, Alek Lukic had been outside in the darkness long enough for his night vision to adjust. There was just enough ambient light coming from the surrounding buildings to illuminate blacked out forms crossing the small section of driveway that ran through the area between the buildings. The commando team was headed for the back parking area and the door that the terrorist cell had used to enter the warehouse, so Alek waited for them to come in. The black clad men had closed half the distance across the parking area in the standard one-by-one spread pattern used by most all professional operators when Alek opened fire.

The good thing about moving in a spread pattern was that a shooter couldn't engage more than one target at a time. This made it easier for the unaffected men to vector in on the shooter and return fire. Alek dropped the first commando with a four-round burst, and the other two men oriented on his location. Rounds rattled off the sides of the steel container and punched holes in the cinderblock wall of the warehouse as Alek instantly tried to make himself as small as possible. To Alek's relief, Zoran

Savić added his gunfire to the situation via the opened man door. His fire took out the second commando in the group. With two of the three-man team down, the remaining commando disengaged from the attack and found cover. Alek moved off down the side of the building, back the way he had originally come. Zoran disappeared from the doorway.

On the opposite side of the building a firefight of Hollywood proportions broke out between a mismatched number of commandos and terrorists as the helicopter dropped in to take the roof. Upon hearing the rotor wash, Zoran grabbed for his radio.

"Everyone get to the van. Out the back door. We have to make a run for it."

Jasna and her cousin Adam Pavlovic jumped from their firing positions and began to run for the doorway. Dunja Pavlovic was readying to abandon her position in the upper window when the lack of covering fire allowed the two functioning commandos to direct all their fire onto her position.

The air around Dunja Pavlovic came alive as 5.56 mm rounds from two Heckler and Koch 416 submachineguns rattled off every conceivable object. The barrage of fire was followed by the thud of a larger round impacting the metal beam next to her. The gas from the MZP-1's 40 mm gas grenade instantly filled the area with fumes. Dunja began to choke as a second round of gunfire ended her life.

Jasna Pavlovic grabbed Adam's arm as he turned back for his wife. His body disappeared into the haze of the gas cloud, and the gunfire fell silent. Zoran screamed for everyone to leave.

Zoran Savić no more than got the words out of his mouth when two of the large rooftop skylights exploded inward sending shards of glass raining down in every direction. The glass and the rope bags falling for the warehouse floor was impetus for everyone to begin running toward the open doorway. Two commandos came rappelling down through the opening in the skylights and instantly began firing. Two more commandos followed on the same ropes when the first two landed boots down. The gunfire that the four men brought consumed the space.

Emil and Zoran Savić took up well-defended positions on either side of the rear door and began to lay down covering fire as the remainder of the terrorist cell escaped to the waiting van. Alek opened fire on the hovering helicopter from the van's driver's door, forcing the pilot to pull off station.

The sudden movement of the ropes by the helicopter sent Eric Garver swinging in a pendulum arc to one side, before he lost grip and slammed side-on into a steel structural beam. To his credit, he hit the ground and was back on his feet instantly and engaging the nearest target.

Zoran waved to Emil to get to the van. Emil produced a compact object which resembled a plastic brick. He pulled the ringed plunger taped to its side and lobbed it toward the commandos. Zoran laid down suppressing fire as Emil slid through the doorway. Zoran was approximately halfway through the doorway behind Emil when a commando round punched a hole through his right thigh. The Bosnian-Serb terrorist screamed in pain as the momentum of his running drove him face-first into the ground.

Zoran Savić had no more than slammed into the ground outside the doorway when the two-pound block of C4 explosive that Emil had lobbed toward the center of the warehouse exploded. Men, shelves, parts and pieces all flew out in a radius from the blast point. The commando closest to the center of the explosion was killed instantly. A second commando was blown all the way across the warehouse's open area. Eric Garver, who was partially blocked by the steel foundation beam he had slammed into, was only blown from his feet.

Emil leapt from the van to retrieve his fallen cousin when gunfire rained down the side of the building from the outside commandos. Emil was grasped by the others in the van and pulled back inside. Aleksander Lukic, seeing no good alternative, slammed the van into gear and sped off into the darkness. The three commandos left outside could not engage the van directly, thanks to Zoran spraying rounds in all directions. Zoran burned through the magazine in his assault rifle and then jammed the barrel into the ground to use it as a cane. He had made it to his knees when a GSG-9 commando's tactical boot slammed into the side of his temple.

In the time that it took Zoran Savić, Bosnian-Serb war criminal and current day terrorist, to regain his consciousness, the world had changed considerably. The sun had cracked the eastern horizon and was shining an ever-brightening hue on the damage that was visible in every direction. Countless polizei officers had arrived and were milling about. The helicopter had landed in the parking area and was sitting patiently. Zoran realized that his leg had even been bandaged. His hands and feet were now physically secured with thick plastic restraints. The plastic dug deep into his skin and took his mind from the searing pain in his leg. But, most importantly, there was a black clad commando looking at him like someone does right before they gut a fish. The blue eyes that shown out of the black balaclava he was wearing said that he really wanted to gut Zoran. Zoran audibly scoffed in his general direction.

"You're conscious? Good."

Zoran Savić made no response.

"We had some time to search out your face while you slept. Though the license in your wallet says Marko Subotić, we know your real name is Zoran Savić."

Zoran Savić made no response.

"Mr. Savić, I am hereby placing you under arrest for acts of terrorism against the Federal Republic of Germany. Sadly for me, you're going to be immediately remanded to The Hague to stand trial in the International Criminal Court for war crimes committed in the former Yugoslavia."

Two commandos snatched Zoran Savić under his arms and pulled him to his feet. The pain from his gunshot thigh screamed through his body. Zoran made not one sound as he was frog marched to the waiting helicopter.

CHAPTER FOUR

THE THREE UNIFORMED men standing to the south end of the Büchel airbase's runway watched wordlessly as a white Gulfstream G550 banked and lined up on the runway's north end. The pilot brought the private jet down on the military runway without as much as a wing waggle. It was obvious to the men waiting on the tarmac that whomever was coming to visit was used to traveling the path of operational authority.

The Gulfstream taxied almost the full length of the runway and made a low velocity pivot on the south end apron, coming to a stop directly in front of the three uniformed men. The two Rolls-Royce jet engines began to spool down as the cabin's passenger door opened.

Doctor Kristin Marie Hughes stepped out onto the door's descending steps and inspected the three-person greeting party assembled before her. There was one German officer, one American officer, and one unidentified individual. It was pretty much the standard package. Doctor Hughes descended the remaining steps to the ground and paused to straighten the wrinkles out of her khaki shorts. Feeling presentable, she strode to the German officer with purpose and extended her hand.

"General Stahl, good morning. My name is Doctor Kristin Hughes. I work for the United States Department of Energy. We would like to have a look at your crime scene."

The German base commander looked into the striking blue eyes of the twenty-nine-year-old, five-foot-six-inch-tall American, and physically bristled.

"Young lady, I have no intention of allowing you access to any area of this base not designated for public tours, without specific direction from a higher authority. I'll answer whatever questions I can, which will not exceed security measures, once the authorization that you have a need to know is established. You will need to have any other questions directed through your government's command structure."

The German general, at a solid six-foot-two-inches tall and two-hundred-forty-pounds, was used to intimidating people with his size and rank. Kristin Hughes was unmoved by his display. She inspected the flecks of grey in his hair and the small scar on his temple and considered her response for a good two seconds.

"A higher authority you say?" Kristin said with a tone that should have told the Luftwaffe officer she was about to ruin his day. "Fine. I can do that."

The young, blond nuclear weapons technician reached into the leg pocket of her cargo shorts and removed a neatly folded piece of paper. She slowly unfolded the quartered sheet and handed it to General Stahl. The big German read the dispatch and blanched.

"The communication which you are holding, which has your specific name at the beginning of it, signed by the chancellor of your government, says that *YOU* will be happy to help me in *ANY* way that I require. As you'll notice, it doesn't say anything about submitting anything through any channels. Nor does it make mention of my need to worry about your inadequate security precautions."

The German base commander blanched again and attempted to formulate a response but couldn't. The two others in the group looked to the tarmac in an attempt to hide obvious smiles. Kristin broke off her stare down with the German and softened her tone.

"I think we're all aware that no one wants any of this splashed about. If you could let me do my thing, I'll be off your base as quickly as I can. Trust me when I say that everyone in both our governments is unhappy and looking for closure."

The Luftwaffe officer turned his head to the unidentified man and made a face.

"She's your problem. Show her what she wants to see."

The third man nodded as the Luftwaffe officer spun on polished boot heels and strode away. Kristin looked at the American officer and shrugged her shoulders.

"Was it something I said?"

The Air Force lieutenant colonel laughed, unable to keep the smile from his face any longer. Kristin extended a hand.

"Colonel Grant, it's good to meet you, circumstances aside."

Lieutenant Colonel Steven C. Grant, detachment commander for the 702 Munitions Support Squadron stationed at Büchel Airbase, smiled warmly at the DOE field operative.

"It's a pleasure to meet you, Doctor Hughes. So, you're Lou Stenson's number one tech? I should say, the rumors don't do you justice."

Kristin blushed. "You're too kind colonel. Do you know Lou?"

"Only by reputation. Not one to be crossed or written off."

"Roger that."

"Our host, the general, was right about two things. If you have any resistance whatsoever, you just tell me and our command structure will make it go away."

Kristin smiled knowingly to the Air Force officer. It was good that he understood the severity of the situation.

"Second?"

"Second," the officer looked over at the third man who was still standing quietly, "our friend here will assist you with seeing everything that you wish to see. I assume you would like to see the bunker first?"

The detachment commander pulled a security pass from his pocket and handed it over to the NEST field operative. She inspected the two-inch by four-inch laminated pass, marked "Top Secret," and then slipped its cloth lanyard over her head.

"Thank you, sir. I am going to have a bunch of questions for you that go well beyond 'Top Secret,' but they can wait till later."

"Whenever you need me, I'll be at Detachment HQ. Best of luck, Doctor Hughes."

The officer nodded to the third man and turned back toward the bunkers. Kristin watched him go and then focused her attention on the third man. The man was standing quietly, just absorbing the situation. Kristin smiled genuinely and extended her hand.

"Hi. I apologize for the strangeness of the greetings. I'm Kristin Hughes, I work for the Nuclear Emergency Search Team, of the U.S. DOE."

"And you track down missing nuclear weapons?"

"And disarm them, yes."

The man nodded his approval. Kristin couldn't shake the vibe she was getting off the guy. He wasn't military. Or, he didn't spend his base time that way. He was either a spy or a commando of some type. Whatever he normally was, right now he was her German babysitter.

"And, you?"

"I work for a section of the Federal Police, and deal with these types of situations as well."

Kristin visually inspected the man. Six feet tall, a solid two hundred twenty-five pounds of athletic muscle, close-cropped blond hair that exposed piercing blue eyes and numerous small scars. The wire-rimmed glasses gave him an almost studious look and covered a naturally investigative gaze. The switch flipped in Kristin's head, and she gave the man her shocked face. She leaned in to talk in more hushed tones.

"You're GSG-9! German Counter-Terrorism and Special Operations."

Eric raised an eyebrow slightly, but otherwise said nothing, which was the universal way operators said yes.

"You guys are legend. I'm definitely getting the royal treatment today. Was it your team that did the intercept in, where was it, Kitzigen?"

Eric Garner let a shadow cross his enigmatic face. His eyes clouded slightly and then immediately turned back to their natural penetrating blue.

"It wasn't our finest hour."

Kristin made a conciliatory face. "You apprehended a long-standing war crimes terrorist. I'd say it wasn't that bad of a day."

Eric Garner made no response. Kristin understood completely.

The pair walked out into the crop fields beyond the security fencing. It was where the story had begun. Kristin laid down in the mass of vegetation and stared back at the fence line.

"They breached the fence line at 1:00 AM, is that right?"

"Yes, within a fifteen-minute window."

"No full moon that night?"

"Correct."

Kristin got back to her feet and straightened the wrinkles out of her clothes. She turned and looked at her counterpart in the German government.

"It would seem that they did their pre-op recon using night vision, or starlight scopes. And from this distance, they weren't the store-bought kind."

Eric Garner cracked a legitimate smile for the first time that day.

"That was our assessment as well. It was probably Russian equipment that they brought with them from Bosnia."

Kristin nodded in agreement and pointed toward the fence line. The two walked quietly to the terrorist group's penetration point and paused. Kristin pulled a pair of glasses from a pocket of her cargo shorts and slid them onto her face. The German inspected the heavy black plastic frames and assumed that it was some type of American fashion thing, though he said nothing. Kristin spent several seconds intensely examining the cuts on the chain link fabric and the cut security wire. When done, she pocketed the glasses and blinked several times.

"Looks like they shorted out the security lead without tripping it, and then painted the fence with liquid nitrogen." Kristin scratched her chin in thought. The statement was more of an investigation question than it was a statement of fact.

"Agreed."

Kristin nodded to no one in particular and continued on through the opening in the fence line. Eric Garner followed quietly behind. In a break from the obvious path back toward the bunker, Kristin broke right and headed toward where the dead security detail had been found. She pulled up at the spot where the site photos had shown the body of the Luftwaffe patrolman and his patrol dog. She inspected the ground looking for something. Eric Garner could not fathom what she was looking for. When done, she stood and slowly turned in the direction of the bunker.

"Question."

"Yes, Fraulein Hughes."

Kristin smiled at the German pleasantry.

"Was the patrol a random patrol, or a patrol working a set route?"

"They systematically covered an assigned patrol area."

"And how long would it take the patrol to go from the bunker to the far point in that patrol area and return?"

The German commando swung his head from the bunker to the far end of the pathway's arc and back. Kristin waited patiently, thinking about other things.

"I would say – approximately nine minutes."

"So, the terrorists waited for the patrol to pass and then continued to wait until the patrol had reached the far end of their route. That would give a solid four to five minutes to breach the fence and make the cover of the bunker before the patrol returned. Once they came back into range, they were dispatched directly."

"That would suggest that they had advanced knowledge of the patrol routes, or that they did sufficient recon from the field before moving on the target."

"Yes. It would."

Kristin headed off toward the bunker/hangar complex at the same cadenced walk she had been utilizing since her landing. Eric Garner stared at the back of the young nuclear scientist for a moment before proceeding off after her.

Kristin was readying to show her laminated pass to the outer ring of German military stationed around the complex when Eric Garner said something to them in a low, but authoritative tone. The troops instantly parted, allowing Kristin access to the building's man door. Both Garver and the German troops nearby kept their distance as Kristin examined the door's control panel and retina scanner. The unit seemed top-notch. The breach of the unit, though carried out in a hasty manner, also seemed top-notch. Kristin removed several photos from a pocket and held them up next to the wall- mounted unit. She flipped them in her fingers until she found an image of the unit as it was found directly after the breach. Kristin nodded at the German commando and waited for him to join her.

"How many digits in the passcode?"

"Ten digits."

Kristin stood and made her way inside. The German followed quietly behind her. She inspected the interior of the hangar in a casual, but deliberate manner, as she made her way through to the second security door. She inspected the door's keypad and retina scanner in the same way as she had done with the outer door. Feeling she had made an adequate examination, she stood and pushed through the security door.

Taking in the size of the bunker's blast door, she paused. She hadn't been prepared for the colossal mass that greeted her behind the hangar's false wall. Kristin turned and took in the camouflaged overhead door that made up the interior false wall, and then made a face.

"Well."

"Most people have had that same reaction." Eric Garner's voice was unnervingly calm.

"This is very well hidden."

"Yes."

Regaining her focus, Kristin walked to the blast door and inspected the damage from the explosive charge that had opened it. The blast looked precise. It was clean, with no over-cooking. It had probably been fairly quiet, too.

"That's a pretty tactical breach, wouldn't you say?"

"Yes."

Kristin looked at her monosyllabic babysitter and made a face before proceeding inside the bunker. She took in the systematic labeling of the contents, every piece inside individually shelved and labeled. The U.S. military really sucked at a couple things, but inventory control was not one of them. She looked down at the wash of footprints in the dusty floor and frowned. There was never anything to be gained from people trampling the scene. She made a slow turn through the bunker, inspecting each row in a uniform manner. Upon returning to the bunker's entrance she found the German commando patiently waiting for her. She smiled at him. He nodded respectfully.

"I'm assuming that they did several rounds of inventory on the ghost ordnance?"

"Yes, fraulein."

"And the only thing missing was a single nuclear device. The MK-54?"

"One MK-54, Tactical Nuclear Weapon. One H-912, Backpack Transport Container."

"Hmm, don't you find that odd?"

"How so?"

"This is a very specific crime. The group did enough research to find a stash of weapons that doesn't exist, and then they did enough recon to successfully enter both the facility and the non-existent bunker. Following this, they breached the unknown bunker, and then stole the smallest nuclear weapon in the inventory."

"Your point?"

"If they wanted to grab something man-portable, why not grab one of the 76s for the Trident?" She pointed to a series of boxes along the bottom shelfs in the nearest row. "Those would stand-down anybody. No. Instead, they intentionally grab the smallest weapon in the bunker. The MK-54 can't be more than five kilotons at best."

Eric Garner narrowed his inquisitive gaze to a razor point.

"So, you're saying that they came here looking for a specific weapon?"

"Yes. A specific weapon, with a specific purpose."

"What purpose?"

"I have no idea. But whatever it is, they want to limit the fallout and the collateral damage."

Kristin Hughes sat down on a nearby crate and pulled her knees up to her chest, setting her hiking boots on the lid of the crate. Her German counterpart stayed stoically standing. Some time passed with Kristin lost in thought before she spoke again. Eric Garver did not inject anything into her silence, as not to disrupt her concentration.

"When you did the takedown in Kitzigen, did you physically see the nuke?"

The German thought for a moment. His expression unchanging as he considered past events.

"No. But we followed two vehicles from the field outside the airfield all the way to the warehouse. They did not stop anywhere for long enough to unload the weapon."

"So, the original group still has the device?"

"As far as I would suspect, yes."

"And your friend, the apprehended Zoran Savic?"

"What about him?"

"Describe him for me, please. What's he like?"

"He's a genocidal killer, and, quite frankly, an asshole."

"Did he strike you as a middleman?"

"No."

"So, a Bosnian terrorist stole a nuclear device big enough to level a small city, but small enough to have minimal fallout. And he didn't steal it to sell it. Which means he intended, or intends, upon using it."

"On what?"

"On whatever he perceives as his target?"

"The Croatians."

"So, they come here to steal the nuke and then sneak back to Bosnia so they can nuke something in Croatia?"

"Your hypothesis matches their direction of travel."

"Hmm, I don't know." Kristin seemed skeptical to the whole line of reasoning. The German just seemed enigmatic.

"It does make some sense, Fraulein Hughes."

"That's what bothers me. Things are seldom this straightforward."

The German GSG-9 commando said nothing while Doctor Hughes thought it all through one more time.

"What did you do with Zoran Savic?"

"He was transferred to The Hague. To stand trial."

"What is your status? I mean, after this is over."

"Why?"

"Feel like taking a quick trip to the Netherlands with me?"

CHAPTER FIVE

THE HAPHAZARD AND botched escape plan worked out to something like a white delivery van from Kitzigen to Rodelsee. Then a blue Mercedes sedan from there to a town called Abtswind. Finally, a medium brown, rusty lorry was acquired at a closed service station, which managed to get the group all the way to the German border.

The group of international terrorists crossed the German – Czech border south of a town called Arzberg. A series of dirt roads and hay fields brought the trip to a pause outside a town called Cheb. Emil Savic pulled the beat-up delivery van into a closed down service station, much like the one it had been lifted from, and parked it out of sight. Alex Lukic exited the van and began to survey the other vehicles in the parking area behind the station while Emil let himself in through the building's rear entrance.

Jasna prodded her cousin, Adam Pavlovic, out of his seat and pointed him toward the open door. Adam had not uttered a word since they had escaped the warehouse in Kitzigen. The grief from his wife's death at the hands of the German commandos was written poignantly over his thickly bearded face. Jasna thought that he now somehow looked much older than his thirty nine years.

Alek came through the service door and hopped up to sit on the service counter. Emil took in the faces of the other three in his group and began to wonder just what had gone wrong.

"Alek, what did you find in the parking area?" Emil tried to keep his voice as calm as possible.

"There is an Opel sedan that will serve us well. Otherwise, they all look like they are in the middle of repairs."

Emil paced back and forth across the small area behind the counter. He was mad. He was very, very mad. He needed to calm down before they all went and did something stupid. *This was what Zoran was always so good at,* Emil thought as he paced. He really should have been paying better attention to him over the years.

"Well, we probably have a couple of hours before someone comes to open this shop. We should rest for an hour or so, and then get on the move before anyone appears. Jasna, can you and Alek take a look around and see if there's anything to eat or drink in this place?"

Jasna nodded her consent and headed off into the bigger part of the shop building. Alek hopped down from the counter and followed her. Adam sat quietly, not saying a word. He just stared at the floor as Emil paced.

In the twenty minutes that Jasna and Alek spent scrounging around the service station, Emil had managed to notice and turn on the small television in the waiting area. As expected, there was absolutely no mention of a break-in at an air force base in Büchel. Nor was there any news about a missing nuclear weapon. What seemed to be making the breaking news on every channel was that Zoran Savić, a forty-five-year-old ex-Yugoslavian, now Bosnian-Serb militia man, had been apprehended after a shootout in a small German town. Zoran Savić, who was still alive, had been transported to The Hague to stand trial for war crimes related to ethnic cleansing suspected during the Bosnian War of 1992 to 1995. It was assured by the newscaster on all the different television channels that the trial of the Bosnian-Serb war criminal would surely be the biggest news story to come out of this year's international criminal court proceedings.

Alek and Jasna returned to the other two with three tins of biscuits and a half-dozen bottles of various soft drinks. Emil stood in front of the television looking ashen. Adam had been pulled from his self-induced coma and also looked as if he'd seen ghosts.

"What is it?" Jasna asked, as if she could hear Czech police pulling into the service station entrance.

"Zoran. He's – alive." Emil could hardly get the words out. The blast and the gun battle had been such that he was sure Zoran had not escaped the building.

"He's what?" Aleksander Lukic said, instantly irate.

37

"He's alive. He was captured by the Germans and handed off to the International Court in The Hague."

"Well, what the hell are we going to do now?" Jasna's statement was cloaked in her own personal outrage in having left their leader behind.

Emil began to pace around the small service area once again. The small limp that he had acquired from a left knee injury years back was becoming more pronounced now that he had been on the move for so many hours. Everyone in the group could see that his dark eyes were smoldering with malice. He knew that he needed to push the malice aside and think clearly. He knew that he was now the de facto leader of the group. He knew he needed to act as such. He could see his lack of schooling was about to become a weakness. Yes, he had the high-tech skills, but he lacked a formal education of any kind. What he had learned about technology, he had learned by doing over many, many years. He had never learned how to communicate clearly or how to think critically. He also wasn't a natural leader, like his cousin Zoran. He was cool under fire. Emil needed to become cool under fire. He needed to become his cousin. He needed to have that happen soon.

"What do we do, Emil?" Adam's voice was solid. It showed no emotion regarding either Zoran's situation or his wife's death.

Emil stopped pacing. He snatched up a grape Fanta from the collection on the counter and calmly removed the cap. Pushing half of the liquid down his throat, he tried to think. He hated grape Fanta. Why the hell had he picked that bottle?

"Emil?" Alek's voice was a bit more forceful than Adam's had been.

Emil Savić pulled his head up level and looked at his remaining comrades.

"It would seem that it all boils down to one of two choices. We can continue our current mission and get the nuke back on home ground. Once there, we dump it on the Croatians, and send that dissident, Marko Juraš, straight to hell. Or, we regroup and go free Zoran."

All three of the others became quiet. Thoughts were just thoughts. Things sounded different when you said them out loud.

"He was taken to The Hague. I would suspect that they are holding him in one local prison or another. We would need to get a look at the situation and find a weak point." Emil was now thinking straight. The sugary beverage had given his brain some much-needed energy.

"First, we would need to get there. The Netherlands is on the opposite side of Germany. We really can't go driving back across Germany with a nuclear bomb in the boot." Alek seemed as clear-headed as ever, so no one challenged him for a moment.

"The Netherlands are coastal. So is The Hague, kind of. We could go around Germany if we had to." Jasna was obviously spitballing, but it made sense.

"How so?" Emil asked.

"Hmm, Alek do you have a map of Europe?"

Alek shrugged at Jasna and went off to find a map. The other three turned their attention to the television screen and its non-stop news about the Bosnian-Serb war criminal. Alek was only gone a minute or two but somehow returned with a map. He spread it out over the counter and everyone gathered around it.

"Considering we're in the Czech Republic now, it would seem the fastest route would be directly north into Poland. We can acquire a boat and pass through Demark, and then out into the North Sea. Once in the North Sea, we can proceed down the coast to the Netherlands." Alek ran his finger around the map surface like a pointer as Jasna spoke, so everyone could follow the path.

"What then – we just pull into the port at The Hague and attack?" Adam gave every appearance that he didn't believe in the half-hearted plan they were developing, but was starting to warm to the idea.

"No," Emil said calmly. "We make land somewhere north of there. We find a place where we can do reconnaissance and formulate a plan. We will also have to get provisions. Whatever we do, it needs to be thought out. It can't be done emotionally, or we're done before we start."

All the others nodded in agreement.

"Let's say we get there. Let's go back to the idea that Zoran is held in a prison. We're going to break into a prison used for the International Criminal Court? That prison certainly won't be like the ones back in Bosnia or Croatia." Alek had made a good point.

Emil rubbed his palms over his forehead and thought. Adam came to his rescue and answered Alek's question for him.

"Attempting to break into a prison would seem a bad idea. The court is in an old mansion or castle in the middle of The Hague. Prisoners that are standing trial must surely be transported from the prison to the ICC at some point. At least once, if not daily. Hitting the convoy is a much softer target, and something we are well-versed at."

"We can spend the trip north and across the sea gathering all the information we can gather. Once we get to The Hague, we can scout the area and formalize a working plan." Emil's voice was much more commanding than it had been previously. The others seemed to take to the change in tone.

"It would seem the idea's sound enough. What's next?"

"I would say that we would need to focus on getting to the Netherlands." Jasna seemed to be thinking as she stared at the map before them.

"Getting to the coast won't be a problem. If the authorities know Zoran's history, then they will assume that we are headed back to Bosnia. That will be the focus of their searching, for both us and the bomb. Going north shouldn't be a major complication. The hiccup will probably come at the Polish coast. We will need a boat and a captain. None of us are sailors. We will need someone to transport us through Denmark and down to Holland." Adam Pavlovic's voice sounded as calm as it sounded on Saturdays in the hometown café, discussing small town politics.

"There has to be someone willing to handle illicit cargo," Emil said flatly. "Right in between Russia and Northern Europe, there is at least one captain, in one of the local ports, which can move contraband. We just need to figure out who that is. I know someone who can help us with that."

Everyone nodded their concurrence.

"I guess the real question comes next."

Everyone looked at Emil expectantly.

"Do we forgo our original mission and go retrieve Zoran?"

"Yes," Adam said flatly.

"I say yes," Jasna seconded resolutely.

"I agree, yes." Alek sounded sure. Still there was something in the background of his voice that was questioning.

"I also agree," Emil added. He nodded to them all in acceptance of the change in plan. He looked at his watch and frowned.

"It would seem we have used up all of our rest time making plans. We should get on our way before anyone comes along."

Again, everyone nodded in agreement.

"Alek, go make sure that the Opel you found has a full tank of petrol. We will take the lorry and drop it in the next large parking area we come to. If you find an extra set of number plates laying around, grab them too. We might want to swap out the plates at some point."

"Yes, sir." Alek turned and headed for the service station's rear door.

"Let's grab the food and drinks and anything else that might seem useful."

Jasna set about gathering up the biscuit tins and soft drink bottles. Adam began to fold up the map. Emil considered the thousand things which could go wrong, and then pushed them all from his mind. One thing at a time.

Alek came back, pausing just inside the service station door.

"We're ready to go. Just one question. What are we doing with the nuke?"

Everyone paused and looked at Emil.

"We take it with us. Put it in the boot."

CHAPTER SIX

K RISTIN HUGHES' COMMANDEERED white CIA Gulfstream G550 leveled out over German airspace and began its northeastern track toward the Netherlands. Kristin exited the main cabin's executive bathroom, having switched out of her Indian tourist garb for dark blue capri pants and a translucent, white sleeveless top. She dropped her gear bag into a chair next to dusty tan hiking boots and then took up a seat across from her guest. Eric Garver took in the change to the American scientist and smiled.

It had taken several hours to get through the DOE's headache of red tape at the airbase. Kristin had wanted to lessen the paperwork, but jurisprudence dictated that it all be completed. The main person of interest in the question and answer session, Lieutenant Colonel Grant, was as genial as possible. It was obvious that he understood all the Washington whitewash which was about to fall at his feet. Kristin knew all-too- well how the detachment and displacement of blame was a go-to tactic around both Capitol Hill and the Pentagon. Lt. Colonel Grant seemed the strong sort. He would probably fare well in the end.

By the time Doctor Hughes had finished her assessment of the situation on the ground, and handled all of the necessary paper entanglements as well as having two different crypto Skypes with her boss, Lou Stenson, and one with CIA DCI Eugene Taggart, a full day-and-a-half had passed her by. She really wanted to be moving quicker, but the hassles of government, which she usually left to others, would not be denied.

The two video calls to her boss at the DOE had been all business. The information she collected was sent straight to the DOE. There it was passed along the necessary channels to appropriate Pentagon and subcommittee groups, to the president, and to "The Group." The Group was good at circumventing the normal Washington bureaucracy and getting solutions to problems.

The call she had made to the DCI had been logistical. She wanted to keep the plane for a while. She had originally been granted use of it, and its pair of ex-military pilots, to get her hastily to the German airbase. She was excited and thankful for the call when it came in, as it had pulled her out of her sightseeing tour. She had flown to Germany assuming it would be an in-and-out affair. But as was her life, she was off on another crazy adventure that could possibly end in tragedy.

Kristin took in her guest sitting quietly across from her. The man gave her the same vibe that her boss, ex-Navy SEAL Lou Stenson, gave her. He was an enigma. She could sense that he wasn't a man to cross or to write off when things turned bleak. He was obviously skilled, but there was something else about him. He was dangerous. She could always sense the dangerous ones right away. They always made her comfortable in harsh situations. It was probably her military brat upbringing, but she could tell the truly dangerous from the pretenders instantly. The man that sat across from her was the real thing. She hoped that they ended up becoming friends. Another dangerous friend would be good to have. Especially one inside GSG-9.

It had taken only a little persuading to get the man to accompany her to the Netherlands. She could sense that he had some type of unfinished business lurking in the background. That didn't bother her. It was always the way with his kind. She understood it all too well. She liked having him here, even if she didn't know what was really driving him.

Eric Garver tilted his head to one side and then to the other. Two audible cracks could be heard as the vertebrae in his neck realigned themselves. He smiled at nothing in particular, seemingly just for self-satisfaction. Kristin inspected her guest for a second time. Close-cropped blond hair and blue penetrating eyes hidden behind wire-rimmed glasses. A crisp white shirt with no tie. A crisp, black business suit and leather shoes. The shoes possessed soles which one could run a good distance in. She was sure that there was a handgun in the portrait somewhere. It would probably be a Sig Saur or a Glock. They were the standard German-issue weapons.

Eric Garver, sensing that the inspection was concluded, decided to break the silence in the jet.

"Question?"

Kristin smiled and nodded. "Absolutely."

Eric Garver pointed toward the gear bag and then waved his hand over her new outfit in a casual, approving manner.

"I was on holiday when the communication of the theft reached me. That was a more appropriate fashion choice for that region. I picked this up before we left Büchel."

"Which region?"

"Northern India."

"Assam or Arunachel Pradesh?"

"Kashmir."

"That's Pakistan." Eric Garver's tone was unchanged, yet instantly curious.

"That depends on who you talk to. Nevertheless, I'm here with you now."

"That you are. And I am here with you. Do you always travel by way of a CIA private charter?"

He was good, Kristin thought. He had obviously done his homework before leaving.

"Normally, no. But there are times and places where it has its inherent advantages."

Eric Garver nodded to her in agreement.

"So, tell me something about yourself, Fraulein Hughes."

Eric Garver's tone was light and congenial, but still probing. Kristin considered his question for a moment, and then thought that they probably should share something of themselves if they were going to work together.

"Well, physically you can see for yourself. Otherwise, I'm twenty-nine years old. I have a doctorate in nuclear physics from Princeton. My dad was in the military and my mom was a family doctor. They both died in a car crash when I was young. My foster parents were also military. They were my dad's group commander, and his family. It was a good fit then, as I spent most of my free time with his kids anyway. I'm single. I live in Las

Vegas, Nevada, technically in Henderson, outside the city. I work for the Nuclear Emergency Search Teams as a nuclear bomb/ordnance disposal person."

Eric Garver absorbed her quick synopsis and pondered each piece of information. He was quiet for several minutes as he thought.

"If you don't mind, what did your father do in the military?"

Kristin smiled a melancholy smile.

"I don't mind. It's the first question that most all military men ask. He was Army. A Ranger."

Eric Garver nodded his approval.

"Well, that explains some things."

"You mean, what's a girl like me doing living a life like this?"

"You have to admit, jetting around the world chasing down stolen nuclear weapons is a fairly niche lifestyle. Not necessarily one that would instantly spring out of a grounded or otherwise conventional upbringing."

"Very true."

The two sat staring at each other for several seconds. Kristin wasn't sure what was going on, but she liked it.

"All right, I gave you something, now it's your turn."

Eric Garver pondered the attractive American woman sitting across from him. He wasn't sure what she really was; operative, delegate, technician, or all the above. He did sense that whatever she was, it was a good thing.

"My name is Eric Garver. I am thirty-eight years old. I have a degree in mechanical engineering from Universität Stuttgart, and am a graduate of the Offizierschule des Heeres, in Dresden. Currently, I am a First Lieutenant in the Luftwaffe on semi-permanent loan to the Federal Police. I have an apartment in Frankfurt, which I'm barely ever in. My parents own an Imbiss, in Wiesbaden."

Kristin took in all the information and processed it in her analytical fashion.

"Interesting. I got the commando vibe right away. It didn't feel like active military, though."

Kristin gave Eric an approving eye.

"I am almost never in uniform. I spend most of my work hours in a suit or black fatigues."

"And your name is Eric Garver?"

"Yes."

"Is it a cover name?"

"No. You seem trustworthy enough to get the real thing. Though I confess telling you that violates my own security clearance."

"Then I will not use it in public."

"You may use it, just not where anyone is going to overhear you."

"I completely understand."

"Now, you know more about me than pretty much anyone else on the planet, barring my supervisors."

"And I will not disrespect your trust, Eric. By the way, what should I call you in public?"

Eric Garver smiled warmly. Kristin was surprised that he had a smile of that caliber.

"I suppose anything that fits the situation. Just never my name."

"No, I understand. I understand that the names of all GSG-9 members are top secret level pieces of information."

Kristin let off a bit of a warm glow, which was obvious to the man across from her. She liked that he would see her as someone trustworthy enough within which to confide his secret. It made her blood warm. Eric returned another warm smile and then became quizzical.

"Just for clarity, Fraulein Hughes, what is your security clearance?"

Kristin Hughes laughed out loud. It wasn't meant to be a joke, but she really thought that the CIA plane would have given it away.

"It's officially listed as Top Secret Plus, with a Presidential Endorsement. In a real-world situational environment, it's listed as, *approved to whatever level is required for access.*"

Eric Garver nodded. "I was just checking."

"I really thought the cool spy plane would have given it away."

"It did."

They both laughed equally. Kristin knew that she genuinely liked the man she was with. She knew very little about him, but she knew that she liked him.

"Out of curiosity, is Kristin Hughes a cover name?" Eric wasn't trying to pry, just curious.

"No. That's my real name. I spend too much time in a public setting to attempt an alias. So, I just do my best to stay low key."

"Hmm, that's what your file said. It just seems an odd life to be living while using one's real name."

Kristin raised an eyebrow that channeled Star Trek's Doctor Spock.

"You have a file on me?"

"As you said, you have spent time in a very public light."

"All time spent for the good of the planet."

"I have no doubt."

The two stared at each other in the way that secretive people tend to do.

"I have one more curiosity."

"Proceed."

"It's noted that you have a small scar on your shoulder. Is the story about how it arrived there accurate?"

Kristin placed her palm against her forehead and pressed. The pressure kept her brain from doing anything rash. She opened her eyes and looked past her palm to the German commando across from her.

"Yes. There is a small scar on my shoulder blade. I obtained it while rock climbing. It has hampered my wearing of a bikini from time to time. Whatever story is in your file I am sure is a fabrication."

Eric Garver studied his host for several seconds. He was sure he had offended her, though her body language had actually given him the answer he was looking for.

"Hmm, yes. Rock climbing would seem a perfectly plausible answer. Nevertheless, while we're together, I can assure you that you are perfectly safe. I have no intentions of offending the Massad by letting such a thing happen again. Fabrications or no."

Kristin pushed her palm into her forehead a second time. Why did every skilled killer she had ever met feel an instant, deep-seated need to protect her? She had a black belt and could shoot straight. She could protect herself just fine.

"That's nice. Now, seeing how we only have twenty minutes of sky time left, I probably should check in with the bosses."

Kristin stood and stepped to her gear bag. She removed a black balaclava and tossed it to the German.

"I'm sure that everyone on this call already knows everything there is

47

to know about you and more, but if it makes you feel at ease? Sorry that it smells like Chanel, I need to do laundry at some point."

"They are all top-level people?"

"Yes."

Eric tossed her balaclava back to her and smiled.

"As you say, they already know."

She stuffed the balaclava she used as a sleep mask back into her pack. Sitting back in her seat, Kristin picked up a remote control unit from a small seat tray next to her and pressed a button. As she replaced the remote, a large flat panel television screen dropped from the ceiling. It almost cut the cabin in two with its size. The chairs they were seated in, and a couple others, pivoted to view the screen. Kristin plugged her phone into a port on her arm rest and hit a number she had pre-punched into the speed dialer.

As the call connected at the other end, the flat screen panel subdivided into eight equal sections titled NSA, FBI, CIA, DOE, NRO, and Secret Service. The boxes marked Justice and Field Ops stayed blank, causing Eric Garver to assume that those people would not be joining in on the call.

"Kristin, my girl, how are you enjoying the jet-setting lifestyle?"

The man from the NSA had a large smile on his face. The television said the man's name was Ed Crowley.

"Well, if Uncle Gene keeps letting me take the plane, I plan to keep taking it."

Everyone on the call laughed. Everyone except the man from the DOE. His expression stayed neutral. Eric Garver stared at the man for a moment. He could tell that the man from the DOE, Lou Stenson, was sizing him up. Garver could also tell that this man was a serious man. No, serious was the wrong word. He was a dangerous man. Yes, that was the word. He seemed about the same as Garver, if you looked past the mileage on his face and the start of greying temples. He had a surety about him. He must be the man that Colonel Grant had been alluding to back in Büchel.

"Herr Garver, we're happy that you could accompany Doctor Hughes on her little side trip to The Hague."

Garver focused on the CIA man who had spoken, one Eugene Taggart, and nodded respectfully. Taggart had the Cold War spy look about him. *Once a spy, always a spy,* Garver thought.

"No offense Kristin or Lieutenant Garver, but I have a subcommittee meeting in thirty minutes. Can we get straight to the SITREP?"

SITREP was standard military slang for situation report. Eric Garver's eyes narrowed at the open mention of his name and rank, which was guarded information that no one knew. The name who had spoken it, one Paul Spenser, from an organization denoted as the NRO, was obviously a well-informed individual.

Kristin smiled at her guest, "they're like this quite often."

Kristin cleared her throat and focused on a point in the middle of the screen.

"Okay, there was a theft at Büchel Airbase, which you already know. A group of undetermined number, but I suspect no more than eight, breached the base security by stealth. They penetrated the maintenance and servicing building, bypassing the electronic security at two locations, and then obtained access to an undocumented and, frankly, very well-hidden ordnance bunker. The blast doors of the bunker were breached by means of a compact explosive charge. It's my estimation the majority of the blast noise was swallowed by the building's heavy concrete construction."

Several nods and exasperated looks could be seen on the TV screen as the NEST field agent spoke. Garver was surprised by the way that the young lady completely held command over the conversation with a group of obviously powerful men.

"An after-action inventory of the facility and the bunker showed that all items were accounted for, save two. One MK-54 nuclear weapon, and one H-912 carry container are currently missing. Everyone involved in the proceedings were supportive and cooperative, though the base commander, General Stahl, started out as kind of a dick."

No one on the TV screen spoke. Each man was processing the information that the doctor had given out. Not one of them looked either surprised or shocked. The man from the CIA cleared his throat and focus returned to the group on the call.

"Alright Kristin, thoughts and assumptions."

Kristin looked at Eric Garver before speaking. She wasn't exactly sure what her thoughts were at this point.

"Well – the group of Bosnian-Serb terrorists that penetrated the airbase were well-trained, well- informed, and technologically proficient.

Considering that their leader is a war criminal, and that they went to considerable effort to steal a single weapon, by-far the smallest weapon in the stockpile, out of an unknown and undocumented stockpile – all thoughts lead to the conclusion they definitely plan to use it."

"Clarify Bosnian-Serb war criminal, please?" Pat Sommers, from the Secret Service, seemed concerned.

"The group of militants that stole the nuke was led by a man named Zoran Savić. He is an ex-Yugoslavian, Bosnian-Serb, who has been running a longtime feud with a group of Croatians. Old wars never really die in the East. Savić was apprehended and properly identified during a gun battle after the theft. He was transported to The Hague to stand trial for genocide and other atrocities. The main body of the terrorist group and the weapon are still at-large." Eric Garver spoke in a clinical manner.

Everyone in the group nodded in an understanding fashion. The DOE man was nodding, but also assessing. He was assessing Garver.

"I read the after-action report on the take-down. Barring the initial outcome, your group did a fine job. Your intel collection and primary response time was outstanding. I'm sorry about the loss of your men, Lieutenant Garver."

The red-cheeked man from the NSA seemed quite sincere in his remarks. But how had he gotten a look at a classified German after-action report? Had Doctor Hughes forwarded him a copy? It was obvious to Garver that this group of people he had become involved with was not to be taken lightly.

"Thank you, Mr. Crowley. It was not our finest moment."

No one said a word, but he DOE man's expression became much less judgmental.

"So, the nuke is headed for Croatia?" Pat Sommer sounded like he wanted to get things moving again.

"That would seem the most plausible scenario, but the weapon's real disposition is still unknown. I would say with good certainty that it is not a U.S. soil problem. Barring that, I don't know. We are heading to The Hague to have a conversation with Mr. Savić right now. Maybe that will help answer some questions and narrow the options."

"Yes, and you're making good time, too," The man from the NRO said smiling, as if he had been tracking the plane in real time, which he probably was.

"You may run into your friend, Mr. Dunn, around The Hague, Kristin."

The CIA man was direct.

"Roger that."

"Kristin, you appear to be in the best possible hands, but be careful. DO NOT go off on a cross-border op chasing war criminals. Especially without a good plan and backup. The nuke may be ours, and that's bad, but if it's not headed back to U.S. soil, then it's not worth risking all for."

The DOE chief's voice was calm and direct. It was authoritative, but it also had concern in it. *Apparently, young Doctor Hughes was a rule breaker,* Garver thought.

"No worries, boss. Besides, I have my very own personal bodyguard on the plane with me."

The statement didn't make the DOE chief smile. Eric Garver didn't smile either.

"Well, the yellow light from the cockpit just came on, so we need to jump off this call. We'll check back in when we know more."

Everyone nodded and mumbled something akin to affirmative and then disappeared from the screen. Kristin unplugged her phone from the port and the flat screen panel folded back up into the ceiling of the cabin. Kristin stretched out her frame and then settled fully into the chair. She closed her eyes and sighed contentedly. Eric Garver sat quietly, processing what had just transpired.

CHAPTER SEVEN

HE GULFSTREAM DESCENDED smoothly along its glide path and made contact on the tarmac of Rotterdam-The Hague airport with only the slightest wheel noise. The pilot took the required exit from the runway after slowing and taxied the private jet out to the hangar area for non-commercial aircraft. It seemed the Zoran Savić spectacle was continuing to make international news, as almost every executive jet hangar was being utilized. The Gulfstream's pilot taxied up to a hangar normally utilized by members of the American government and pulled to a stop. Eric Garver looked out the window and inspected the plane already in the hangar. The American flag and obvious government tail marking indicated that an American presence was already present. Kristin stood properly and retrieved a small clutch, which had sat next to the dusty gear bag.

"What do you think? Want to go chat with your boy, Savić?"

"Why not."

Eric Garver stood and followed the nuclear scientist down the aisle of the main cabin. She stuck her head into the cockpit and talked with the pilots for a few seconds, then made her way out the plane's cabin door. Several ground crew members paused to take in the chic blond woman exiting the plane. They also took in the man exiting behind her and automatically assumed he was the bodyguard. It was a natural sight at executive airport hangars. The ground crew returned to their previous duties unbothered by it all.

"Doctor Hughes." A proper dressed man standing next to a sleek black Mercedes sedan called out and raised a hand.

Kristin turned and headed off toward the Mercedes. Eric Garver followed along quietly. Kristin opened the Uber app on her phone and checked the photo to make sure she was getting into the right car. Eric caught a glimpse of the iPhone's screen and made a quizzical face.

"You use taxis?"

"The U.S. Government has an alternate account with Uber. The pool of drivers is fully vetted and have security clearances. It costs a lot more, but I tend to like it. They call it Uber Double Black."

The German commando shook his head, smiled, but said nothing. The driver opened the door and smiled as he assisted Kristin Hughes into the car. The larger man moved to the opposite side and slid into the backseat next to her.

"You're headed to the ICC, yes?"

"Actually – could you take us to the detention center at the prison in Scheveningen, please?"

"Yes, ma'am."

The driver pulled the car away from its designated parking space in a professional manner and proceeded toward the airport's private vehicle exit. Kristin retrieved her phone and punched a number in the speed dial. It rang two times.

"We're on the ground and headed to the prison. Is there any way that you could have someone from the ICC meet us there, to smooth the introductions and such?"

Kristin paused for five seconds, listening to the person on the other end.

"Thanks! You're the best."

Kristin killed the call and banged her fingers on the phone's screen to send out a text. Eric said nothing as he watched her out of the corner of one eye. Kristin smiled at her phone screen, in lieu of smiling at the commando.

"The call was to the director of operations, FBI. The text was to my boss at DOE. They can be helpful at times. And my boss gets moody if I don't let him think he's in charge."

Eric Garver reflected on the image of the DOE chief and then made another quizzical expression.

"I don't believe moody is the word you're looking for."

Kristin turned so she could look at her comrade straight on.

"His look during your call was one of concern and a need to take action. That I understand all too well," Garver said.

Kristin turned away from Eric Garver and looked out the Mercedes' window. Their driver had made his way out of the airport and was already headed north on the A13. A sign for the town of Delft passed by in a blur.

The three in the car rode the remainder of the way to the prison quietly. The detention center for the International Criminal Court was in one of the wings of the Scheveningen prison, in a suburb of The Hague. Unofficially known as The Hague Hilton because of its relatively luxurious conditions, the actual Scheveningen prison appeared to resemble a revamped castle.

The complex sat on a raised section of ground, surrounded by a tall cut stone wall. The double tower affair with a gated front entry point was really only missing the portcullis to finish off the theme. The upper building sections that could be viewed above the exterior wall looked of the same cut stone construction as the defensive wall. Upon closer observation, Kristin could tell that the structures father back in the prison complex were of brick construction, but the front end was still old stone. It looked entirely too nice to be a prison.

The driver pulled up to the main gate. Standing in front of the thick wooden entry doors, which remained tightly closed, was a solitary individual. The driver exited and opened the door for Kristin.

"I'll be waiting in the car park area when you're finished, ma'am." The driver pointed a thick thumb over his shoulder at the parking area next to the entrance road. Kristin smiled and nodded.

"That sounds great. Thank you."

Eric Garver and Kristin Hughes made their way over to the waiting gentleman, with Garver about a step ahead of Hughes.

"Herr Becke, we weren't expecting you back."

The German commando nodded and extended a hand. The Belgium security officer took the hand and shook it.

At five foot-ten inches tall, and maybe two hundred thirty pounds, Thomas Claes seemed kind of fat to be a security guard at The Hague. Kristin guessed he was maybe forty-five years old, but it was a little hard to tell. The man had an obviously large amount of mileage on his body. Brown hair with flecks of grey, and light grey eyes, spoke of an intelligent man. Red veins in his cheeks spoke of excessive alcohol consumption.

Kristin guessed that both were probably true. She turned to Garver and smiled.

"Herr Claes, might I introduce Doctor Kristin Hughes of the American Department of Energy."

Thomas Claes waited for Kristin to extend her hand, and then shook it in a chivalrous manner. He seemed nice enough at first glance, but they hadn't gotten to the jurisdictional boundaries yet.

"The Department of Energy?" The Belgium seemed to be wondering why the Americans would care about a Bosnian war criminal.

"Yes, sir. The Nuclear Emergency Search Team, to be specific. I would like to have a talk with your new inmate, Mr. Savić, about some of the activities which preceded his incarceration."

The Hague official's eyes narrowed like a hawk zeroing in on a field mouse. His demeanor was instantly cooler.

"That explains the call from the United States government official. What exactly do you want to question Zoran Savić about, Doctor Hughes?"

And, we have officially established the boundary lines, Kristin thought. The man in front of her was almost bristling now. Kristin looked to Eric Garver for some direction. The commando gave the slightest of head nods, indicating a no response. Kristin put on her happy to be here, political face, and readdressed the ICC official.

"Herr Claes, I can assure you that it's nothing sinister. The facility that he was caught looking around contained both American and German interests. I just happened to be in Germany on some other business and received a call asking if I could assist in the interview. That way, the FBI could tie up its red tape without a bunch of expense. The U.S. has no real interest in an ICC war criminal from Bosnia, other than to help with justice where we can."

The German commando nodded. The security officer calmed and smiled. Kristin took it as a good sign. She smiled back warmly. Her comrade's expression was unchanged, as usual.

"Well, in that case, the ICC would be happy to assist you with your interview."

Kristin Hughes and Thomas Claes smiled at each other uncomfortably. Well, at least Herr Claes was uncomfortable.

It turned out that the process of gaining entrance into Scheveningen prison was surprisingly easy. Kristin almost wondered if she had made a mistake by including the security man, Thomas Claes. Once the prison personnel had gotten a good look at her attire, Doctor Hughes was all but personally escorted to Zoran Savić's cell. The bored and under-utilized security personnel at the prison facility fell all over themselves to help the attractive American. Kristin had experienced the sensation many times before, so she played along. If it got them through to the prisoner faster, she wasn't going to complain.

This specific reaction to her all-American good looks was one of the reasons that she enjoyed living in Las Vegas. There were so many attractive women in Las Vegas that she mostly went unnoticed. Being anonymous was nice, and it allowed her to unwind after her more stressful assignments. She had been planning such a wind-down when she returned from the India adventure, but this whole Zoran Savić affair had cancelled her plans. Oh well, Sin City would always be there waiting for her to return.

Eric kept Thomas Claes from getting in the way, as the prison staff ushered the group straight into the meeting area. Kristin took up her position on one side of the steel table and adjusted her chair. A mirrored window took up the entire wall behind her and separated the meeting room from its observation area. Kristin gave a quick head nod to the window and then made a slashing motion across her throat to Eric Garver. He nodded in return and stepped from the room, dragging Thomas Claes with him.

A minute or so went by quietly before Zoran Savić was escorted into the room. He was attired in a standard issue prison jump suit, along with a body belt and handcuffs. The handcuffs were repositioned to secure his hands to the large metal table. Once secured, the two prison guards escorting Zoran Savić exited the room. Kristin sat quietly for a time, just taking in the war criminal. His weight, maybe two hundred and forty pounds, with a barrel chest, spoke of a forceful man. The numerous scars about his neck, forehead, and right eye, combined with a large scar on his left arm, spoke of war. His full head of dark hair and smoldering dark eyes spoke of malice. If she knew nothing else about the forty-five-year-old Serb than what she could see from across the table, she would have enough to know that he was where he needed to be. Some men were just evil. Kristin wasn't sure that Zoran was actually evil, but she was sure that he was no friend to humanity.

Two distinct knocks came through the glass window signifying it was time to get on with things.

"You speak English, yes?"

Zoran took in the even tone of the American woman and smiled.

"You mean you don't speak Bosnian?"

Zoran Savić's English was broken, but passable. Kristin made a note on her paper.

"No, I don't. So, we'll continue in English, seeing how yours seems adequate."

The Bosnian war criminal settled back into his chair and garnered a smile similar to that of a used-car salesman. Kristin was instantly annoyed. She made another note on the paper.

"I would like to talk to you about your activities the other evening, before your apprehension."

"You mean about breaking into German base?"

"Yes."

"It wasn't difficult, once small reconnaissance was done. How do you say, we let ourselves in?"

"How many is we?"

"More than me."

Kristin made a note on her paper.

"The after-action report estimated a group of eight people. Is that accurate?"

Zoran shrugged his beefy shoulders, but didn't respond. It was okay, Kristin could tell from his body language that her estimate was close.

"Why would you leave your normal operating area, an area that keeps you safe from justice, to break into a military base in another country?"

Zoran made a disgusted face at the use of the term *justice,* and Kristin could tell that she had found a raw nerve.

"I think you know the answer to question."

"To retrieve a package, which is now missing from the inventory?"

Zoran smiled. Kristin made a note on the paper.

"You mean nuclear weapon which is missing?"

Kristin was now hoping that Eric had killed all the recording devices.

"Yes, I do. You stole a portable nuclear weapon from the annex. I would like to know where it is? And, what you plan to do with it?"

Zoran smiled his car salesman smile again. Kristin made a checkmark on the paper.

"Do your friends still have the weapon?"

Zoran shrugged.

"What is your plan for the weapon?"

Zoran shrugged.

"Are you planning a Chernobyl type event in Croatia somewhere?"

Zoran pondered the image in his mind for a moment, and then shrugged. Kristin made a note on the paper. She considered calling Eric Garver into the room for support, and then changed her mind. The tactics that would loosen Zoran Savić's tongue weren't Eric Garver's domain. *Nor would they be condoned by the ICC*, she thought. She wished she could transfer him to a CIA Black Site for a couple hours, even while knowing most all the Black Sites had been dismantled after the whole Gitmo fiasco. But at times, Black Sites and their advanced interrogation methods were exactly what was required.

"So, you actually do plan on using the weapon on some target in Croatia or some other nearby territory?"

Zoran returned his expression to neutral and shrugged.

"They tell me that you used to work in a factory in Sarajevo, before the conflict broke out?"

Zoran's expression turned quizzical.

"And that both of your parents died in the shelling of Sarajevo."

Zoran's expression darkened visibly.

"I can see where one's decisions, from that starting point, could lead to genocide."

"You know nothing."

Zoran was obviously put-out now. Kristin made a note and a check mark on the paper.

"I know that whatever happens with your merry band and their stolen goods, you are going to die in a prison. Die as a convicted war criminal. You're not a victim. You're not a hero. You're a terrorist."

Kristin did everything she could do to keep her tone level and her manner neutral, but it wasn't easy. The more she talked, the more Zoran became irritated. When she finished, he was glaring across the table at her. The contempt he harbored was obvious.

"You know nothing. This place not hold me for long. In end, I come looking for you. After I do your Chernobyl to those that oppress me."

Kristin tried to remain calm. She had been threatened by ruthless men before. But, with Zoran's agitated state, she couldn't dismiss the possibility that he believed in his dark heart what he was telling her was the truth.

"You're going to rot in prison, and then, hopefully die for your crimes. Your friends may carry out your initial plan, but it won't be you doing it, it will be them."

Zoran clammed up, but only for a moment.

"Either way, I win."

Zoran smiled and leaned back in his chair again.

"Where are your friends?"

Zoran smiled broadly.

"I don't know. If I did know, I not tell you."

"What is the plan for the nuke?"

Zoran shrugged.

"What is the target for the nuke?"

Zoran shrugged. Kristin knew that her window of opportunity with the man had come and gone. She made a note on the paper and stood.

Kristin made her way from the table to the reinforced metal entry door. She rapped on the door twice with her knuckles and waited for the guard to open it. Stepping into the threshold, she turned back to look at Zoran Savić.

"Goodbye, Mr. Savić."

Zoran Savić smiled at her coldly.

"Yes. Until I see you again."

Kristin exited the room. She didn't speak a word on the way out of the prison. Eric Garver and Thomas Claes were still arguing about the legal ethics of shutting off all or the room's recording devices. The Hague security man was being bureaucratic. The German commando wasn't being baited by it.

Once the whole group had passed the exterior walls and was free of the prison confines, Thomas Claes quickly said good day to them and headed out to the car park area. Eric turned and looked at his young American comrade. She was not as jovial as she had been upon entering the prison. He had seen that type of reaction to detainee questioning before.

"So?" Eric's tone was supportive, not probing.

"So, I think that if he ever gets out of there, and figures out who I am, I'm in serious trouble."

Eric's expression grew clouded but stayed calm.

"They tend not to get out of Scheveningen Prison, independent of its minimal appearances."

"That's good."

"Did he give up anything useful?"

"Logistically, no. He was a big pompous pain in the ass. I would say he believes his group still has the nuke. And whatever they stole it for is in or around Croatia."

"So, you're off to Croatia?"

"I don't know. He carried the whole conversation like he was going to get sprung at any moment."

"Sprung?" The German looked puzzled.

"It means to get broken out of jail."

"So, you think that his group is headed here?"

"I – I don't know."

Kristin twisted a piece of hair around her finger and made a face.

"I think I'm going to stay here for a day or two and see what happens. I'll have the pilots run you back to Germany."

The German GSG-9 commando smiled softly. It was warm and comforting in a way that Kristin really needed.

"I think I'll stay here as well."

"Then I will just tell the pilots to stand by."

Eric Garver nodded.

"One question."

"Yes."

"Herr Becke?"

"The people at The Hague and the ICC know me as Herbert Becke."

"Nice to meet you, Herbert."

"And you."

Eric pointed toward the Uber driver waiting in the car park area. The two wandered off in that direction.

CHAPTER EIGHT

THE SUN HAD risen several hours back, and still Kristin Hughes lounged in an eternally comfortable king-sized bed. The hotel, which was situated on the coast of the North Sea, was luxurious and provided an excellent view. She had been pointed in this direction after conferring with The Group and wasn't the least bit surprised when she arrived to a waiting reservation. The suite, on retainer to the FBI European Section, was way too nice for Kristin to afford on her own. She hoped that her new friend, Eric Garver, wasn't judging her by what he was seeing of how she lived.

Kristin rose from the bed and slipped into a thin silk robe brandished with the hotel's initials. A pair of slippers from under the writing desk went on her feet and she was padding out into the living area between the two huge bedroom suites.

"Eric?" Kristin's voice was light and casual.

"He's not here."

Kristin Hughes froze in her tracks. The voice, though definitely not Eric's, was familiar. It seemed to have come from the terrace. She reoriented herself toward the open terrace door. A light breeze blew through from the opened door and gave her a slight shudder. Even though it was midsummer in Europe, the frigid North Sea was still the North Sea.

Kristin broke through the opening and inspected the man sitting in the bright morning sun. A sturdy two hundred twenty-five pounds, six feet tall, with a Mediterranean complexion that had become well-tanned by the European summer sun. A crisp black Armani suit and tie, with grey dress shirt and Gucci shoes. He was as well-dressed as ever.

"Robert!" Kristin's voice came out full of joy.

"Good morning, Kristin. The morning light does you justice." Robert Dunn, CIA field operative attached to The Group and Kristin's assassin of choice, smiled broadly and tipped his coffee cup in her direction.

"I won't ask where you've been, so *how* have you been?"

"Quite well. Handling the usual affairs. And you?"

"I'm as good as can be expected."

Kristin took up a seat at the table across from Robert Dunn and situated herself. Dunn poured her a fresh cup of orange juice from a carafe on the table.

"Not to be a bore, but what operational brief did you get, and how long can you stay? Oh, and how did you get in without anyone noticing?"

Kristin was smiling a smile she saved for her favorite people. Robert Dunn was trying not to laugh. Because, it was really all jest.

"How did I get in? Really? It's what I do, sweetness. As for the other two, no brief, and as long as you need me."

"That last part is nice to know."

"Why?" Robert Dunn was curious. "You seem to have picked up your own personal bodyguard somewhere along the way. A fairly good one, too, from the looks of him."

"You met Herr Becke?"

"No. I watched him exit the suite and head out toward the beach, I assume for a run. He seemed very situationally aware."

"He is —"

"But?"

"I don't know. He's like Stenson in a lot of ways."

"Better yet, a *real* operator."

"He is that. In every respect."

"Well then, I'll be as nice as I can be."

Kristin laughed out loud at the statement. She wore a smile on her face that was unconcealable.

"No, you won't. You'll be you, as always," she said.

"Probably true."

Kristin couldn't believe that she had become such good friends with Robert Dunn. She had assumed that their awkward meeting, on an Italian beach outside the town of Pisa, would have led to an awkward working relationship. In all respects, it easily could have. Fortunately for everyone concerned, the two had taken to each other quite firmly. It wasn't a romantic relationship, but a strong friendship. They had found, once they had passed by the initial awkwardness, that they genuinely liked one another. This had made all the senior members in The Group very happy, because field agents who didn't fit in were quickly eliminated from the team.

Robert had called on Kristin to utilize her expertise on several occasions. Kristin had taken comfort in his shadow during a small stay in Uganda. Having your own assassin/bodyguard was useful to a woman with her lifestyle.

"So, do you want to give me the skinny on what's going on?" Robert still sounded playful, but it was getting-back-to-business time.

"Why don't we wait for Herbert to return? That way we can do introductions and brainstorming at the same time."

"That's fine by me."

The two had discussed nothing in particular for approximately twenty minutes before Eric Garver made his way back into the suite. Kristin called the concierge and requested a full breakfast be sent to the room. It arrived as Eric was finishing his shower. He made his way to the terrace and casually took a seat between Kristin and Robert. Robert Dunn took in the German's fluid movements and his choice of seat, and then smiled. He liked this man already, though only professionally. Kristin looked at both men and cleared her throat.

"Robert Dunn, meet Herbert Becke. He works for the German Police."

Both men shook hands and gave each other a quick assessment.

"Yes. GSG-9, isn't it? Mr. Garver?"

Robert had a face that said he didn't like the ruse of the alias.

"Dunn? A company wet work man operating primarily in Europe, right?"

Eric held the same stern expression for a moment, then both men laughed before offering each other a proper hello.

"Well, that charade didn't last long." Kristin just shook her head at them both.

"We're spies. It's what we do," Robert said matter-of-factly.

"True," Eric Garver added for affect.

Robert reached out and grabbed the coffee from the serving platter on the table. He swung it from upright to the pour position and filled his cup without spilling a drop. He gestured with the carafe to the others. Both Kristin and Eric declined, so he returned it to the serving platter.

"So, what do you say the two of you fill me in on why I'm at The Hague?" Robert's tone was relaxed, but businesslike.

Eric and Kristin looked at each other. Eric nodded and gave her the "it's your show" look.

"Okay, it goes a little something like this."

Kristin spent the next thirty minutes running through the series of events which had brought them together. The break-in at the German airbase was followed by the theft of the nuke. A very specific nuke. A nuke that was also no-longer supposed to exist, much less be in a country that it was not supposed to be located in if it did exist.

Eric picked up the conversation and explained the tracking and apprehension of Savić in the town of Kitzigen. He continued to explain the prisoner transfer to the ICC, and the reason people were calling him Herbert Becke.

Kristin took over again after deciding on a cup of coffee. She went over the meeting that they had conducted with Zoran Savić at the prison the previous day. Then she dug into the now marginally warm hotel breakfast in front of her.

Robert Dunn took in the whole story, making small mental notes as each of them talked. He thought the whole thing through once, and then a second time, before he spoke.

"First question. What is the working yield on the weapon?"

"Inventory paperwork puts it at around two kilotons." Kristin's voice was smooth and analytical.

"Second question. What were the capabilities of the team that stole the nuke?"

"Tactically, and technologically speaking, very good. They work as an effective team and possess all of the requisite skills." Eric's voice was colder, but still analytical.

"Working belief is that they plan to detonate the nuke?"

"Yes. People that steal ten nukes, sell ten nukes. People that steal one nuke, blow it up." Kristin was very matter-of-fact.

"Suspected target?"

"Guessing somewhere in Croatia?" Eric said it as a question, but it was probable.

Dunn nodded. "The boys in The Group tend to agree."

"It seems the realistic idea," Kristin added.

"Now, Zoran. What is his current, real world control on the terrorist cell, now that he's in prison?"

"What do you mean?" Eric Garver was instantly curious. Kristin could see the analytical wheel in his mind spinning behind his wire-rimmed glasses.

"How weak are they without him? How will they react now? Will they continue on like good little troops, or will they unravel?"

"Not knowing the other members of the cell and their backgrounds, it's hard to say how they will react. Seeing how they are, by nature, a secret cell, I would think that they would easily continue on."

Eric sounded as though he was thinking and talking at the same time. They both turned to look at Kristin, whose expression was extremely suspect about at least part of it.

"What?" Eric asked.

"I'm not sure that they're going to continue on with their original mission. They have always acted as a group. Or, I suspect that they have. One of their team was killed and another captured. It is safe to say that Zoran Savić is the leader of the cell. He definitely has the personality to be."

The other two stayed quiet for a second or two before Dunn prodded her.

"Keep going."

"Two out of probably eight or so people. We put a dent in their total number, plus took their leader. They may not have enough people to do whatever it was they originally planned. Or, Zoran may not have relayed the complete plan to them. My gut tells me that something isn't what we think it is."

"Why?" Robert Dunn asked in a concerned voice. He'd seen the look she was displaying before. It never led to good places.

"Because of Zoran."

"What do you mean," Eric asked.

"All the time I was talking to him yesterday, he gave me the impression that he wasn't going to be in prison very long. He basically said as much. I think that he thinks his crew is going to spring him."

Both men looked at her suspiciously.

"I'm telling you, that's the play at work here. At least Zoran thinks it is."

They both continued to look at her suspiciously, though their hardened expressions were softening by the minute.

"Now, I have a question," Kristin said, looking at Dunn.

"Fire away."

"What is The Group's stance concerning the nuke itself?"

Robert looked at Eric Garver and then shifted in his chair. He returned his gaze to Kristin with an expression that said *in for a penny, in for a pound.*

"As long as the nuke doesn't go off in the U.S., or in some NATO country, and as long as it doesn't take out one of us by accident, they have no vested interest in it. The big boss implied that he would deal with the political fallout as it came."

Robert Dunn turned to look at Eric Garver again.

"I assume that means shifting as much blame as possible to the Germans."

Robert shrugged, as if to say that was just the world that they live in. Eric nodded in understanding. Kristin smiled wryly.

"So, if I continue to chase my theory that the terrorists are coming to break Zoran out of prison, that's okay?"

"I should think so. Is that your plan?"

Robert Dunn now had an expression that seemed to show her new agenda worked well for him. That made Kristin suspect. Robert looked over at Eric Garver again. The German commando had shifted back into his anonymous observer persona. He was obviously going wherever Kristin was going. That made Robert happy. The girl really could find trouble in the most unlikely places.

"Okay, Kristin, so your merry band is coming to the Netherlands to spring their genocidal leader out of prison. What are they doing with the nuke?" Robert had that devil's advocate sound in his voice.

"They are bringing it with them." Kristin Hughes' tone was sure.

"Why?"

"Because. Because nobody is going to hide a nuke. Because they also can't trust giving it to any one they know, that's as untrustworthy as they are. No, if they went to all the trouble to steal a man-portable nuclear weapon, they are going to take it with them wherever they go. Definitely."

"The logic makes sense, I guess."

Robert Dunn looked like he had slowly come around to Kristin's way of thinking. By following Zoran Savić, in some strange way, they were tracking the nuke. It was definitely an unsound theory, but it made a strange sense. Robert nodded in approval.

"If that's your plan, then I need a small favor."

Kristin was wary. Dunn's favors could be expensive.

"Yes?"

"Can I borrow your plane?"

Kristin raised a Spock-like eyebrow at her friend, the assassin.

"What? You didn't bring your own plane?"

"I was close by, so I drove up. It seemed easier. I need to take a small trip. I think I know someone who will be able to shed a bit of light on your merry band of terrorists. It's just he's too far away to drive to quickly."

"So, we trade our plane for your car? Seems legit. It will let me get rid of the Uber driver."

Robert Dunn laughed out loud.

"Are you still using those Uber guys? You really need to call me when you come to town."

Kristin gave him her *"whatever"* face.

"Where are you headed?" Eric asked.

"Sarajevo."

Robert reached out and retrieved the coffee again. The other two just looked at one another.

CHAPTER NINE

MIL SAVIĆ STOOD against the rail of the fishing boat as it sliced through the unusually calm waters of the North Sea. The water below them was as black as night and reminded Emil of the large coal mines he had seen outside of the village where he grew up.

Emil was happy that the sea was calm. He was not a natural ocean-going man, having been much happier in the highlands of his home country. The North Sea had a reputation for being treacherous to cross, and Emil was happy the weather condition during their journey was not the norm. He had heard stories of a passenger ferry capsizing recently, and the stories had made him apprehensive.

Fortunately, the cell's trip had been without incident. It had given Emil time to sit and think. Any plan to get Zoran out of The Hague would need to be well thought out. Yes, they would need a solid plan.

His first thought was to use a "bump-and-run." A bump-and-run was Bosnian mob slang for causing an accident with a target vehicle, stealing what you wanted, and then escaping in an alternate vehicle. That tactic no longer worked all that well in Bosnia or Croatia. *Probably used too many times*, he mused. But what about in the Netherlands? These were proper people. They didn't have unruly traffic. A good bump-and-run might be exactly what could be utilized in this situation.

Emil figured that the drivers would pick up Zoran at the prison and transport him by a direct route to the court building in the heart of the city. The drivers would have made this trip many times. They would be used to the normal flow of traffic and be unprepared for an unexpected calamity.

As he thought about other ways to spring Zoran, the bump-and-run came to be the best option. There was no way that they could raid the prison. They couldn't do that with twice as many men. The prison was out of play.

The other end of the equation wasn't any good either. The International Criminal Court would surely have good security. It would also have television people reporting news. The number of eyes and cameras would be a problem, even without the large security measures they must have in place. That point was also out of play.

But if they intercepted him between the prison and court, they had a chance at success. They would still need to recon everything, so they knew where the pickup point and the transport route would be. *That was doable*, Emil thought.

So, the route between the two points appeared to be the weakest link in the chain. There would be traffic and traffic cameras to deal with. There would probably be more than one transport vehicle as well. That was okay. Worst case scenario was a series of three vehicles, one of which was armored to protect the prisoner. That was an attackable target.

They would need to get a look at the transport vehicles. Then they would need to case the route and find a blind spot. There was a blind spot in every route. Then they would need to acquire a vehicle big enough to either disable or force the transport vehicle off the roadway. Those vehicles were always available if you searched hard enough.

Cracking open the target vehicle, if it was armored, would be a bit of work. Handling the internal guards wouldn't be an issue. At best, they would be armed with submachine guns and sidearms. That was easy enough to deal with. They would need to find an arms dealer in The Hague once they arrived there. Emil was sure that there would be at least one. He would put Adam on that hunt when they landed.

Jasna Pavlovic approached Emil from the cabin door and took up station next to him on the rail. The breeze blew through her long black hair and pushed it around her face. She swept at the wayward strands to remove them, but it was in vain. Her dark eyes were hidden behind sunglasses. Emil could tell that she was enjoying the boat ride.

"The captain says that we should make our landfall in about an hour or so. He's headed for a private set of boat docks, just north of the city. He says they are unbothered and will do well for us entering without issue."

"That's good, Jasna. Very good."

She smiled and looked out over the North Sea. The smile stayed on her face as she inspected the dark waters.

"How do we stand for a vehicle when we land?"

"That should also not be a problem. He knows a couple of people who will happily look the other way."

"Very good. Has Adam talked to the captain about helping out again, when we leave?"

"About that. He said that he is not real excited about partaking in the exit. Too much heat. Too many people hunting an escaped fugitive. However, he does know a man who will, most likely, be interested. He will put us in contact with that man when we land."

Emil nodded to her in understanding, and then smiled softly.

"Each needs to look out for his own. It makes perfect sense to me. We'll meet with his new captain when we land."

Emil turned his gaze back to the blackness of the sea. Jasna stayed a moment longer, and then wandered slowly back to the fishing boat's main cabin.

The trip from the small Czech town to the country's border had been obstacle free. They had found a place to cross into Poland that was quiet. Traveling north through Poland was calm. They had stopped for petrol several times and did their best to stay out of the service station CCTVs when doing so.

Somewhere in the middle of Poland, Emil had made a phone call to a friend back in Bosnia. It had been only an hour or so before a return phone call was received. Emil's contact had given them the name of a captain who operated out of a town called Kolobrzeg for the next leg of their journey.

Finding the captain, and coming to an arrangement, had been easy enough. The captain was a man of limited morals, but reasonable ethics. He would handle the illegal job from time to time but was never one to talk about the deal. Emil had liked him immediately.

The fishing boat captain explained to them that the only sticking point would be getting through the Strait of Odense. The strait had a lot of traffic, and that could be an issue. Otherwise, the trip should be problem free. Since the European Union had formed, the waterways restrictions had significantly loosened. The captain had said that they could navigate the passage through by Copenhagen, but that section of waterway was tighter and more heavily watched, so they would instead head for Odense and blend in among the other boats.

The trip from the port of Kolobrzeg up through Denmark and out into the North Sea had been smooth and easy. No other vessel had given them as much as a second look and no authority had hailed them on the radio. The captain had piloted his vessel without issue, giving Emil time to think and his friend's time to rest.

The captain had raised an eyebrow as Aleksander stepped aboard carrying a large duffle over his shoulder. The captain, for his part, went about his business without a question as to what sort of object the duffle was concealing. That was good, since poking his nose in would get him killed, and no one in Emil's group knew how to captain a boat.

Currently, everyone was rested and ready to break their leader out of prison. For not being a leader, Emil was starting to feel good about his abilities. Like many things in life, one learned how to do things by doing them.

The ship arched to port and the mainland came into view. The change in the boat's direction had not changed the smoothness of the sea, and the fishing boat sliced through the water without restraint. Emil smiled at the black water. *Maybe he would learn to fish one day*, he thought.

Emil hopped the rail onto the dock behind the captain and followed him onto shore. The remaining members of the terrorist cell all drew weapons and waited. It was only a short wait before both men came back down the dock with a leisurely sense about them. Emil thanked the boat captain and the two men shook with a solid clench of hands.

"At the end of the dock there's a black, four-door Audi."

Emil tossed Alek the keys and everyone in the cell headed down the dock. Alek put the duffle bag in the trunk and climbed in behind the wheel. Emil took up the passenger seat. Adam and Jasna sat in the back. The captain watched the Audi disappear behind a building, sighed, and went back to his fishing boat. The bunch was quiet and well-mannered, but still, some East Europeans weren't too trustworthy. This group was up to something that he was happy to know nothing about.

On the drive south from the town of Katwijk, Emil explained his plan. Everyone in the car would find a safe place to hole up once they reached The Hague. Emil had been given an address by his contact when he was discussing the boat, but it was not a sure location. They would need to check it out. Once they were stationary, Alek and Jasna would recon the route from the prison to the court building. Adam would help Emil find proper vehicles for the ambush, and then they would find out when Zoran was to be transferred. Once done with surveying the route, Alek and Jasna would lay out the path from their hideout to the get-away point at the city marina. Emil would go make contact with the new boat captain and set up an exit strategy. Adam would be responsible for any last-minute items that would need to be acquired.

Once everyone was ready, they would free Zoran and escape to the sea. If all went well, they would be gone before anyone could muster a response. If not, well, they would deal with that when it happened.

As Emil talked, everyone else in the car listened. The plan made sense. It was sound and had a minimum of moving parts to deal with. All in all, it was good.

Alek pulled the Audi into a quiet section of town, down in the south end of the city. An austere, wholly anonymous building sat in front of them on Karperdaal. The street front of the building was uniform and allowed no good places for police to stage for an ambush. Or to attempt and surround them. To the rear of the building, there was a canal between the building and the local highway. Better yet, the building had a large garage door for service deliveries. It looked like it would do nicely.

Alek pulled the Audi into the garage after Adam had looked around and found a door key under a potted plant. The four terrorists circled a coffee table inside as Emil laid out a map of the area that they had acquired earlier. The new boat captain that Emil needed to meet with was generally tied up at the Marina Ter Heijde. It appeared from the map that the safe house was about halfway between the court building and the marina. To Emil, that was a good omen.

He had considered that everyone in the Netherland's law enforcement system would expect a direct departure after a jailbreak. Holing up and waiting a day seemed to make good sense. It would give the police time to circulate Zoran's picture to the locals, but that wasn't a big problem since it had been up on all the news channels almost daily since his arrest. Television coverage and newspaper articles about the impending trial appeared to be everywhere. Waiting a day would allow the police to canvass the marina and move on. Then, the whole cell could just ease out and move along behind all of the police searches.

Adam pointed out the location of the prison and the location of the ICC on the map. An obvious route could be seen on the map between the two facilities. Alek traced it with his fingers. Jasna and Emil nodded in agreement. The path had a couple of blind turns which might be able to be exploited. They would need to see the route first hand. The Audi had local license plates and would be a good vehicle to do a route recon in. It was as anonymous as any other commuter car in the city.

Looking at the route on the map, it was starting to look like they would need a vehicle of good size to break up the convoy. They would probably need one to block traffic as well. Two large vehicles could be tougher to acquire than one. Maybe it would and maybe it wouldn't. They would need to look around and see what there was to work with.

Emil looked out the window and noticed that the sun had tipped. There were still many hours until darkness, but there was no reason to rush into action either. They would need to be ready, both physically and mentally, not just logistically. There was no reason to get crazy about things now. The first order of business really seemed to be food. They should all get a good meal. They could do their individual tasks in the morning.

"Jasna, why don't you and Alek go out and find some food. If you pass a grocery, it might not hurt to do some shopping. Food and water for a couple days. It might also be good to get some first aid supplies, just not all in one stop."

"We'll go get supplies," Alek said. He looked ready to do something, or maybe anything.

Emil looked down at the duffle sitting on the floor next to the table.

"We also need to find a safe place for that thing."

Alek nodded and smiled.

CHAPTER TEN

E RIC GARVER POWERED the midnight blue Six Series BMW down
Zwolsestroat with commanding authority. Kristin Hughes sat in the
passenger seat and looked out on the northern suburbs of The Hague
as they whizzed by in a blur. The throaty 650i convertible was purposely
built to both respond to the road and make those in it look good. It was
a natural choice of vehicle for a man like Robert Dunn. Kristin's long
ponytail tossed in the wind and made Eric Garver pleased. Even if they
never found the nuclear device or the terrorists that took it, he was enjoying
his time with the American scientist very much.

The BMW hung a right onto Pompstatimsueg and cruised leisurely
past the entrance to the Scheveningen Prison. They proceeded south down
the main road and entered Nievue Scheveningse Bosjes. Garver slowed
the car as they crossed through the public park looking for good points
where one might set up an ambush. The split, two-lane road they were on
collapsed to one lane and the pair exited the south end of the park with
no good options.

The convertible continued south past the Nigerian Embassy, and the
embassy of the Republic of Kenya, before it found its way to the river.
Turning left, the two proceeded along the waterway all the way to its
connection with the N440. The Hubertus viaduct, as it was known to the
locals, ran back along the other side of the waterway. The two sightseers
were almost back to the embassies before the road turned south and
dropped down into The Hague.

Eric Garver swung the BMW left through the traffic intersection and
the two headed east along the Scheveningseweg. Kristy made a mental

note of the large Starbucks sign on the corner as it receded from view. The two skirted the northern side of the Zorgvliet as they cruised down the main road.

Eric brought the car to the right at a split in the road and then pulled into the outer entrance for the International Criminal Court. He continued past the driveway for The Hague Academy for International Law and steered the car out around the outside of the palace that the ICC was housed in.

All in all, it was a pretty direct route from the prison to the courthouse. There were minimal weak points in the route. It had no real blind intersections and few areas that provided good concealment. Even the areas where the route made its way through parks or alongside gardens, the route was wide open and had few intersections. There was no good place to conceal an attack vehicle or set up an effective ambush. It really was as clean of a transport route as one could ask for.

Eric and Kristin completed the route two more times and were attempting a third when Kristin pointed at the Starbucks sign and made a "pull it in" sign with her thumb. Eric nodded and hung a right instead of a left at the intersection. He ended up shooting past the first parking garage but arrested the big BMW in time to make the second one. It was a lovely day in the Netherlands city, and the walk back to the coffeehouse was pleasant. Kristin Hughes wore a happy expression on her face as she walked, and her tan Born Eryka flat sandals made a small click-clack noise on the sidewalk as they strolled. Eric could sense that she was right in her element. She seemed so content walking the streets of Europe or being driven around in a nice car. He suspected that her actual life was quite the opposite. Most people's lives were not a reflection of what they showed the world.

Eric opened the door to the American beanery so that Kristin could enter. He nodded a gesture and proceeded in behind her. The flashy American coffeehouse would have been his last choice in the upscale neighborhood. The coffee was not what any civilized European would consider paying multiple euros for, but lady's choice was lady's choice.

Kristin made her way straight to the counter where the barista stood and ordered two double espressos. Eric Garver stood quietly and made a face that suggested he was pleased. The two made their way outside and found a small table where the whole intersection was visible. The barista followed shortly after and placed two small espresso cups on the table with them. Eric thanked the young lady and she wandered off, seemingly pleased with herself.

Eric and Kristin sat quietly and waited for the small doses of caffeine to cool. Eric took in Kristin's fashionable attire a second time. She was quick with finding shops to buy clothes and seemed unbothered by traveling bag free. It was probably just another reflection of her lifestyle. He thought about that for a moment, and then considered that her credit card bill must be outrageous. He considered again and concluded that it must be part of her compensation package. Americans were famous for such things.

Kristin Hughes took in the traffic coming and going through the intersection onto Scheveningseweg. It was almost midday and the traffic was still fairly light. Anywhere in America, it would be gridlock at this time of day. She didn't miss the traffic in the U.S. It could be a pain, especially in downtown Vegas. She usually made her way around the outside of "America's Playground" just so she didn't have to deal with traffic. Whenever she wanted to go down to The Strip and have a little fun, she called an Uber. It was way easier to be dropped off in front than it was to park and walk. If you have the unfortunate experience of parking all the way at the far end of the MGM Grand parking garage for fight night, which she had, it was an easy half-mile walk just to get to the casino. Well, it certainly seemed like it was that far. No, being driven up to the front door was worth every cent you paid for it. And being driven around Europe by a handsome German man wasn't too bad, either.

Kristin turned her head gracefully and inspected her counterpart. He was inhaling the first half of his espresso. A crisp black suit, a crisp white shirt, no tie, and a neutral expression. The same package she had been introduced to on the runway of the airbase. As near as she could tell, he had two suits. They were the same suit, matched to the same white shirt. The shoes were complementary of the suit but built for running and fighting. She assumed that somewhere in his ensemble there was a weapon. Well, actually, she knew that there was a weapon. She just didn't know where it was currently holstered.

Kristin liked that the close-cropped blond hair and wire rimmed glasses made Eric look studious. It was appropriate. He seemed to be studying the situation around him continuously. She also liked that all his numerous tiny scars didn't detract from his natural good looks. They also failed to make him look like a mercenary. She was always drawn to good-looking and capable men. She seemed to collect them.

Kristin Hughes was a great many things. She was capable, she was intelligent, she was well-spoken, she was sexy, she was immensely calm and capable under great pressure, and she was non-judgmental. Those were great qualities. But, all those things aside, she was not the one thing she really needed to be in most of the violent situations she seemed to continually find herself in. She was not a competent operator. She could fight masterfully while wearing a karate gi. She could shoot exceptionally well on a range. She had adequate stealth and good situational awareness. She just didn't think that in her brain she had *it*. She could hold her own in a street fight or gun battle, but she didn't do it naturally. So, she collected operators like other women collected jewelry.

Pretty much every commando, assassin, mercenary or soldier that she had worked with had tried to get her to go that last little bit of the way along. None of them had completely succeeded. Her boss, ex-Navy SEAL and still active operator Lou Stenson, had concluded that at her core she didn't possess the violence of action necessary for a person of such a specialty. He knew, as every other instructor on the planet knew, that you couldn't make someone violent without imposing other problems. It was better to let it go, if violence wasn't in them. Kristin could be quite violent, but she wasn't a violent person. Operators, by their own nature, were not violent people. They did, however, need to be able to instantly employ the violence of action inherent in them.

As soon as her boss had come to this conclusion, Doctor Kristin Hughes was no longer let out on her own. She was escorted. Between the DOE, FBI, CIA, Secret Service, and a host of foreign country security agencies that owed her favors, there was always someone to watch over her. Sometimes having a keeper made Kristin chafe, but there wasn't much to do about it. Currently, that position was being filled by the enigmatic German GSG-9 commando, Eric Garver.

"So, what do you think of the route?"

The German's voice pulled Kristin from her meditation.

"Which part?"

"All of it. I think that it allows for only two or three weak points."

Kristin thought about all the driving they had been doing. Apparently, she had started to just watch the countryside go by while they drove. Her due diligence to the task at-hand had escaped her. But she had paid enough attention at the beginning to be able to answer his question. That was good.

"The parks seem to be out. They're too wide open to be useful. The section by the embassies, on the north side of the river, was good enough. They would need a good escape plan to utilize that area. Frankly, the intersection in front of us is as good as it's going to get. If they wait until they are down by the ICC, the whole place is too congested."

Eric took off his glasses and rubbed a spot off the left lens. Sliding the glasses back on his face, he smiled.

"That was pretty much what I was thinking also."

He smiled at her again in reassurance. He wasn't exactly sure why. She wasn't sure about it, either, but she liked it. Kristin finished off her coffee and sat the cup back on its napkin in a gentle fashion.

"So, you think it could be done here, too?"

"Well, it has merits. You could conduct a good hit-and-run and be on your way fairly quickly. Where the embassy area is good for the box-in attack, this area is good for the smash-and-grab."

Kristin laughed, though it came out as more of a giggle.

"You call them smash-and-grabs over here, too?"

Eric Garver smiled broadly for the first time since they had met.

"I'm pretty sure that they call them that everywhere."

Kristin made a face, as if to suggest that she was being made fun of. Eric Garver smiled again, as to suggest she was right.

"What do you say that we take one more trip around the circuit, and then go visit our friend Thomas Claes for a quiet conversation?"

"That sounds good. After that, we can find a nice café and have something to eat."

Eric stood promptly and assisted Kristin with her chair. It was her assessment that most hardened men were also quite gentlemanly. The two sides of the social coin naturally complemented one another. Kristin stepped off, as to start the walk back to Robert's car.

"By the way."

"Yes."

Kristin paused too quickly, like a high school girl waiting on a compliment. She instantly chastised herself for it.

"All the cafés are in France."

Kristin squinted and squinched her face to protest being picked on, and then began walking again. Eric followed along with an unassuming look on his face.

The final trip around the circuit showed no new ideas or attack options. The two stopped and wandered around the embassy area north of the river for a time. They did some casual window shopping to blend into the crowd. Eric Garver could see some options in the area, but not as many as he had seen in the main intersection they had been at earlier.

The two drove the rest of the route and pulled into the main entrance for the International Criminal Court. Eric Garver parked the car and put the top up. The two made their way to the front receiving area of the palace-like building. Kristin looked at the information board and the endless list of offices that the place contained. The board was almost as tall as the wall it was on and seemed to be broken down alphabetically.

Thankfully, Eric Garver had been to the ICC before. He knew where he was headed. He collected up the American scientist and headed off down a non-descript, yet ornate hallway which looked like all the other hallways. The German led her toward the rear of the building and up a wide set of stairs to the second floor. At the end of the hall they were in was a large series of doors marked *Security*. Eric Garver made his way to the fifth one of the uniform doors and paused.

He rapped on the door twice, and then opened it. A stylish receptionist sat properly behind a desk in the middle of a square room and smiled as Herr Becke and his guest entered.

"Good day, Herr Becke. Are you here to see Herr Claes? I don't believe he has anything on his schedule for the next several hours."

"Yes, please. I apologize for stopping by without a proper appointment."

"That is no problem, Herr Becke."

Herbert Becke introduced Kristin to the secretary named Emmanuelle, and the two exchanged pleasantries. Emmanuelle picked up the phone, pointed at the door to the next office, and smiled. Both Herbert and Kristin nodded and proceeded in that direction. Entering the security man's office, the two found Thomas Claes. He seemed much more suspect to their appearance than his secretary.

"Doctor Hughes. Herr Becke. How are you enjoying your continued stay in The Hague?" Claes said it in such a way as to impart to the two that he was surprised that they were still there.

"Your country is lovely. I'm enjoying it very much, thank you."

Kristin spoke in a touristy voice. She sounded happy to give a good review. Herr Becke sat in a chair quietly next to the one she had taken up.

"Well, that's very nice. Now, what brings you here today?"

Thomas Claes' voice was level and smooth, but it had an undercurrent of annoyance to it.

"We would like to discuss a theory that has been developing since we last spoke."

Herbert Becke's voice was all business.

"Proceed."

"We have been revisiting all of the information that has been collected to date, and we have a theory about the near future. One you might find disturbing."

Becke was trying to be direct, but coy.

"And that theory would be?"

"That the group Zoran Savić is associated with is on its way to The Hague to break him out of his incarceration and then flee the country."

Kristin watched studiously as Thomas Claes turned pale and then bleached white. He started to physically shake, which made his fat jiggle and begin to ripple his frumpy suit. She was pretty sure that he was going to melt down if he didn't arrest his agitation quickly. He attempted to do just that. It took a moment for him to calm.

"A prison break? From the International Criminal Court?"

"Yes. Most likely, it will occur during the prisoner transfer from the prison facility."

"Are you insane? This is the International Criminal Court. We don't have prisoners escape us!"

"Herr Claes, I can appreciate that it sounds suspect. But these people are the type to attempt such a feat."

Kristin's voice was clinical, but her professional tone did nothing to curb Thomas Claes' belligerence.

"Madam. This is the Netherlands. It is not America. We do not tolerate such things here."

"Herr Claes, one question."

Thomas Claes focused on Herbert Becke, who was still sitting calmly in his chair. His calmness was opposite that of his now more-animated American counterpart.

"Yes, Herr Becke."

"When is Zoran Savić scheduled to be brought to the ICC for arraignment?"

"In two days. At just after the lunch hour."

"Thank you for your time, Herr Claes. We won't keep you any longer."

Herbert Becke stood promptly, in the standard German fashion. Kristin Hughes followed suit, though slower and with reluctance. They made their way to the door and left quietly. Kristin was sure that, as they made their way across the parking lot, Thomas Claes was still fuming.

CHAPTER ELEVEN

ROBERT DUNN'S APPROPRIATED Gulfstream made a slow decent into the Sarajevo International Airport and touched down without as much as a gallop. The private jet rolled down the well-used runway and turned off on a smaller taxi path that led to the non-commercial hangars on the far side of the airfield.

Dunn stepped off the plane with the two pilots and gave the place a good hard once over. To his pleasant surprise, the war-torn capital didn't look nearly as bad as he had suspected it would. The airport terminal was freshly painted and in fine repair. The runway was the same. The Jerusalem of the Balkans, as it was known in some circles, had done much to repair the devastation suffered from the Bosnian war of the early nineties. The post-war construction he was seeing had been money well spent.

The city and its surroundings rested deep in the Sarajevo Valley and was not as big a city as the 1984 Olympic television coverage had made it out to be. To Dunn's trained eye it looked almost sleepy. Maybe the information he had glossed through on the Lonely Planet website was up to date? He hoped it was. He didn't want to have to shoot his way out of Eastern Europe.

Robert Dunn separated himself from the pilots and headed for a nearby taxi stand. The relatively new looking lead taxi fired up its engine upon seeing him head in its direction. He climbed into the back seat and smiled at the driver.

"English?"

"Yes, I do."

"Dragic Bakery. On Ploča."

The taxi driver thought for a moment and then nodded his head vigorously.

"Yes. It's north of the Vajećnica."

"Could you take me there, please?"

The taxi driver nodded and dropped the car into drive. The car sped off from the taxi stand with reckless abandon and headed out of the airport gate into traffic as if it all would simply stop for him. Dunn considered putting on his seatbelt, but decided against it.

"CIA?"

The taxi driver looked at Dunn through the rearview mirror with a big smile on his face.

"No. Why? Do I look like CIA?"

"A casually dressed American, arriving in a private jet, wanting to get a loaf of bread. You're not a backpacking college student, no?"

Robert Dunn laughed happily. "All right, you've got me. I'm CIA."

"I knew it. What are you in Sarajevo for?"

Dunn gave the taxi driver a conspiratorial look and smiled a shifty smile.

"Can't say. You know how it is."

The taxi driver laughed and switched lanes. He continued his push through traffic and switched the conversation over to something about the influx of Syrian refuges coming from the Middle East conflict. Apparently, the large mass of displaced Muslim men has been doing as much damage in Sarajevo as they had everywhere else. It was a sad state of affairs.

Dunn replied just enough to the cabby's conversation to keep him fixed on the Muslim issue. He had been accused of being CIA on several occasions. Oddly, every time it had been in Eastern Europe. He blamed it on the slow uptake of the television. Eastern Europe was still a couple decades behind current U.S. programming. Okay, maybe not a couple decades, but they were definitely behind everyone else.

As the taxi driver weaved in and out of the heavy traffic, Robert Dunn watched the scenery outside his window. In deference to the driver's backpacker comment, there did seem to be a lot of Westerners walking the main sidewalks and gardened areas of the city.

The online guidebook Dunn had looked at during his flight east from the Netherlands had mentioned that the city of Sarajevo had been nominated as the European Capital of Culture for 2014. It seemed that the tourist trade had locked onto that bandwagon. Sarajevo was also mentioned on the list of best cities in the world. Dunn had assumed before he arrived that the city's inclusion in the world's best list was a mistake. Now the idea seemed to have some merit. The official buildings still had that cold Soviet feel to them, but behind that one could feel the influence of the Ottomans and the Austria-Hungarian Empire that once resided here. Really, the place didn't seem that bad.

The taxi driver was still going on about something in his semi-broken English as he continued to weave through traffic. The city was full and busy. The car came to an abrupt stop and slid into a parking spot on the west section of the street. The section of town they had stopped in seemed too commercial to Dunn for a bakery, so he gave the driver a quizzical look.

"Dragic Bakery, yes?"

"Yes."

The taxi driver pointed to an alleyway, just visible through the maze of traffic on Ploča.

"Bakery is at end of alley there. It is actually on corner of Mlini, across from guesthouse."

Dunn looked at the driver with curiosity.

"So why didn't you just take me to Mlini?"

"You ask for Ploča specific. I figure you come here before."

"Fine. Stay here. I'll need a ride back to the airport in a little bit."

"You pay euros?"

The taxi driver smiled in that way that most Eastern Europeans do when they are extorting someone.

"Deal. Euros."

"I'll be right here when you are done."

Robert Dunn peeled off a hundred euro bill and gave it to the taxi man.

"I will be back in thirty minutes or so."

"Yes, sir." The taxi man smiled and pocketed the note.

Robert Dunn crossed the busy street and made his way to the alley. Moving slowly into the opening, he was relieved to see that it was a fairly wide walkway with shops on either side. Locals came and went from the shops in an everyday sort of way. Maybe this section of town wasn't so removed from the residential section of town he had imagined.

The CIA assassin made his way down the alley to the far end in a leisurely, but straightforward manner. No one seemed to notice or care that he was there. No one at all. That made him comfortable enough to proceed inside the shop when he came to it.

The bakery looked like it had been in the same location forever. It was the absolute picture of lived-in space. Two young women went about setting out loaves of bread and conversing with customers. The customers seemed the type of people who frequented the shop every day. They came in and picked out loaves, exchanged some chit-chat, and then left. The smell of the fresh bread was intoxicating and made Dunn instantly hungry. One of the young women came over to where Dunn was standing and said something to him in what he guessed was Serbian. He smiled back at the young lady pleasantly.

"English?"

The woman smiled kindly and nodded.

"Yes, sir."

Robert Dunn returned her smile with the same warmth she had shown.

"Ranko Dragic?"

"He is the store's owner."

The woman's voice was pleasant and unassuming.

"May I speak with him?"

The young woman turned instantly suspicious, but her pleasant countenance stayed intact.

"This way, sir."

Robert Dunn was led into the rear of the bakery, where an older man was pounding out a big wad of dough with his fists. Flour puffed up in the air each time he beat his hand into the mound. The flour hung in the air for a moment and then settled back down to evenly cover everything in the area. The man went about his work in a repetitive way that put Dunn instantly at ease.

The young woman spoke something to the man in their native language, and he stopped his work. Dusting off his meaty hands with a cursory whack on his apron, the man turned to face them both. The young woman smiled and turned, heading back the way she had come in. The two men now stood alone in the bakery's kitchen.

"Mr. Ranko Dragic?"

The man slapped his apron a second time, a large puff of flour wafted into the air around him.

"Yes."

"My name is Robert Dunn. I have it on good authority that you are the man to talk to about *private matters* from the old Yugoslavian days."

Dunn's tone and countenance were both measured and moderate. Ranko Dragic looked at him sternly for several seconds, taking in his measure.

"You're CIA. No?"

Robert Dunn didn't answer the question. Instead, he gave the man the slightest of shrugs. The old baker took in his measure a second time, before waving his hand at a table and chairs to one side. Both men sat and Ranko retrieved two glasses and a water pitcher from the table.

"The bakery has been here for three generations. It is because of the water. This water is the best water for bread making."

Robert Dunn picked up the glass and downed about a third of the liquid. The water had a definite taste to it. He presumed it was from minerals natural to the water table.

"So – what may I help you with, Mr. Dunn?"

"I was wondering what you could tell me about a man named Zoran Savić. It's rumored that the two of you worked together in the past."

The man rubbed the bridge of his nose with a meaty hand and thought.

"Zoran and I were in the same military unit during the Bosnian-Croatian conflict. I left the service and came back to the bakery. He went in another direction."

"That's what I am interested in most. That other direction. What's his recent activity like and what are his associates all about?"

The old Serbian baker stared at Dunn sternly for another short time, deciding what he wanted to say.

"You want to know about the Sons of Sava? Hmm, must be that business on the television."

Dunn was instantly curious.

"The Sons of Sava?"

"Zoran Savić's group. The name Savić means son of Sava. Since there are two Savićs in the group, they are known as the Sons of Sava."

Robert Dunn's hunch had paid off. He had found the right man.

"Actually," the old baker continued, "they're all relatives of one person or another. That's the way such things go in these lands. There is Zoran, he is the definite leader of the group. His cousin Emil Savić is second. Emil is somewhat of a hothead, as you Americans say. A construction worker by trade, both of his parents died during the conflicts. Then there is Adam Pavlovic and his wife Dunja. Adam and Dunja are also bakers. They also have no parents left, due to the conflicts. Adam is Zoran's cousin as well. Jasna Pavlovic is Adam Pavlovic's cousin, and a schoolteacher, I think. Again, no parents left alive. And then there is Aleksander Lukic. His is the youngest of the group. He is an auto mechanic over in the north suburbs for most of the time. His father is still alive. He lives in one of those houses for the pensioners."

Dunn processed all of the information as the old baker spoke quietly. He scribbled down the names of the group members as the old man went along and just stored the rest in his head. After sufficient time, Ranko continued.

"The group never seemed to be able to let go and go back to their old lives. Too much war, I think. They gather and then clash with groups from across the border. There are men and women to the north that are the same way. Zoran has spent the last several years combating with a Croatian dissident named Marko Juraš. Juraš leads a small band of ultra-right wing, pro-Croatians. It is rumored that he's mad that he was displaced from his family lands in Bosnia. His family supposedly had lands to the north, over by Doboj."

Dunn finished scribbling notes and caught up with Ranko Dragic's pause. They both drank some water before Ranko continued on.

"Zoran and his group are the same as Marko Juraš and his group. They cannot see that they fight for nothing. The borders have been drawn where they are. Time has moved on."

Ranko rolled his hands in a way that implied that it was all for naught.

"So, they want to unite Yugoslavia or something?" Dunn's question was earnest and Ranko gave him no rebuke.

"No. That's not a possibility. I don't think that it would work out, even if it could be done. There is too much misery in the soil now. Frankly, I don't know what they fight for."

"Do you think they are the type to use heavy weapons?"

Ranko's eyes narrowed on the CIA man.

"What type of weapon?"

Robert Dunn scanned the room quietly, making sure that there was no one hanging out next to a door or window.

"Nuclear weapons. Small nuclear weapons."

Ranko's expression escaped his face for the briefest of seconds, before he recovered.

"Are there any small nuclear weapons?"

It seemed like an honest question, though more rhetorical than actual. Dunn nodded anyway.

"Yes, there are. Zoran Savić and his group stole one from a military base in Germany a couple days ago."

Ranko Dragic's face turned ashen for several seconds. He drank his water and then refilled his glass. As he spoke, he didn't look at his guest, but kept his eyes on his water glass.

"This explains all the news on the television."

"Zoran was captured and sent to The Hague to stand trial for war crimes. One of the women you mentioned was killed in a gunfight. The rest of his group and the weapon are missing."

Ranko continued to look at the water glass.

"Mr. Dunn, I would think you should find this group, before they do something that cannot be undone."

"I agree. That's what brought me here today. Are his comrades the type that will want to free Zoran Savić? Do they have blind loyalty?"

"Yes."

"Do you think they will use the weapon?"

"Yes. Men and women such as this will use whatever they can find. At whatever the cost."

"What would you think is their next move?"

"If they returned without Zoran, they are holed up in the Tuzla area, north of the city. If they did not return, then they are in the act of freeing Zoran. To be honest, I would think it to be the second one."

"You think they will go free him?"

"It is that blind loyalty that you spoke of."

Dunn finished his notes and placed the note pad in his pocket. Ranko

Dragic broke his vision away from the water glass and drank some of the liquid.

"Mr. Dunn, you seem like a hard man. These men and women are also hard. I would not give them any leniency. They live double lives and are good at being manipulative. I would not take them at face value."

"That's good advice, Mr. Dragic. I thank you for taking time to speak with me."

The two men stood and shook hands. Ranko Dragic's meaty hand swallowed up Robert Dunn's. The CIA man turned and headed for the door, pausing after several steps.

"Should I leave a certain way or avoid anyone on the way out?"

The old Serbian baker smiled broadly. It wasn't the soviet block any longer, but he appreciated the man's caution.

"No, you will be fine. As will I. Stop and buy some loaves of bread as you go. You'll find them quite expensive, but hopefully worth your journey."

Robert Dunn smiled knowingly at the old baker. Nothing in life, or intelligence work, was ever free. He nodded in agreement and turned for the door.

"I'm sure that whatever they cost; they will be worth every penny."

CHAPTER TWELVE

ALEKSANDER LUKIC AND the blue Opel puttered down the street at a respectable pace for city traffic. In the passenger seat, Jasna took pictures of the scenery with a stolen camera. The two looked the same as every other tourist couple out seeing the sights. The weather was beautiful, with blue skies and none of the customary onshore breeze.

Alek made his way north up the coast. The day had brought many a native out to the Scheveningen beach, and the area around the beach's entrance was uncustomarily full of traffic. Jasna shrugged her shoulders at Alek as he maneuvered through the small bit of congestion, as if to say *be happy we're not downtown.* Alek nodded his head and weaved through the traffic without any rebuttal.

The two Bosnian sightseers turned inland and headed for the prison. Sitting on a raised piece of land and denoted on numerous street signs, it wasn't really a problem to find. Both Alek and Jasna wondered if the prison wasn't something of a tourist attraction. It seemed too good an idea not to explore, so Alek turned the Opel up the drive and headed toward the main parking area. Stopping in front of a large information billboard they read all the signs one at a time. No casual visitors. No guests allowed in the prison block. Identification necessary beyond the main gate. And others denoting items that were not allowed on prison grounds. It appeared that enough other people had wondered the same thing and had stopped to ask, so prison officials were forced to put up the big signs. Well, it had been a stretch to think they might have just walked in.

Alek noticed another couple in the parking area taking pictures of the prison and pointed them out to Jasna. She instantly nodded in agreement.

Alek put the car back into drive and pulled it into the first available parking space in the open parking lot.

The two Bosnian terrorists exited the car and casually strolled to the far end of the parking area. In the middle of a grass section off the end of the parking was an informational poster, like the kind used at European historical locations. Jasna took a picture of it. She took another, being sure to get the words on the poster in focus. Alek walked a couple of feet to a low railing which blocked a path running from the observation area to a door built into the fortress wall. A fair piece of the prison was originally a fortress, and the spot where Jasna was standing offered a good view of the prison wall and the main entrance. Jasna snapped off numerous pictures of Alek with the real target in focus in the background. Deciding that they had stayed long enough, the two turned and made their way back to their car. No cameras from the prison turned to follow them. No one came out to ask them any questions. As they got back into the Opel, another couple was getting out of their car with a camera and a cheap hotel map. Jasna and Alek eyed the couple at the same time and laughed.

The two made their way back down the main drive and turned onto the road to continue their sightseeing. Working their way south through a park, they came to an area just north of the canal. Alek pulled the car into a parking space and Jasna wandered a short way down the sidewalk to feed change into a parking meter. The two did the tourist stroll through the middle of the area. They took pictures in front of some of the shops, obtaining good photos of both the Nigerian Embassy and the Kenyan Embassy. Walking back to the car, Jasna commented that she liked the Kenyan building better than the Nigerian building. It was older and more pleasing. Alek added some comments and, for a moment, forgot that he was an internationally wanted fugitive.

The pair hopped back into the Opel and continued on their way. The drive out and around the canal onto the Hubertus viaduct was industrial and of no use to their needs. When the pair reached the intersection of the main roadway and Scheveningseweg, the road which led off to the International Criminal Court, Alek pulled off and brought the car to a full stop. He looked in all directions as quickly as he could and decided as the traffic light changed that it needed to be looked at more thoroughly. Pulling back into traffic, he made his way through the traffic light and then doubled back at his first opportunity. Alek took a wide arc around the intersection the second time and ended up coming at the intersection from a different direction.

The intersection of the two main roads was wide and heavily traveled in all directions. Alek maneuvered the Opel into a parking garage and the two got out to take a walk. They walked out of the garage at street level and paused at the intersection to wait for the pedestrian crossing signal. Alek propped himself against a low concrete retaining wall and pulled out a map he had found in the Opel's glove box. Jasna took numerous pictures of the intersection and pointed out different interesting items, as any tourist might do.

While Alek fiddled with the map, he looked over top of it and inspected the traffic traveling through the intersection. The traffic contained vehicles of all shapes and sizes. He spent most of his time paying attention to the larger vehicles. They seemed to be coming primarily from the south behind where he was sitting. Not nearly as many came from the viaduct or up the street where the court was located. Alek seemed pleased with what he saw as he stood up. Jasna snapped a couple more pictures and turned to look at her partner in crime.

The two made their way back to the garage and retrieved the car. It took a moment for traffic to clear enough for them to get out onto the street. They headed east along the wide main street which led to the International Criminal Court. As they had expected, the roadway offered no real places of opportunity for the team to ambush the prison transport vehicle. It was basically just a straight run from the intersection they had scouted to the entrance of the ICC.

Alek puttered on by the main drive to the palace which the ICC was housed in and kept going. Jasna looked over at Alek as he passed by the entrance turn. He shook his head and kept driving. Making a wide swing around the outside of the sprawling court complex, they headed west back toward the intersection where they had previously stopped. Aleksander Lukic took a little time and drove through the intersection from all four directions. He wanted to get a feel for how the traffic lights changed and how the vehicles moved. The more he made his way around the spot, the more he became convinced that it was the right location for what they were planning. It had a good hit point and a good avenue of escape once the chaos started. It was the most functional location they had seen all day. It was the right spot.

Alek slid the Opel into an open space along the edge of the street and shut the engine off.

"What do you think?"

Jasna looked over at her friend and gave him an inquisitive expression.

"You mean you're finally curious enough to ask, Alek?"

"Funny, Jasna. Funny."

"I think this intersection area is the best location. We need to make sure that the transport is actually going to come through here, but otherwise I would think this is the best place."

"Me too. We lay in wait, and when the transport vehicles come into the intersection, we take them head on. Once they are immobile, we free our comrade and head out the same way we came in."

Jasna nodded her head as Alek spoke. His outline made good sense to her. She could see it all play out in front of her as Alek brought it to life with his words. The crumpled metal, the smoke and screeching sounds, the gunfire, and the engines of the get-away vehicles. It looked just like a movie scene as it came to life in her imagination.

"I like your idea. This plan is a good plan." Jasna spoke with reassurance.

"It seems sound. We should go back and tell it to the others. I think they'll agree."

Jasna Pavlovic seconded his statement by shaking her head. It all appeared to be quite sound. They would liberate their imprisoned leader and then go home, where later they would nuke their neighbors to the north. Jasna smiled a thin and distant smile.

Alek put the car back into gear and waited for several cars to pass before pulling out into traffic. He moved along as any tourist would, looking at the sights sliding by the window.

CHAPTER THIRTEEN

ERIC GARVER STOOD in the middle of the hotel room's large terrace and looked out towards the North Sea. He was a natural early riser. He could tell that this was not the style of his American counterpart. That was fine with him. Doctor Hughes sleeping in gave him quiet time to think things through.

Eric was naturally an analytical type of person. He found that thinking through everything he planned allowed him to find less obvious avenues which might be exploited. Alternate means of looking at whatever problem he had in front of him. He liked being analytical. It kept him cool under fire. Mostly because the process of thinking things out presented him with multiple options.

On this particular morning he had been analyzing alternate avenues of approach. Not for himself and Doctor Hughes, but for the prisoner transport from the holding facility to the International Criminal Court. He had studied the maps of the city in detail and could not discern a better route than the one they had driven the day before. None of the other available paths through the city seemed to offer a more direct or comfortable route. The one they had initially worked out still made the most sense to him.

Just to make sure, he called Thomas Claes' office to check with him. Claes was also an early riser and liked to be in his office before others. It probably allowed him to get work done in an unbothered manner. Eric had found today's Thomas Claes to be somewhat more accommodating than he had been in previous meetings. That was a great way to start his day in and of itself.

After allowing the Belgium security man to drink his espresso and entertain some general conversation regarding the weather, he confirmed the travel route and that the transfer was still being planned for tomorrow at midday. The security man seemed almost jovial as he explained that the notice of transfer had been released to all the local newspapers and would be part of their morning circulation. He explained that it was standard practice to inform the shop owners and city folk of the increased police patrols in the area while the transfer was happening. Sometimes people would wait and watch the procession pass. Sometimes crowds would gather at the ICC building to see the prisoner being led in. It was all a pretty standard affair in The Hague.

Eric Garver, a consummate professional, cringed at the idea of news articles and crowds, but thanked Thomas Claes for his help. He was staring out at the North Sea as Kristin Hughes came gliding out onto the terrace. She was wearing a silk robe emblazoned with the initials of the hotel.

"Good morning, Eric. You look deep in thought?" Her voice was soft and made the seasoned professional smile.

"Good morning, Kristin. I was just going over the transit route in my mind, looking for missed possibilities."

Kristin sat and poured a large cup of coffee from a carafe on the table. Situating herself in the chair, she leveled a conspiratorial gaze at her German comrade.

"You suspect that there is a better way for the prison transport to make its way through town?"

"No. I talked with Herr Claes this morning and he confirmed the route that the transport will travel. Apparently, they even feel comfortable sharing the information with the local newspapers. Netherland's efficiency."

Kristin sipped at the top of her steaming mug but waited a second or two to give her response. She sensed that the last part was bait. If so, she wasn't taking it.

"Well, at least the route is confirmed. That's some good news."

"I suppose so."

"What say once I'm properly attired, we go out for a drive? You know, just to calm your sense of impending dread."

Kristin lowered her coffee cup and smiled up at Eric in a way that little children or lovers tend to do. It made Eric Garver equal parts happy and uneasy.

"We have already driven the route."

"True. But one more time won't hurt anything and maybe something will have changed overnight. It can't hurt. Besides, sitting around waiting isn't good for anyone."

That was true. Eric Garver knew it. Waiting was something mandatory in his business. It was also something that did nothing but exacerbate problems. Waiting was always bad for the hunter and good for the prey.

The German commando looked out to the sea. He knew that she was right. He just didn't want to admit it for some reason.

"What about the weapon?"

"What about it?" Kristin asked, wondering why her counterpart was changing the conversation.

"Your real goal is recovering the nuclear weapon, yet you seem focused on a man already in custody."

Kristin sat her coffee cup on the table and looked at the German man's back in a suspect fashion.

"The nuke is most definitely with the terrorists. If the terrorists are here to free their leader, then the nuke is also here with them. When we find the terrorists, we will find the nuke. If, for some reason yet unknown to us, they have offloaded the weapon to a courier, then Robert is in the best place to intercede. Since we have not received any flash traffic from Robert, the nuke is here. Find the group. Find the nuke."

"How is it put in your country? You seem to be giving them a lot of leash to run around on."

"Without a door-to-door, racially profiled search of the city, I really don't see how that can be helped."

"I suppose you're correct."

"I don't know that I'm right. I just hope that I'm not wrong."

Eric Garver turned and faced her wearing an expression of compromise.

"Valid point."

Kristin Hughes nodded at her counterpart in a way that suggested equal compromise.

"Thank you."

Kristin stood and shoved her chair back under the table.

"Let me get properly attired and we can go see the sights."

Eric Garver nodded and smiled. Kristin turned and disappeared into the hotel room. Eric turned and looked out toward the sea. The sky was blue and cloudless. The water, as near as he could tell, was calm. None of the scenery had the look of a terrorist smash-and-grab or of a potential nuclear catastrophe. That was usually the case with such things. Things were always quiet at the beginning.

Garver walked over to the table and poured a small cup of coffee. He would rather have a cappuccino at this time of day, but there seemed to be none without room service. He made a face at the American-style black liquid in the white china cup, then tossed it into his mouth. It would just have to do for now.

To Eric Garver's complete surprise, it only took a reasonable fifteen minutes for Dr. Kristin Hughes to reappear in the hotel room's main salon looking completely stunning. He had no idea where she had procured the blue sundress or the wide brimmed white hat, but they suited her. Kristin smiled politely as her German friend presented his shocked face. She was a traveler. She knew how to pack a bag for all situations.

The two made their way back to the car they had borrowed from Dunn and headed out into The Hague. They were working their way along Stratenlaan when Kristin's iPhone chirped. She pulled the secure cellphone from her catch and poked the home button. The home screen of the smartphone displayed a text alert from Robert Dunn. Kristin tilted her head to one side in an Audrey Hepburn "Roman Holiday" sort of way. The gesture caught Eric Garver's attention.

"What is it?"

"I just got a text from Robert."

The German looked over at her as he slid the car through the morning traffic. Kristin poked the text icon with her finger and waited for the display to refresh.

"It says that he found out what he went to Sarajevo for and is headed back our way. He hopes to have more information for us by the time he gets here. He has to check with The Group first."

Eric Garver slid the BMW over into an outside lane to pass a slower moving Citroen.

"That sounds good. It also sounds like it substantiates your hypothesis about the weapon being here."

Kristin really liked that he was a trained killer but was still able to use words like hypothesis. She stuffed the phone back into the small catch and snapped the clasp closed.

"It would seem so."

Eric Garver expertly maneuvered the sleek BMW back to the Scheveningseweg intersection from the water side and pulled it into the valet parking line at the Crowne Plaza Den Haag Promenade. Kristin made a quizzical face as the crisply dressed valet descended upon the passenger door. Her well-spoken driver pointed back at the Starbucks sign and smiled.

"It's called a cappuccino. American coffee is awful."

Kristin smiled politely and stepped out of the vehicle. The morning sun had warmed the city and a light breeze coming in from the ocean was now a welcome addition. Kristin adjusted her sun hat so the wide brim shaded her eyes. It was a cloudless, blue sky day.

The two retrieved drinks and made their way to a large terrace that looked out over the now full intersection. Vehicles of all shapes and sizes appeared and disappeared as the traffic signals cycled through their stop-and-go rhythm. Eric found an empty table out by the roadway and pulled out a chair so Kristin could be seated. He took up station in an adjacent seat and the two watched the traffic as they waited for their beverages to cool.

Across the Scheveningseweg from the coffeehouse, Emil Savić watched the two sit. For some reason he couldn't explain, the two made him nervous.

"What is it Emil?"

Adam Pavlovic looked at the terrorist cell's de facto leader and waited. He could tell that something was off, but he wasn't sure what had just changed.

"The two that just sat down at that American coffee shop across the street. The man and the woman. I don't know. They make me concerned."

"Do you know them?"

"No. I've never seen either of them before. It's just how they carry themselves. Unless I miss my guess, the man is military. And the woman, she's no casual tourist."

Adam Pavlovic picked up his 35mm Pentax camera and pushed the lens out as far as it would go. The two were far enough away so that they were at the end of the camera's focal length, but the image finally managed to come into focus. He blasted off a half-dozen pictures of the two and then sat the camera back down.

"They look okay to me, but we'll find out who they are anyway."

Adam Pavlovic seemed to lack the concern of his counterpart, but Emil shook his head in rebuke.

"There is something about them that's off."

Adam gave him a quizzical look.

"This is The Hague. I'm sure that there are any number of random ex-military and black coats lurking about."

Adam had heard the term black coats on a television show about spies as a child and had come to use it whenever possible.

"I'm sure there are, Adam. Somehow, I think this is something different."

"How so?"

"I don't really know how. I just sense it. Even when we were boys, Zoran always said to trust my instincts. He would say, 'your gut knows when things are off.'"

Adam nodded to Emil. He had heard Zoran Savić say the same thing in the past. Zoran always knew when things were going off. He just did. Well, up until the last time.

"Relax for now, Emil. We'll go back and find out who the two of them really are. Then we'll know what to do."

Emil nodded and Adam Pavlovic turned and walked away from the intersection. As they walked, Emil looked back over his shoulder at the intersection and the two strangers drinking coffee.

"Aleksander has a good eye. This spot will be perfect for our plans."

Adam nodded his approval.

"I agree."

CHAPTER FOURTEEN

THE EARLY MORNING air in suburban Alexandria, outside Washington D.C., has a sweet scent and a dewy texture. The type of dew that left a thick film on your car's windshield. Nathanial Baker, United States District Court chief justice, District of Columbia, observed the other cars in the driveway as he parked. Each of them had sat long enough to develop that thin film of dew. It would seem he was late.

Justice Baker made his way through the internal door's ID challenge and retina scanner and proceeded up the stairs to the second floor. Another series of key codes and scans and the heavy blast door in front of him swung free. The opened door allowed him entrance to the secured meeting space.

The game room, as it was known to the men that utilized it, was a repurposed FBI safe house. When it became a de-listed cold war property, the director had grabbed it and black booked it. It was transitioned into an extra-secure meeting place for people of proper clearance. The repurposing had been done at the behest of the president and was now the home base of operations for The Group.

The Group had been a brainchild of President Jackson. In a post 9-11 world, where the United States intelligence community had become utterly bogged down in a sea of jurisdictional and authoritative turf wars, something had to be done. It was originally thought that the creation of the Director of National Intelligence, would solve this problem. In reality, the DNI, one Mr. John Hudgens, only made things that much worse.

So, being a doer, as all great presidents are, the commander in chief simply circumvented the whole arrangement and created a new way for all the necessary intelligence offices to interrelate to each other without the jurisdictional problems. This was when The Group was created. One trustworthy individual from the upper level of each of the necessary security agencies, along with a select field team member, were brought together in secret to share information and resources openly and without the need for bureaucracy. They were set up to work outside the system, answerable only to the president. It was a Cold War solution to a twenty-first century problem. In truth, it just seemed to work better.

Though not a member of any intelligence agency, Nathanial Baker had been introduced to The Group at its inception. Being a high-level justice, he was at the table to give voice if any operation had major jurisdictional or international political or boundary issues. He had initially recognized the situation as emotionally compromising but had since come to understand its desperate need. Currently, it was a position that he viewed as essential to the country and its security.

Justice Baker waved in the direction of the poker table as he entered. The banter in the room was not that of impending doom. It had all the hallmarks of a fraternal order, with joking and personal ribbing among members. He made his way to a handcrafted mahogany side table and placed his cellphone and car keys into the open area marked "Chief Justice." A quick glance at the table showed every one of the green, felt-covered spaces was full of cellphones, PDAs, car keys, radios, and weapons of all varieties. Nathanial turned and proceeded to the poker table.

It seemed from the people present that he was the last to arrive. All sitting members of the group were in attendance for this meeting. It was a very select crowd. Pat Sommers, head of the Secret Service protection detail for the president. Bob "Pepper" Sloan, Director of Operations for the FBI. Paul Spencer, the Senior Systems Director for the National Reconnaissance Office. Ed Crowley, the Senior Systems Analyst for the NSA, and one of The Group's senior statesmen. Lou Stenson, Department of Energy NEST Operations Chief, and still operational ex-SEAL. And Eugene Taggart, the DCI for the CIA, and the other senior statesmen in the crowd. They all looked generally pleased with themselves. Well, everyone but Pepper, who was losing money.

Nathanial Baker took in this cross section of perhaps the nation's most powerful men and smiled as they poked fun at each other. Now that he'd arrived, they could begin discussions. The Group tried to meet with all parties involved being in attendance. The field team members were seldom at the meetings but were brought in via teleconference when necessary. The Group's three field team members were FBI Special Agent Bob Donewoody, CIA Asset Robert Dunn, and NEST Field One, otherwise known as Dr. Kristin Hughes. The field members were seldom physically present, as the state of the planet required their being in other places. They were the eyes, ears, and muscle of The Group. The action element, as it were.

The Chief Justice placed a water bottle in the poker table's cup holder and sat in his designated seat. Pat Sommers was in the middle of explaining some shooter stand-off situation that the Secret Service had become involved with a couple days back. Pat made video game hand gestures to the others at the table. Lou Stenson, the real trigger man at the table, returned his own hand gestures for added effect, which made everyone laugh. Nathanial Baker decided to just sit and wait it out.

It was an odd rarity that everyone showed up to one of these gathering in a good mood. The state of domestic and international tensions was usually taut enough to be causing someone some amount of headache. Fortunately for all, United States affairs had been quiet lately. There was the issue of the missing nuclear weapon in Europe, but that was in Europe. Right now, things for the homeland were looking fairly good. And everyone secretly involved in keeping it that way was taking five minutes to relax.

The conversation turned from the stand-off to some story in the news. Several members of The Group accused Ed Crowley of manufacturing the story and planting it in the media stream. He laughingly denied the affair, stating that if he was going to make up news it would be better news than what they were currently reporting. Of course, everyone laughed.

The cards were shuffled and dealt again. There was a round of betting and a card exchange. The game - five card draw - was a standard choice at the table. More money went into the kitty and the cards were flopped onto the felt. Once again, Bob Sloan made a scowling face and muttered under his breath. It was odd to the Chief Justice that Bob Sloan, an absolute expert at terrorism and counter terrorism strategy, could be so consistently lousy at poker. It just seemed counterintuitive.

The pot broke and everyone anted to start again. Nathanial Baker threw his ante into the pot and Paul Spencer dealt him in. He checked his cards and saw nothing that would be remotely useful. Oh well, such was the course of his day. The closed-door session at court to consider different merits of the landmark case they were arbitrating had gone several hours longer than necessary. All the justices had left the session in a churlish mood, himself included. He had gone and had some breakfast, and then done his bit to try and shake it off. Sadly, the drive down from the capital had been predictably bad. It was the time of day for bad traffic. He had tried not to let that add to his increasingly bad mood, but he could tell he failed.

Sitting amongst these men, however, was helping. The lighthearted gossip and comradery of the group was enough to draw anyone out of a bad mood. He could feel all of last night's tension slowly loosening as he sat and listened to the men joke with one another. The accusations of inappropriate card play being bandied about were enough to make anyone's spirits lift. Nathanial Baker had almost completely tuned out when Gene Taggart drew him back to the here-and-now of the poker room.

"You look like you've had a long night, Nate. Tough go at Justice?"

Gene's tone was congenial and seemed to be as much a greeting as it was a question. It was at this point that he realized that he hadn't actually spoken a word since he had left his chambers back in the capital.

"Oh, sorry. Just lost in thought, I guess. It has been a long night."

"They finally find Jimmy Hoffa? You need to go in and set bail?" Bob Sloan smiled broadly at the obviously tired chief justice. Nathanial Baker returned a lopsided grin.

"Last I heard, Pepper, Jimmy was your guy's doing."

Everyone at the table laughed heartily, including Pepper. It was a long held conspiratorial belief that the FBI had done away with the problematic union boss, at the behest of the mob.

"Yeah, Pepper, is Jimmy really buried under the Meadowlands?"

Lou Stenson's question was genuine in tone. A departure from the remainder of the morning's conversation. Sloan squinted and focused a couple times but retained his smile.

"Strictly conspiracy theory. The Teamsters handled that whole affair in-house, as far as I know."

"Okay, then. Who's buried in Grant's tomb?"

Bob Sloan raised an inquisitive eyebrow at the big ex-SEAL.

"Seriously?"

"Seriously."

"Some dude named Grant."

The entire table erupted into animated laughter. Even Nathanial Baker, ever the stoic entity in the gathering, found great humor in the response. The volume of noise lasted a solid thirty seconds. By the time it had subsided, new cards had been distributed to the players and everyone was either checking or betting.

"Seeing how everyone is here, we should probably talk a little shop. If that's not going to darken the mood in the room."

Gene Taggart's tone was measured, but it definitely wasn't a question. Around the table, one by one, heads nodded in agreement while cards were exchanged.

"I had an extended conversation with Mr. Dunn. He took a hop to Sarajevo and met with someone who could shed some light on our terrorist group. I passed the conversation on to both Bob and Ed for analysis."

Ed Crowley leaned down toward the floor and pulled a manila envelope out from under his chair. With administrative efficiency, he laid out pictures of different individuals on the table for all to see. Everyone sat their cards down and began studying the photos. All the photos were eight by ten, photochrome color, like they had come from some long-shelved archive file. All were unretouched action shots, save one which had "Deceased" stamped on it in red ink. The ink looked new.

"It actually didn't take much digging to find out who they are. The cell has been operating raids into Croatia for some years now. The photos are courtesy of a woman we know in the Croatian embassy."

Ed's tone was analytical, as it usually was when discussing business. It was an obvious side effect of too many years at the NSA.

"Do the Croatians know why we wanted the pictures?" Nathanial Baker's tone was direct.

"Yes. It seemed better not to lie to them. You know, in case this thing goes south."

Everyone nodded in Ed Crowley's direction. It was only right that the Croatians be allowed to prepare. Pat Sommers picked up the photo with the red ink on it to inspect it further.

"Why does this one say deceased?"

"Dunja Pavlovic," Ed said, adjusting his hand of cards sitting on the table. "She is, or was, Zoran Savić's cousin. She was killed in the Kitzigen warehouse shootout, while the cell was fleeing with the nuke. She was the one that the GSG-9 team took down when Zoran was apprehended."

"She looks like someone's wife or something, not an international nuclear terrorist."

Ed pointed to another photo on the table. It was of an otherwise unassuming man.

"She was married to this man, Adam Pavlovic."

Pat Sommers sat the photo back down on the felt tabletop and leaned back in his chair.

"Ed, what's the status of this information? Has it been transmitted to our people in the field yet?"

Lou Stenson was half all-business, and half lost in thought.

"Not at this time. We wanted to vet it first."

"Has that been done?"

"Yes."

"Okay, we should get all of this out to Kristin and her GSG-9 counterpart."

The NSA man nodded at the DOE chief and started to pick up the photos.

"What is Dr. Hughes' status, Lou?"

Gene Taggart asked the question that everyone seemed to want answered.

"Currently, they're in The Hague. Her and Eric Garver, her GSG-9 escort, that is. They're working an idea that the cell members are actually going to spring Savić before they make a final run back to Serbia with the nuke."

"Spring Zoran Savić from The Hague?"

Nathanial Baker sounded surprised. He had done guest appearances at The Hague's law court to hear and review testimony. It just wasn't the kind of place you busted out of.

"I know, Nate. I said the same thing when I heard it. But if you hear Kristin lay out the logic, it has a ring of merit to it. Good enough to have convinced Garver, too. And the hit at The Hague is why Dunn took his hop to Sarajevo."

Gene Taggart raised an interested eyebrow at the mention of his operative's name. Dunn hadn't explained to him why he had gone, just that he had gone.

"Does it actually make any sense in the field or is it speculation?"

Pat Sommer's analytical mind was humming. He could see a prison transport in heavy traffic and a shootout.

"Hard to say. They've determined that the only real way to have success is to boost Zoran in transport. The Hague ICC and Scheveninger Prison are out of the question. They think they've nailed down the most-likely hit point as well, but they're still assessing the situation."

Pat Sommers nodded as Lou spoke. Everything he was saying made good operational sense.

"Whether the Zoran emancipation theory is real or not, I completely agree with Kristin's tracking. Wherever the cell goes, the nuke goes. If they haven't returned to Bosnia, then they very well may be in the Netherlands. Either way, find them, find the nuke."

"I agree," Ed added after Lou finished speaking.

"So do I," Gene Taggart added.

Nathanial Baker chewed on Lou Stenson's use of the term emancipation when referring to Zoran's escape. It somehow conflicted with his African-American heritage, though it did seem perfectly accurate. Maybe he was just overly tired. He had been awake most of the night.

"Ed, when you send the photos and whatever intel we're sending to the field team, could we pass it along to the good people of The Hague as well?"

Ed Crowley nodded at the chief justice.

"I'll get it all out the door as soon as we're done here."

"Sounds good, Ed, now – whose bet is it?"

CHAPTER FIFTEEN

ADAM PAVLOVIC SAT in front of the laptop computer they had acquired during their scouting mission and typed away on the keyboard. The encrypted Instant Messenger site he was using was linked up with some people that they all knew back in Bosnia. He refused to think of it as Bosnia and Herzegovina. That was only a designation some politicians had given it. Those people knew nothing about the place, its people, or its history. They were outsiders. People like the ones at the International Criminal Court who presumed to sit in judgement over everyone else.

Normally, it was Zoran's duty to handle communications between the very independent cells still operating inside Bosnia and Croatia. The old guard of men and women who fought to retain their homeland.

It seemed to Adam that everyone who had come to their land, had tried to rule it. The Macedonians, the Ottomans, and lately, the Soviets. The Soviet machine had done its best to impose rule over the land, but failed. So, they left, and anarchy followed in their wake. The Bosnian Serbs had risen up to reclaim the lands they had so long been denied. The fighting had been long and bloody. It had fractured the area into new and different states. The lines on the maps had been redrawn yet again. Still, no one was satisfied. That was the way with such longstanding conflicts.

Adam tapped some more text into the keyboard and waited. He had been in the conflicts for as long as he could remember. He was just a child when the initial skirmishes broke out. He had sided with his kind. He was Serbian. Correct that, he was a Bosnian Serb. He was not a Croatian

Serb. He wasn't even sure if there were any real Croatian Serbs. They were really just confused people who refused to connect with their real heritage.

Confused or not, they did fight well. The resistance to the Bosnian cell's activities by the Croatian cells across what was currently recognized as the border was fierce. They, too, were men and women of the land. They all knew how to smile in the face of tragedy and oppression.

Unlike others in the secret community of resistance fighters, Adam Pavlovic held no animosity toward his assumed enemy. They were all just people doing what they saw to be right. It was the same as what his group of people were doing. Everyone was out to advance what they saw as best for them.

The conflicts hadn't really brought any sense of deep despair to Adam. Both of his parents had died in the fighting between Bosnians and Croatians. That was probably what had propelled him to join up with his cousin, Zoran, and become a freedom fighter. Even though the fighting had killed his parents and led him to this path, he didn't hold any hatred in his heart for anyone. A great many non-combatant people had died on both sides of the fighting. Weapons were indiscriminate at times. Nevertheless, even his own parents who had died due to the fighting had lived long lives. They had enjoyed their time on Earth. Everyone had to die at some point. That was their time to die. Small-town people held a different view of death than their counterparts in the big cities. City people were detached from the land. Adam hoped that he could make it out of life still holding onto his non-hateful views. He had seen too many people consumed by their hatred. He didn't want that.

He looked up at the small calendar on the wall above his computer table. Someone who had used the room in the past had left the calendar behind. The picture on it of a little girl eating pasta made him smile. He focused in on the basket of rolls on the table. They looked fresh from the oven. He could just tell.

He missed the smell of fresh bread from the oven. The sight of flour in the air and the sounds of the people going past the open window of his bakery. They had been away from Tuzla for some time now. He wondered how the people in the small town were getting on, with his bakery closed for so many days.

Adam ran his hand through his thick dark beard hoping that some stowaway flour would fly out, but none did. He had moved to the small town of Tuzla after fighting had consumed the city of Sarajevo. He had fought for a time, but then decided to leave instead. He had found Tuzla to be warm and welcoming. He settled in, and soon was undistinguishable from the locals. Even though he had no experience in such things, he decided to open a bakery. The early years had been a struggle. But once he learned how to properly make dough into rolls and loaves of bread, he carved out a place in the little village.

He had met his wife Dunja during those early years. She, like Adam, had gone there to escape the fighting in Sarajevo. They had bonded almost instantaneously. She helped him learn about the baking. They had helped each other through the pain and the loss.

Adam paused his thoughts when he realized that he would have to return home alone. How was he going to explain the loss of his wife to the townspeople? That was, of course, if they hadn't already heard about it from the international news channels. How was he going to be able to return to the bakery when there would be such a void in it now? Dunja Pavlovic was as much a part of the bakery as the stone walls, or the flour, or the water. How was he going to continue?

The computer let out an audible ping for a third time before it pulled Adam Pavlovic back to the present. He looked up at the little girl on the calendar and smiled. He would both grieve and worry at a later point. Right now, there were other things that needed doing. He looked down at the computer screen to find a picture of the woman from the coffee shop. He made a quizzical face and began to read the text that followed the image. The picture on the screen was not the picture that he had sent his contact, which was what had made him curious. The picture on the screen showed a woman in cargo pants and a desert sand-colored top wearing a ballistic vest. She appeared to be in a military area of some kind. Even with the dark sunglasses and her hair pulled back from her face, he was sure that it was the same person.

The text under the image started by saying that they had no idea who the man was. He appeared to be European, but no one in their network could identify him.

Adam Pavlovic scratched at his thick beard and thought. There had been something about the man that had seemed familiar to him. His movements maybe? He wasn't sure. There was definitely something. The woman, however, he was sure that he did not know her. She looked and moved like no one he had come across before.

The text went on to say that the woman was American. Her name was Doctor Kristin Marie Hughes, from Las Vegas, Nevada. She worked for the American Nuclear Emergency Search Teams as a weapons specialist.

Adam Pavlovic's eyes went wide. What? How? How could she be here? How was that possible?

He continued to read the text. It went on to detail her education and her exploits in some high-profile situations. Apparently, she possessed a knack for getting in the middle of situations and mucking them up. She seemed possessed of a talent for derailing terrorist activities. That just would not do here.

Adam stood and grasped the laptop computer with both hands. The others needed to see this information and understand what was going on outside their safe house. He turned and strode into the next room with a purposeful gait.

Emil looked up from his newspaper and took in Adam's entrance. He seemed agitated. Emil sat the paper down and waited for Adam to start on about whatever was bothering him.

"We have a problem."

The words came out with the anticipated sense of impending doom which Emil had been expecting.

"Define problem," Emil said calmly.

Adam sat the laptop computer on the coffee table in front of Emil and turned it so that he could see the screen.

"The woman from the coffeehouse yesterday? She is an American. She works for the American's nuclear search teams. She is supposedly a bomb technician."

Emil rubbed his face and then read the entirety of the text conversation while Adam paced around in a tight circle. Alek came into the room at the notice of raised voices and took in the image of the two men. He took a seat in a chair by the doorway and waited for the anxious discussion to continue.

"They don't know who the man is? That strikes me as strange. He carried himself as military, or maybe a spy."

"I agree. I was also suspicious of his mannerisms. I get the feeling that we've crossed paths with him before. There's something unexplainable about him."

"You have a friend that knows people inside the prison, yes?"

Adam nodded his head. The different operational cells had cultivated many useful contacts over the years. All one needed to do was make an inquiry.

"Contact your man. See if their contact has any information about a pair of people, a man and a woman, visiting Zoran in the last several days."

Both Adam and Alek looked at Emil oddly. Emil was starting to become a lateral thinker. It gave him a good feeling. He wondered why he hadn't started to do so earlier.

"Why would we want to know that?"

Aleksander was a little behind in the conversation, not knowing that the others had encountered the two people at the coffeehouse. Emil waved a hand at Adam Pavlovic and he pulled out his cellphone. Emil turned his full attention to Alek as Jasna padded into the room.

"We ran across two suspicious looking people seated at a coffeehouse while we were out doing reconnaissance on the traffic intersection you selected. When we returned, I asked Adam to see if he could identify them. The intersection, by the way, does look like the best location to hit the transport. Good work."

"And the people? Who are they?"

Jasna had also come to the conversation late, so Emil stayed stoic. He was amazed how he had been able to keep his annoyance in check over the last hours.

"We're still working on that. It appears that the woman is some type of American bomb technician. She works for their NEST team. The man is, as of yet, unknown."

Both Alek and Jasna looked at Emil wide-eyed. Emil glanced up at Adam, who was in the doorway of the adjacent room speaking in hushed tones.

"The Americans know that we're here? How can they know that we're here?"

Jasna's voice was almost at the panic level. Emil put up a hand to calm her. As with a small child, she calmed, or at least quieted. Emil looked to Adam as he finished his phone call.

"They'll check with their contact and get back to us. They said that ICC prisoners get very few visitors, so it shouldn't take long to get a response."

Emil nodded as he spoke, "good, now we just need to stay calm until they call back."

"Stay calm?"

Adam was calm, but he knew that they couldn't just sit there. They needed to be doing something. Moving forward with their plans.

"Yes. Stay calm," Emil said in a fatherly tone. "We don't know who the man is or why the two of them are here in The Hague. They may be nobody to bother with. And besides, they don't know where we are. We should gather some facts before we make a plan."

Adam heard his words, but Jasna did not.

"But the Americans? They know that we're here, Emil!"

Emil sighed.

"No, they don't know. If they knew that we were here, then they would have put a military lockdown on the city and began to look for us."

Jasna calmed somewhat, but still wasn't buying it.

"They don't know that we're here. They may think that we might be coming this way and are just speculating. They may also be here for some completely different reason. The information from the man at the prison will tell us much."

"How so," Alek asked.

"If they're here for us, then they will have visited Zoran by now. To visit a prisoner, they would have had to pass security and sign into the logs. So, we will be able to identify the man with the NEST woman. Also, if they went to see Zoran, then it's safe to say that they'll be attempting to determine what our movements have been since Zoran was captured. They'll be trying to figure out where we are now and what we might be doing."

"And if they are after us?"

"Then we'll need to deal with them."

Emil was calm. He was calmer now than when any of the others in the group could remember. He was reminding them of his cousin, Zoran.

"Deal with them how," Adam asked. His tone carried a suspicious quality.

"That would depend upon how they're going to complicate our plans. Frankly, if we can avoid contact with them completely, that would be best. We have managed to do that thus far, so we may be able to continue as planned for the time being. The fact that we encountered them while scouting the intersection where we plan on making the hit could be complete coincidence. We have to complete our plans and get the required equipment ready to free Zoran. We can do that while we wait for more information."

"Coincidence?" Jasna was incredulous.

"Yes, coincidence, or unlucky timing. Who knows for sure? I do know that Zoran is going to be moved from the prison to the ICC tomorrow at noon. I also know that we have work to do between now and then."

"What if they get in the way tomorrow?" Adam was calm and level. He was also raising a question which everyone wanted answered.

"We kill them."

Emil sounded detached, like he was discussing making a bank deposit or the day's weather. He had made the transition from obvious second-in-command to ruthless leader in a surprisingly short amount of time. Adam was internally taken aback by his new callousness.

"What if they warn the people at the court, or the prison guards that are transporting Zoran?"

Alek, like Adam, seemed calm, but there was something in the way the question came out that made Emil suspect he wasn't.

"They probably already have notified them, if that's what they're here to do. To be honest, I don't see the people at the prison complex getting too excited by their alerts."

"Why not?"

"The Hague's ICC has never lost a prisoner in its custody. Europeans are pompous people. Europeans with a 100 percent success record are even more pompous. I would bet that they were polite but didn't actually give the American woman the time of day."

Both Alek and Adam nodded in unison. Jasna stewed on it for a moment longer, but finally agreed as well. Western Europeans had a naturally instilled sense of superiority that irritated everyone on the planet.

It irritated the Eastern Europeans more than most. To the lands of the East, all Western European history could be summed up as a never-ending series of conquests and crusades. There was always someone from the West with an army who was attempting to instill their own form of civilization. That was until the Soviets showed up. Western Europeans were pompous, but they weren't crazy. They had no interest in fighting the might of the U.S.S.R.

Adam's phone vibrated in his hand and he stepped out of the room to answer it. Emil watched him leave and then refocused his attention on the other two. They seemed to be complacent enough for the time being. It wasn't that their concerns were unjustified. It was that Emil seemed to be grasping that being reactionary was only good for their competition. They needed to have a plan, and an escape path, before they engaged the enemy. If they didn't, they would certainly come up short, especially in foreign lands.

Adam came back into the room. He looked a little ashen. Emil sensed that things were about to take another bad turn. All three looked to Adam and waited for him to speak.

"The two visited Zoran at the prison, day before yesterday. The guard confirmed that the woman spoke with Zoran and that her name is Doctor Hughes. Supposedly, she questioned him about the theft of an item stolen from a German military base. I guess she didn't like the answers she was given."

All four people turned their heads and looked into an adjacent room where the stolen nuclear weapon sat quietly on a countertop.

"And?" Emil said stoically.

"And, the man's name is Herbert Becke. He is a German policeman of some variety."

Emil looked solidly at Adam. He was amazingly calm.

"Do you think he is part of the group that attacked us at the warehouse?"

"Yes. There's something about him that I find familiar. It would explain a great deal if we had encountered him before."

"So, how did they find us, Emil?" Alek was asking before Jasna could go off on a rant.

"They haven't found us. Not yet anyway. But it does appear that they might think we're here or headed this way and could be looking for us."

"Why? How would they know to come here?"

"The same way that we came here. The path of least resistance, I would think. They needed answers and they chose the most obvious place in which to start."

"So?"

"So, we continue with our original plan. If we need to alter it along the way, we will."

Adam looked over at their de-facto leader and gave him a knowing expression. They would definitely need to alter it later on.

"Emil, when we end up altering the plan, I like your idea of killing them both. For Dunja."

CHAPTER SIXTEEN

HREE LOUD KNOCKS thudded through the hotel room door. Eric Garver instinctively drew a Model 20 Glock pistol from a waist holster and half-racked the slide to check that there was a round in the chamber. Kristin wandered out of her bedroom on the opposing side of the large suite and gave Garver an inquisitive eye.

"Someone at the door?"

"Oh, that's what that sound was."

Kristin made a face and padded to the door so that she could put her eye against the site glass. The image of a well-dressed man in room service attire appeared in the little site glass.

"All right. We have breakfast."

Kristin Hughes swung the door open and smiled broadly. Without a request for entrance, Robert Dunn pushed the service cart into the room and nodded to them both.

"Good morning. Breakfast, with compliments from the staff."

The CIA man made a flourish while removing a silver dome cover on a plate to reveal a large pile of eggs and bacon. Kristin smiled like a child at Christmas. Eric Garver nodded politely. Dunn had suspected a cool reception.

"Hmm, hard to please some customers. Okay then."

The CIA man removed a second, smaller cover to reveal an extra-large cappuccino. This time, the GSG-9 man smiled. Dunn gave a look of satisfaction and started pushing the service cart toward the terrace.

Robert Dunn, CIA assassin and Kristin's normal field protection, had landed several hours before. Since it had still been nighttime in The Hague, he passed the time reviewing the information package that The Group had sent out. The information helped him to make sense of some things that the old baker had told him in their conversation.

The loaves of bread he had been obligated to purchase at extortionist prices had been given to the crew. Well, all but one of them. The smallest loaf he chewed on as he read. It was just bread. There was no butter or jam, but it was excellent. The old man was an accomplished baker. That was something Dunn could respect.

The bread and the information had made the time pass quickly. Dunn had gone over each person's bio from front to back. They were all easy enough to figure out. People brought together from the ashes of war and pushed toward some higher purpose. Well, if you could call the continued killing of other people from their own homeland a higher purpose. The nature of the conflict hadn't been the strange part to Dunn. Every nation or territory had its own story of lingering conflict. The fact that it hadn't been conceded after it was obvious that it was finished was what struck the assassin as strange.

The conflict that had torn Yugoslavia apart was now decades old. The people, for the most part, had moved on. Even the grand old Olympic city of Sarajevo, which had been all but completely decimated, had been rebuilt to the point where the city could be put back on the tourist map. One had to look hard to see the scars of the war years. It was sad that all the college-aged backpackers he had seen wandering the streets hadn't taken the time to see the city's gritty underbelly while they were running from one restored café or museum to another. That was the way with the passage of time. It whitewashed things and made them viewable again.

The fragments of armies and militias leftover from the war – the ones who couldn't let go and continued their fight – was what Dunn couldn't wrap his head around. Why would anyone continue to fight for a lost cause? Why bother? There was obviously no going back. The past had already moved on without them. They couldn't bring back those days now, no matter how hard they tried.

To Dunn, it was obvious that they were no longer fighting for a homeland. The new country lines were drawn on all the maps and the ink was very dry. New countries had risen from the ashes of war and established themselves. This meant that the terrorists he was now searching for were just fighting out of principle. Principle? That word was a problem for the CIA man.

Robert Dunn had known many principle-driven men during his career. Robert Dunn had killed many principle-driven men over the course of his career. People who operated out of principle all had one underlying problem: At some important moment they all became blind and stupid.

There were no great causes. There was no justifiable situation that would make people stop and go back to the old ways. There was no better time, or farmer's pride, or tie to the land, or sense of place. It was all well-crafted lies. Everyone, deep down in their bones, knew it was true. It was one of the great lies of civilization.

In reality, we were all still nomads. The human race was still a big gaggle of hunter-gatherers. How could people justify the endless resources and money that had been invested into international travel if not for this restlessness. People traveled more now than they did at any other time in history.

Of the terrorists that he was traveling after now, Dunn had spent the majority of the dark hours pondering over Emil Savić and Adam Pavlovic. Zoran Savić was of no consequence. He was in prison. At least, he was currently in prison. Aleksander Lukic was young. He probably still believed all the stories he was told. Jasna Pavlovic was easy enough to figure. She had lost family and then found a purpose in revenge. Her skillset was obviously useful to Zoran and the cell that he ran, but she was still just a soldier.

It was Emil and Adam that he found interesting. Emil Savić, though the obvious second-in-command, had never been a real voice inside the group. According to both U.S. intel and the old Bosnian baker, Zoran Savić was the only voice in the group. With Zoran now out of the picture, how would Emil handle his newfound role as leader? And, if he was good at it, why would he bother trying to free Zoran? If he did free Zoran, would he willingly go back to being in the shadows? Or would this situation create a rift inside the cell? No matter which one of these questions came up with a negative answer, there was obviously potential for turmoil building inside the cell he was chasing. It was a turmoil that Dunn might be able to exploit.

Adam Pavlovic, now he was another problem altogether. Adam

himself, his skillset and knowledge, that wasn't the problem that Robert Dunn saw in the data. The fact that the GSG-9 team had killed his wife right before his eyes was the real problem. How would he react the next time they were put in a similar situation? Grief was an unexplainable game changer. Grief caused the most seasoned soldiers to do the dumbest things during times of extreme stress. Truth be told, there was no predicting how he would respond the next time there was a gunfight. This caused Robert Dunn to think.

As an assassin Robert Dunn generally didn't like unpredictable situations. Nor did he like unpredictable people. The vagaries of chance played a big enough part in his life already. Dealing with situations was best done in a methodical way. Attempting to respond to people's individual unpredictability gave things a layer that Dunn really tried his best to avoid. Many in his line of work had died by not accounting for some random detail or event.

Robert Dunn was normally a situational killer. He liked to enter those situations with a working plan. His plans tried to predict how someone was going to act based upon how they had acted in the past. Things like grief had a tendency to muddle things up.

He had finished both the bread and the information review by the time the sun broke the Eastern horizon. He had thought about the Bosnians for as long as he cared to. It was time to go find his favorite doctor and her new German sidekick and see what they had been up to in his absence. He was sure that it would be as interesting as anything he had done.

Dunn made his way to the hotel and gave his taxi driver a heavy tip. A stop at the lobby bar had produced the room service tray and the food. Another substantial tip to the barman made sure that no one on the staff was going to care. That's how Dunn had made his way to the doctor's room, where the three now took up station around the table on the suite's terrace. The space had become the team's temporary home base. Robert Dunn removed a manila folder from a shelf on the tray and sat it in the middle of the table. Eric eyed it suspiciously. Kristin paid it no notice and continued devouring her breakfast.

"I've been a little out of local affairs as of late. When do they plan on moving Savić from the prison so he can stand trial?"

Robert clipped the end of a Cuban cigar and rolled it around in his hand to find its balance point.

"Tomorrow, at midday. We have also confirmed the route they plan to use, along with the most probable strike point."

Robert lit the cigar with a beat-up Zippo lighter and nodded professionally at Eric Garver.

"Do you know what kind of transport they plan to use? And do they plan to clear the route?"

Eric's expression became clouded. Robert Dunn could instantly tell he had found the weak point.

"We don't know the details of the transport, but it will probably be a standard three vehicle arrangement, with Zoran Savić in the center vehicle. It is the method they prefer."

"Yeah, and they released the transport time on the damned TV over here."

The sentence fought its way out of Kristin's mouth full of toast, but it was still legible. Robert Dunn adjusted his gaze toward the world's number one bomb technician. He couldn't understand how she could eat the way she did and keep the body that she had. She had to have a high metabolism and good genetics, but still. Kristin picked up a slice of bacon and stuffed it in her half-full mouth as Robert reflected on her statement.

"Well, that could be good or bad. We won't know until it plays out."

Eric Garver nodded in agreement. Robert took a long, slow pull of the cigar and blew a smoke ring straight up into the air as not to ruin the atmosphere at the table.

"Okay. What's in the folder?"

The statement was much more audible and clearer. Robert assumed that Kristin had finally swallowed. He looked down at the folder. It still lay right where he had dropped it. He had received it at a late hour. He had assumed that Kristin had received hers at the same time. Washington time was behind them by a good seven hours. The group had probably sent the intelligence packet in the middle of the afternoon, once it had been thoroughly vetted.

"That would be the work up on your Bosnian terrorist cell. It's full of interesting things."

Eric sat stoically, as if he was waiting for a dissertation on the material inside. Robert Dunn found his response to be curious. Kristin, however, was eager like a schoolgirl. It was her standard "zero or one hundred" response paradigm. She reached out and flipped open the folder. She laid out the pictures so all of them could see them and then produced a page of handwritten notes. The writing appeared to be Robert Dunn's.

"You've both met Zoran Savić. He's the number one henchman here."

Robert pointed to a picture in the middle of the group, and the other two around the table nodded.

"He is the group leader, major event planner, and by all accounts, completely guilty of everything that the high court is charging him with."

The other two nodded again.

"The second in charge, and person most likely to be running the show now, is his cousin Emil Savić. He's not as seasoned a leader as Zoran, and the more hot-tempered of the two. Where Zoran came up through the war college system, Emil has no formal education to speak of. He works odd jobs and construction work. That being said, he seems to be the established 'tech man' of the cell."

"Age? Parents?" Eric asked.

"Mid-forties. Both parents' dead. He tends to live in central Sarajevo."

Eric Garver nodded as if he were taking mental notes.

"You may recognize her," the American assassin said to the German commando as he pointed to another photo. "She's the one that your team took down in the Kitzigen standoff."

Kristin leaned in to get a better look at the woman. Eric knew what she looked like. He also knew what the GSG-9 commando she had killed looked like.

"She may still be playing a part in this whole affair. Her name is Dunja Pavlovic. She is reported to have had a high school level education. She lived in Tuzla, Bosnia, where she ran a bakery with her husband Adam."

Robert Dunn pointed to the picture of Adam Pavlovic. The others' eyes followed his finger as it moved across the table.

"Adam Pavlovic, another cousin of our boy Zoran, is a couple years younger than his wife. He made it most of the way through high school before the conflicts destroyed that idea. Both started out in Sarajevo and migrated to Tuzla at some point. Both sets of parents are dead, due to the conflicts."

Eric Garver studied the picture of Adam Pavlovic. The big beard, the piercing blue eyes, and the sturdy build. He might be a problem.

"The rumor is that he is the voice-of-reason and cool head amongst the individuals in the cell."

Eric Garver raised a suspicious eyebrow at Robert Dunn.

"That's what I thought when I read it, too. Now, the other woman, Jasna Pavlovic. Yes, there are a lot of Pavlovics. She's mid-thirties, with a college degree. She teaches fourth grade in central Sarajevo. Both parents died in the conflicts. She is Adam's cousin, and the explosives person of the cell."

Robert shifted pictures and continued without interruption.

"The kid's name is Aleksander Lukic. He's a twenty-eight-year-old mechanic out of some Sarajevo suburb. High school, no college, but clever and smart. The dad lives in an old age home. His mom is dead from the conflicts. He is Zoran's nephew, as near as we can tell."

"So, they're like a big unhappy terrorist family?" Kristin didn't mean for the statement to come across as funny, but her upbeat tone pushed it that way.

"Yes. Which substantiates your hypothesis that they are here to break Zoran out of prison."

"Any thoughts about the nuke, which is the reason that we're here."

"The Group agrees that if the cell members are here, so is the nuke. It is most-likely just being carried around at this point. Once they free Zoran, they will take him and the nuke back to Bosnia and do whatever it was they were originally going to do with it. The stories say that the cell has been in some long term spat with a Croatian bunch of about the same size. That merry band of terrorists is run by a man named Marko Juraš. I don't know anything about him. End of the day, he and his cell are probably just as upstanding as this bunch is."

Dunn waved his hand over the pictures on the table and pulled a lung full of smoke off the cigar. Kristin stared at the picture of Emil. Eric Garver looked at each picture for several seconds and captured their images fully.

"Where did you get your intelligence?"

Eric Garver wasn't questioning the CIA man as much as he was being diligent.

"The base information came from a man named Ranko Dragic. He's a baker in central Sarajevo and a compiler of information on the seedier parts of Bosnian-Croatian history. He also baked the bread that made your toast."

Robert pointed toward the crumbs on Kristin's plate.

"He's a forthright man. The rest of it came from various files inside U.S. intelligence."

Eric Garver sat and digested all the information that Dunn had provided. Kristin was still looking at the picture of Emil Savić. She was trying to find something in his countenance that would tell her what he planned to do with the bomb. Sadly, divining information from the ether was not one of her strong points.

"Did your source-tell have anything to say about how they might go about freeing Zoran?"

The German was going to make it all come together in his mind, one way or another.

"Negative. I'm sure that they do this type of thing from time to time, but it doesn't seem to be anything that they're known for. They will probably hit the convoy at some point between the prison and the ICC. A smash-and- grab operation of some variety. But that's conjecture, not intelligence."

Eric Garver nodded and returned another look at the documents before him. A moment passed as he processed information before he spoke.

"We think we have the most plausible scenario figured out. And we know the timing."

"Well, you're the counter-terrorism expert in the family, and she's the bomb expert. Since I'm just the assassin, I'll happily tag along with whatever plan you two have mustered up."

CHAPTER SEVENTEEN

EMIL LOOKED OUT the window of the safe house at the well-maintained canal behind it and thought that they were going to need a backup plan. The primary plan was fine, but it lacked the thing that well-organized teams called surge capacity. It wasn't capable of expanding to meet new situations.

The primary plan, for its part, was pretty simple. They would station an observer several blocks up the street from the impact intersection to notify the team when the convoy approached. That would be Jasna's job. When the convoy approached the intersection, a large vehicle would block it and pin the lead vehicle in place. That would be Adam's job. A second large vehicle would come up from behind and fix all the convoy vehicles into the kill box. Vehicle number two would be Alek. Once squeezed together; Alek, Adam and he would come in, pop open the transport vehicle and free Zoran. They would all climb into Jasna's get-away van and exit in the direction of the lead vehicle. That direction would have the least residual traffic. They would drive to the safehouse, retrieve the nuke, and switch to a clean vehicle. Then, together they would head to their exit boat that would transport them out of the country.

It was a good plan. It didn't have a lot of moving parts. It didn't have a lot of things that could go wrong. Fewer pieces meant a higher success rate. They needed to obtain the vehicles and drive the route one last time. Otherwise, they were ready to go. That was the primary plan. However, a backup plan would go a long way toward quieting the voices in Emil's head. The American and the German showing up wasn't helping him stay calm.

The remainder of the cell walked into the room and took in Emil staring down at the canal.

"What's wrong Emil? What is the problem?" Jasna sounded concerned, as always.

"No, no, Jasna. Everything is well. I was just thinking that a backup plan would be useful."

"The plan we have is a good plan. It has worked well for us in the past." Adam was sound and sure.

"I agree, Adam. I was thinking more about the escape part. A second route away from the scene toward the safe house. Or, a second route from here to the boat."

"You're worried that the Netherlands will react like the Germans did." Adam had a calm voice. It kept the others calm.

"They did react much quicker than was expected. And there are a lot of cameras in this damned city."

Adam and Emil looked at each other in a knowing way. The others remained quiet, letting the situation play out.

"We do have a little time left," Adam said casually.

"No. I'm just being overcautious. Our plan will work fine."

Everyone looked at each other with a look that tried to reassure whomever they were looking at.

"We have just under a day before they move Zoran. Let us get out of here and do what needs doing. Adam and Alek, head to the construction site by the intersection. Find us a pair of heavy trucks. Dump trucks or cement trucks would work best. Jasna and I will head to the other side of town and find a proper place to hide the van so we can spot the oncoming convoy. We will meet back here when we are complete and discuss whatever changes present themselves along the way."

Everyone nodded, but no one spoke. They all just turned and headed for the door. They knew what needed doing. Now, they had to go do it. In a little more than a day, they would be headed back to Bosnia with their leader.

Across the city, another conversation had about the same level of surety. Kristin, Eric, and Robert had managed to finish breakfast but not the discussion.

"Let's say that everything in your gut is right on, Eric, that means that everyone will be at the intersection when the convoy goes through."

"Yes. So?" Eric Garver had thought the whole affair through so much that it was starting to become mush in his mind. The CIA man's questions weren't helping.

"So, we grab one of the grabbers and make them tell us where the nuke is. I say we grab the young guy. He's probably the least seasoned to getting interrogated."

"What about the prisoner escape?"

"What about it? The reason that we are all here is to recover a stolen U.S. made nuclear weapon. It is NOT to handle The Hague's prisoner transport issues."

The German commando glared at the CIA assassin and instantly realized that he was right. Somewhere along the way the notion of killing Zoran during the raid had also become an unspoken operational idea. He softened his expression and looked at the tile on the terrace for several long seconds before he spoke.

"You are completely right. I seem to have become invested in the idea of Zoran Savić receiving some type of justice."

Robert Dunn took a good look at his German counterpart. He wanted justice for his team. Dunn understood that. It was what was right.

"Don't worry, Herr Garver. I also want Zoran Savić to get some justice for your comrades. And he'll see it, whether it's at The Hague or somewhere else."

The two men passed a look that made Kristin Hughes' skin turn cold. It was never a good idea to get on the wrong side of violent men. She knew that, even though she thought she was seeing a deeper side of that now.

No one spoke for a couple minutes. They all just sat and looked out over the city toward the North Sea, waiting for the deep sense of dread to pass.

"Okay. Onto more current business. We seem to have just over a day before Zoran gets moved across town. What parts of the idea have we yet to explore?"

Kristin decided that she would answer this one. Maybe a feminine voice would help soothe some tension.

"We've found the appropriate intersection. And we have informed the authorities at The Hague. I suppose that we need to find out where they would stage for the hit? And where they would procure the blocking vehicles from?"

Robert Dunn made an agreeable expression. That made good sense. They would need to steal the vehicles from someplace close to their safe house or the strike point.

"They will need a lookout to notify the intercept team when to go. That lookout will need to be stationed ahead of the strike point, at least several blocks."

Dunn could tell that Garver was back to thinking like a commando leader.

"They could steal the vehicles from several different places. Sales yards, manufactories, or construction sites would all be likely. To check them all would take more time that we have. Tracking down the survey point seems the best use of time. There may be two or three prime locations from which to survey it."

"I agree. Without the survey point, their whole plan is for naught. Finding that point would definitely be time well-spent."

"Well, that solves that then," Kristin threw in for closure. "Let me get some sensible shoes and we can be off."

Robert Dunn stood as Kristin stood. Eric Garver was already standing, so he nodded politely. It seemed they had come up with a useful plan for their day.

The sun was high in the bright blue sky by the time they made it into the city. A lack of clouds and the breezes along the shore that usually accompanied most summer days in the Netherlands was pushing up the mercury. The day was on its way to being downright sticky.

Dunn parked the BMW in the crown Plaza valet for the second time, and the three walked outside to face the intersection. Traffic came and went from all directions at a constant pace. Business was always being conducted in the little city, and traffic reflected that.

The threesome strolled down along the Hubertusviaduct and Van Stolkport on a wide promenade. The foot traffic in the park was light at midday, presumably pushed indoors by the summer heat.

At the base of the Indisch Monument, Robert Dunn brought the stroll to a halt. Numerous paths in the park intersected at the monument's location. Benches around the area gave a good view of the grass lawns and a small lake in the background. But if one turned around, the benches also gave a good view of the Professor B.M. Teldersweg Motorway. A pair of tunnels built into the road construction allowed the walking paths to continue under the motorway to the opposite side, where they transitioned back into city streets.

Eric Garver took up a spot on the bench nearest to the monument and began to survey the motorway. This definitely was a good place to direct other people in the cell as the convoy appeared. They weren't more than three or four blocks from the main intersection and there was nothing between here and there.

Kristin wandered over to where the walking paths passed through under the motorway. Large square concrete drainage sections had been used to create a tunnel under the roadway. She had seen this design many times back in America. These particular tunnels lacked the customary graffiti that American tunnels usually contained. Their cleanliness was strange to her.

Kristin looked back at Dunn and Garver. They were pointing toward the monument and talking. Kristin waved a hand and pointed toward the tunnel. Robert Dunn nodded and waved back, before returning to his conversation.

The air inside the tunnel was cool on Kristin's skin. The change in temperature made her smile. She walked through it in seconds, appearing on the far side of the motorway. As she had expected, the area on this side of the motorway was sectioned off into a parking area for the end of the street. Small shops and buildings filled the streets, but not in the claustrophobic way which the high-rises of the city center did. The small shops along the streets created a comfortable everyday neighborhood within the larger city.

Kristin wandered the distance of the parking area before turning around. The parking area was sparsely filled, so she wondered how much of this area was the domain of bicyclists.

A man and a woman came out of the shop behind her and started toward the parked cars. Kristin glanced over her shoulder at them out of habit, then went back to looking at the cars. She had no more than focused on the cars again when her instincts began to tell her something was wrong. She turned again to look at the couple, but now only the man was present. He walked toward her with a deliberate gate. She had seen him somewhere before, but she couldn't put a finger on it. He was Eastern European, maybe?

"ROBERT!"

Kristin Hughes managed to get the scream out at full volume before the butt of Jasna Pavlovic's Makarov pistol slammed against her temple from behind. The impact of the handgun had the desired effect, knocking Doctor Hughes to the sidewalk. Emil Savić increased his pace over to the American and hoisted her up as if he were carrying a sleeping child.

Robert Dunn was running for the tunnel before he knew why he was running. Eric Garver was only one full step behind him. They were both unholstering weapons by the time that Dunn's brain processed that the scream he had heard was his name. Emil Savić was closing the rear door of a red Peugeot when the two intelligence officers came bursting through the tunnel opening. Gunfire erupted instantaneously.

Two rounds each were expelled from Dunn's and Garver's weapons in a proficient manner. One of Garver's shattered the rear windscreen and the other seared its way through Emil Savić's triceps muscle. Dunn's two rounds impacted the driver's side window and sent glass flying in all directions.

Emil let out a howl as Jasna Pavlovic returned fire on the two men. She emptied the Makarov PM compact 9mm, letting eight rounds go in a sprayed-out fashion. The returning fire caused both Dunn and Garver to dive for cover. Her return fire allowed time for Emil to crawl inside the car. Jasna abandoned her shooter's position on the far side of the auto and climbed behind the wheel. The car was already moving when Dunn came off the ground and started firing once again.

Robert Dunn leveled his .45 Auto Glock at the rear windscreen and focused. He thought he saw two heads, which meant that Kristin was probably across the rear seat. He adjusted his aim and started squeezing off rounds at the car's rear tires. He was running and shooting. He could vaguely hear a second handgun with an altered rate of fire. It wasn't until he ran out of rounds that he realized Eric Garver was running next to him and also firing his weapon the whole time.

The two men ran at absolute speed, following the get-away vehicle around one corner and then another. All the time they ran, the car pulled farther and farther away. The car veered a hard right onto Ver-Huëllweg and accelerated away down the wide main street.

Both Dunn and Garver arrested their run at the intersection. What the hell had just happened? They were talking about good places for dinner, and then they were in a gun battle and Kristin was gone. Gone? No. Kidnapped. She was kidnapped by a Bosnian terrorist cell. What the hell had just happened?

It was the police sirens in the distance that brought the two men back to reality. The Hague police force was on its way. Garver was sure that they had been spotted by one street camera or another during the exchange of fire, as CCTV was everywhere in the city. Dunn was sure that neither of them could be here when the police arrived. The sirens were growing louder.

"We need to go! Now. Leave the car where it's at."

"We'll meet again in a couple hours at the World Forum."

And with that, the two men turned and ran off in different directions. Dunn went back the way they had come for a couple blocks and then turned off into an alley. Garver followed the direction of the car for another block and then turned in the opposing direction.

As the two men ran at full speed, it seemed that one police siren multiplied into dozens. The whole city police force had been woken up and was now out on the hunt. Robert Dunn flagged down a taxi and hopped in.

"Mesdag Panorama, please."

The cabbie nodded and headed southeast toward the gallery. Traffic in that direction was light and Dunn was out of the immediate area in no time. He thanked the cabbie as he climbed out of the car at the queue for the panorama and took his place in line. He waited for the cabbie to disappear completely before walking away toward the south.

Dunn pulled his phone out of his pocket and dialed a number from memory. It rang twice.

"Sir, we have an immediate problem. The terrorists we were tracking just kidnapped Doctor Hughes."

He paused.

"Yes, sir. You heard the SITREP correctly. Both myself and the German engaged the cell, but had to disengage with police arriving."

He waited.

"Yes sir."

Dunn pocketed the phone and wondered if he hadn't just put a bullet in his own head.

CHAPTER EIGHTEEN

UGENE TAGGART, CIA DCI, slammed down the phone and swore. He marked the time on his watch and wrote it on a notepad. He added time zones in his head to establish the current time in the Netherlands and then stared at the number for a good five seconds.

Not waiting for the desperation of the situation to sink in, he started digging for his cellphone. As he was retrieving his cellphone from his suit pocket, he noticed the long crack in the handset of his desk phone. Oh, well, there goes another phone.

Scrolling through the numbers in the cellphone's contact list, he settled on a Cayman Islands number and dialed it into the desk phone. One set of clicks on the CIA end and another set of clicks with a screeching sound from the other end told Taggart that the call was both encrypted and scrambled. The phone rang three times.

"Good morning. You're in early. What's happening up in the good old US-of-A that has you reaching out to me?"

Eugene Taggart paused for two seconds to formulate a sentence.

"Do you have a team in Europe, or can you get one there immediately?"

"Yes. We have a five man insert working a long-distance op in Spain. Why?"

"Doctor Kristin Hughes was just abducted in The Hague. I need her back."

"When, exactly."

"Forty-four minutes ago. Center of the city. Broad daylight. She had a company man and a German GSG-9 asset for an escort."

There was a pause on the other end of the line.

"Gunfire?"

"Yes."

The man on the other end of the line made some notes on a pad. Taggart could hear the scratching of a pencil on paper. He could also hear the sound of waves on the beach and knew that it had been too long since the two of them had talked face to face.

"Okay. What exactly was she doing there?"

"She was tracking a Bosnian terrorist cell that stole a U.S. made man-portable nuclear weapon from an airbase in Germany. The terrorist leader, one Zoran Savić, was apprehended in a shootout with a GSG-9 team in a town called Kitzigen. It was Hughes' belief that the cell went to The Hague on the way back to Bosnia to retrieve Savić when he is transferred from the holding cell at the prison to the ICC. They were doing recon for the boost when it all went south."

The man on the other end of the line made some more notes on his pad.

"And the nuke?"

"It is assumed to be in The Hague with the terrorists."

"Roger that."

There was some more pencil scratching before the man spoke again.

"Tell me exactly what you want for an outcome."

"I want you to do *whatever* needs to be done to retrieve Doctor Hughes, mentally and physically sound, from the terrorists."

"And fallout?"

"At any cost."

"I understand. We will be underway immediately. How long until they move this Savić to the International Criminal Court?"

"Tomorrow. Midday. Standard three vehicle prison convoy."

"Roger that. Anything else?"

"Don't waste any time."

"We seldom do."

And with that, the line went dead. Eugene Taggart set the handset back down in its cradle. He looked out the standard sized window in his standard sized office and wondered what must have happened to let a top-level field asset get abducted from under the very noses of the company and the Germans. This definitely was not good.

The DCI scrolled through the numbers in his cellphone contact list a second time until he came to Ed Crowley's number. He pressed the button and waited. It rang two times.

"What's up Gene?"

"The last number that I dialed from my office phone. Make it go away permanently."

"Which line?"

Gene Taggart looked down at the phone and realized that he didn't have any idea which one of the encrypted lines he had just used. He made a face. He must be getting old.

"Not sure. Do every line."

"No worries. Consider it taken care of."

As the Senior Systems Director of the National Security Agency, one of the easiest things in Ed Crowley's day was making digital information permanently disappear. When he got done pressing buttons, it simply no longer existed.

"Done. What's going on over at Langley?"

"We have a massive problem Ed. Kristin Hughes was just abducted while in The Hague."

There was a long pause before the NSA man could formulate a response.

"Exactly when? Exactly where?"

"Say, forty-five minutes ago. The Hague city center."

"Scenario?"

"As far as I know, she was with Dunn and the GSG-9 man, Garver, at the time."

There was another pause.

"Is she intact?"

"Unknown. There was an exchange of gunfire. They drew some blood, assumed to be one of the terrorists. They had to E and E before the locals arrived."

"I understand. We'll make her priority one. Main room. I'll get ahold of Paul Spencer and see what kind of assets the NRO can shift our way."

"Thanks, Ed."

"We'll get her back."

"We're going to get her back, and someone is going to pay."

"Has anyone told Lou yet?"

"He's the next call."

"He doesn't know?"

"Dunn called me direct. I made a call. I called you. Now, I'll call Lou."

"I understand Gene, I'm just saying –"

"Yeah, I know."

"You know he's going to want in."

"I know. I've been rolling that around in my head for a couple minutes now. Him in the field could be good or bad."

"I'm pretty sure that I can get him there quick, if you can have Dunn meet him."

"How?"

"I've got an Air Force general who owes me more favors than he can repay in a lifetime. A quick Atlantic hop shouldn't be a problem to arrange at short notice."

"You happen to know where Lou is right now?"

"Yup. He's here. He was up on the hill yesterday. Subcommittees."

"Good. Set it up."

"I'll call him directly with the details."

"That sounds good, Ed. Thanks."

And the line went dead. Gene Taggart drew a breath and scrolled down the contact list to the S section. Toward the bottom was one Lou Stenson, DOE operations chief for NEST. Gene hit the green button on the screen and drew another long breath. The phone rang one time.

"Hey Gene, you caught me with my phone in my hand. Damned thing won't stop ringing today. I'd say we should catch a drink later, but I'm scheduled to have dinner with the DOE high command."

"Lou, Kristin Hughes was abducted in The Hague, approximately one hour ago."

There was dead silence on the other end of the line. He could imagine the range of expressions playing across Lou Stenson's face. Then he could hear the gears in his head turning.

"I'm going to need to borrow one of your fast jets."

"The NSA is already setting up something faster than that. Robert Dunn will meet you at the airport in Rotterdam."

"Can you send me all the intel you have. Straight to my phone."

"Roger that."

"What is her status?'

"Unknown. There was an exchange of gunfire before the scene became untenable. We can only assume that she is otherwise unharmed."

"Roger that."

Eugene Taggart heard something in the back of the big SEAL's voice that he wasn't even sure the man was able of possessing. It was apprehension.

"Lou, not to sound like your dad, but cooler heads tend to prevail."

"Roger that, Gene. My head's in the game. Besides, I have a whole plane ride to calm down and look at the situation tactically."

"I just wanted to say it once, out loud."

"I understand."

"Lou, we'll get her back. You hear me. We'll get her back and people are going to pay."

"That's a fact."

The apprehension was gone. It had been replaced by a cold edge that Gene Taggart was sure he liked even less.

"Oh, one more thing."

"Go."

"If you run into a set of mercs, they're on your side."

Lou took a second to digest the sentence. The covert intelligence agencies of the world often used mercenaries and private contractors to handle operations that they could not be formally tied to. As far as Lou knew, the United States didn't employ mercenaries on any level. They hadn't since directly after the first Gulf War. The CIA director must have been making calls to old friends.

"I read you five-by-five, Gene."

"Good. Now where exactly are you?"

"On the hill. The Capital Building, sublevel three.

Gene Smiled at his desk before he could stop himself. There really was no taking the military out of a military man.

"Okay. Head for ADW. Use the back door. They know to expect you, or they will by the time you get there. Ed Crowley is setting up a supersonic Atlantic hop for you. You'll get the data package in route."

"Roger that. Thank Ed for me. I'm moving now."

Lou Stenson hung up his phone and stuffed it back in the pocket of his suit jacket. Looking at his watch, he puzzled out how to best get through the horrendous D.C. traffic.

ADW, otherwise known as Joint Base Andrews, was the military complex that took up a large section of acreage to the southeast of the capital. Sitting just outside the beltway, it was the station that every military member hoped they didn't get. Lou wondered what type of favor Ed had done for someone to get him an invite through the backdoor without eight layers of paperwork done in triplicate. Whatever it was, Lou wasn't asking any questions.

The big ex-SEAL smiled at the receptionist guarding the door he was standing outside of and asked her to explain to those who asked that he had been called away on an emergency. He didn't wait for the young woman to respond before he was already halfway down the hallway.

Hitting the beltway, Lou was happy to see that all the traffic on the route was still headed into the city. Everyone was on their way to another day of mundane bureaucracy. The routes heading out and away from the capital were all but empty of traffic. He made it down to the signs for I-495, or the beltway north. He glanced down at the speedometer as he slid under the street sign and saw that the meter was registering a mild ninety-two miles per hour. Lou lifted his foot off the gas pedal and backed the rental car down to a respectable eighty-five.

It was an interesting idiosyncrasy of the nation's capital that you were more likely to get pulled over for speeding at ten mph over the speed limit than you were for thirty mph over the speed limit. He just figured that the local police assumed that if you were going that fast, it must have something to do with national security. Most times that was true. But, still.

Lou slammed down on the brakes and whipped the rental off onto the exit ramp leading to ADW. Maintaining a civil speed, he made his way south around the perimeter of the base and across the golf courses located just outside, where he pulled up to an unmarked gate on the backside of the base. The gate guard recognized the NEST Operations Chief without needing identification and opened the gate. Lou Stenson thrust his government identification out the driver's side window as he came to a stop.

"Mr. Stenson. Good morning. We've been told to expect your arrival.

Just follow the guys in the patrol car. They will escort you directly to your plane."

"Thank you. I appreciate the assistance."

The gate guard took a look at the small Avis sticker in the corner of the window.

"You want that we should return the car for you?"

Lou looked at the young marine quizzically.

"You can do that?"

The guard smiled conspiratorially.

"We do things like that for the people we like. Congressmen and senators? We let those sit. And aides, aides are the worst. Those get parked in the bad spots."

Lou smiled broadly at the Marine. He knew exactly what game was being played here.

"I would appreciate it if you could drop it off at the rental car company. If not, just don't park it next to the aides' cars, please."

They both laughed. The jokes played at military installations never really changed.

"No worries. Now, you have a hop to catch."

Lou nodded and stomped on the gas. While he made his way out to the flight line, at a brisk fifteen miles per hour, he pulled out his phone and made an audible note to take care of the gate team at Christmas.

CHAPTER NINETEEN

UGENE TAGGART BOUNDED up the stairs inside The Group's safehouse with a pace that was new to the various security details stationed around the building. Clearing the ID pin pad and retina scanner, he yanked the door to the game room open and proceeded inside. Forgoing protocol to place his cellphone, electronic devices, and weapon in his designated holder, he strode straight to the collection of men gathered in a loose circle before the sofa's coffee table. Taggart paused to take in the expressions on the men's faces. Bob Sloan, Paul Spencer, and Chief Justice Nathanial Baker looked at him with varying degrees of concern. He knew where Lou Stenson and Ed Crowley were currently located, so where was Pat Sommers from the Secret Service? Just as he considered the man's location, Pat came bounding through the door in much the same way that Gene had just done. Pat wore much the same expression as everyone else in the room. Gene refocused on the collected group as Pat slid into an empty space in the circle.

"Good. We can get right to it."

"I think that would be a good idea," Bob Sloan said in a conciliatory manner.

"Shouldn't we wait for Ed and Lou," Nathanial Baker asked.

"They're currently occupied with this very situation. They already understand the broad strokes of what we're going to discuss."

Taggart smiled weakly at the Chief Justice and then looked at his watch and did a little math in his head.

"Approximately three hours and forty-five minutes ago, Kristin Hughes was abducted while in The Hague. She was with Dunn and Garver at the time the abduction took place. There was a substantial exchange of gunfire at the scene. Both Dunn and Garver engaged but had to exit the scene before the local law enforcement arrived."

Pat Sommers looked around and took in each of the men standing in the circle.

"Where's Lou? Does he know yet?"

"He knows," Gene said calmly. "He's on his way to The Hague now. He caught a hop out of Andrews."

"There's gonna be hell to pay when his boots hit the ground in Europe."

Everyone looked over at Pat Sommers. Most all of them had thought it, but no one was going to say it out loud. Well, no one but Pat.

"Not to question the man's acumen, he is par excellence at the operational game, but what is one man going to contribute when we already have two such men there?"

Nathanial Baker was an excellent justice, but not yet completely familiar with paramilitary operations. He had learned much in his time with The Group, but still viewed parts of the system from a Hollywood viewpoint. His question wasn't meant to be condescending, and it wasn't received that way by the other men.

"Lou actually brings a whole host of operational skills to the team over there. I'm sure that he'll be instantly advantageous to them."

Paul Spencer spoke with the surety of a military man, which he was when he had started out in his adult life. In a post-911 world however, a place such as the National Reconnaissance Office was a much better fit for his high intellect.

"What is the current status in The Hague?" I mean, where are The Hague police in all of this?"

Pat Sommers was pushing the conversation forward, which Gene appreciated.

"As of right now, they're basically stumbling around in the dark," Gene spoke like someone who had been watching it all live. "They responded to the scene with standard Netherland's efficiency, but since everyone involved fled in various directions prior to them arriving, they've basically been chasing their tails since the start. It seems that they questioned some shop owners and put up a bunch of roadway checks in random places, all of which have produced nothing. Everyone involved has evaded quite successfully."

"What's the status of Dunn and Garver?"

Pat was keeping it on-point. Gene Taggart could sense Pat's agenda item coming.

"Is the old man worried, Pat?"

"Yes. The nuke was a big-enough headache to deal with. Now he has shootouts between terrorists and assassins to potentially deal with. He is significantly concerned about both Doctor Hughes and the huge political nightmare this will create if it keeps going sideways."

Everyone in the circle of men knew that the president was a patriot. That being said, he was also a politician. Sometimes he looked at doing what was best for the country, and himself, politically. Those decisions usually ran counter to what was good for the intelligence community.

"I can appreciate that the president is justifiably concerned, Pat. I think everyone here has a sense of what is at stake."

"In that case, the old man would like to pose a thought."

Everyone stared at Pat Sommers. The president almost never commented on the activities of The Group. It was the way that he kept deniability of the shadowy, immoral, and illegal things that were required in certain black operations.

"Go ahead."

Gene Taggart's suspicion was palpable.

"There are several elite military units in the area. Both Delta and Navy Special Warfare are available. He would be happy to reassign one of them."

All of the intelligence men looked at the floor. Justice Baker looked confused. Paul Spencer looked over at Pat in the way that a boss looks at a junior employee who thinks he has come up with a great idea.

"Where a SEAL team would sound like a great idea on paper, they are not an actual clandestine operational asset. You know that America is said to go everywhere the American military goes. Verified American military personnel would create more problems than they would solve, especially set loose in a political thorn patch like The Hague. There are better ways to proceed."

"There are?"

"Yes. Tell the old man that we will be rerouting satellite traffic, and to keep the Joint Chiefs off of our backs."

"Done. What about firepower? Are we leaving it to the three of them to rescue Doctor Hughes and handle the nuke?"

Gene Taggart sighed. Everyone stopped talking.

"The three of them aren't necessarily alone."

Pat Sommers' look said that he didn't understand the statement. Nate Baker didn't either, but he knew enough not to ask for clarification.

"What do you mean, Gene," Sommers asked without the same concern.

"Stenson, Dunn, and Garver have all the firepower and gear to do what needs doing. Plus, there is an outside entity in the city also actively looking into Doctor Hughes' part in the matter."

"What kind of outside entity?"

Everyone in the intelligence game knew that outside entity was an operational euphemism for mercenaries. Why it hadn't registered with the Secret Service man, Eugene Taggart wasn't sure.

"No answers, Pat. That's all you get on this one. The CIA is handling CIA business as the CIA sees fit."

Nat Baker cleared his throat, which paused an obvious escalation in tensions within the men.

"I submit that Gene is correct here. Just because we interact well together does not mean, nor should it imply, that we would be ignoring obvious jurisdictional boundaries. The CIA does what it does internationally. They do it the way that works best. Prying into how, and why, only compromises all of us."

Eugene Taggart nodded at the chief justice with approval.

"Sage advice as always, Nate." The Director of Operations for the FBI, Bob Sloan, knew that he didn't want to know what he now understood.

Since the very foundation of The Group, there had always been a problematic jurisdictional interplay between the FBI and the CIA. Where the FBI was a federal policing agency with postings in various countries of note, the CIA was a clandestine intelligence and operations entity. The two had very different missions, utilizing very different levels of moral flexibility to achieve them. Both Gene Taggart and Bob Sloan had done their level best not to impugn the other. Nate Baker had been included into The Group to smooth and clarify the ramifications of this working relationship.

"Okay, that topic aside, what is our planned response?"

Pat Sommers knew that he had to have something to take back to the president. It didn't have to be something good, but it did have to be something tangible. This time it was Bob Sloan who answered the Secret Service question.

"Our operational plan is unchanged, as of right now. The primary mission is to find the terrorists, and by proxy, our lost items with them."

"How so?" Pat Sommers asked suspiciously.

"Simple. You find the terrorists and you find Kristin Hughes. You find the terrorists and you find the nuke. It's all A plus B equals C type math."

"That's Lou's operational plan going in," Gene Taggart said in a calm and quiet tone. "He's focused on personnel retrieval. Find the terrorists and follow them to the doctor."

"What are we planning for Zoran Savić or the nuclear weapon?" Nathanial Baker asked.

"Nothing to both items," Gene responded. "The situation with the nuke is unchanged, independent of its location. If it isn't coming to U.S. soil, then it's a political issue. As for Zoran Savić, he wasn't our problem to begin with. If he ends up escaping, then he ends up escaping. If he doesn't, well he doesn't. The Hague will be handling their own business on that front. That was the last thing Lou and I discussed on his way out."

Gene looked around the circle of men.

"Lou is geared up for a reconnaissance and recovery operation. Handling whatever goes sideways during the op will be considered a field-level decision."

"So, there's a scenario at play here where Zoran Savić walks free and blows up The Hague?"

Nathanial Baker was being analytical, but he had also spent time in The Hague. Paul Spencer decided to field the question. It would be easier for him to answer it than it would for his CIA counterpart.

"The short answer is yes. The long answer is no. In our very real world of blood and revenge, none of those three men over there right now is going to let Zoran Savić or any one in his terrorist cell walk away from this alive. A bridge has been crossed that cannot be uncrossed. As for the bombing of The Hague? As much as I would applaud them if they blew up Brussels on the way out of town, the EU's surveillance policies are a right pain in my ass most days, it realistically isn't going to happen to either the Netherlands or Belgium. The cell originally stole the nuke to blow up something in Eastern Europe. Presumably some target of opportunity in Croatia. They aren't going to waste a nuke that took so much blood to acquire on a random target. They are going to take it back where they came from and use it there as planned."

"Anywhere in Croatia is better than The Hague, but still." Bob Sloan smiled weakly.

Pat really wanted to hear one of them say that we were going after the nuke, too. His boss was known for asking exacting questions. He didn't like to knowingly lie to his boss. Paul Spencer could feel Pat's internal conflict from across the circle.

"Well, since they're done filming Game of Thrones, Croatia's a better target area than anywhere in Western Europe." Paul tried smiling to lighten the mood in the circle. "I wouldn't worry, too much. Lou Stenson isn't going to let them leave the area with the nuke. I'm sure that once Doctor Hughes is back in our positive control, recovering the bomb will be his next immediate priority."

Pat nodded. "That makes good sense."

Gene Taggart turned from his position in the circle and walked to the bar cart stationed next to the heavy wooden table which normally collected all of the men's phones, electronics, and weapons. He retrieved a bottle of water and a bottle of Heineken, and returned to the other men. Opening the beer, he handed the bottle of water to Pat.

"Here Pat, you're starting to look a little parched."

The Secret Service man took the bottle, but didn't open it. Gene tossed back about half of the beer and smiled.

"Tell the president not to overly worry. It hasn't gone so wrong that it can't be fixed. Even if, for some yet to be explained reason, we can't get Doctor Hughes back intact, as we all desperately want to, there will definitely be a bloodbath following up her recovery. With both Dunn and Stenson on-station in country, I'm betting all of my Vegas money that the bloodbath will be epic."

Pat Sommers scowled. The president had enough problems right now, with China being belligerent and Russia helping Saudi Arabia flood the market with cheap oil.

"Well, that will certainly create a political disaster. But it is better than the alternate scenarios."

"Don't worry, Pat. We've gotten the boss out of bigger political disasters than this one."

Bob Sloan looked over at his Secret Service counterpart and smiled. Pat Sommers knew that the statement was a direct reference to The Group's involvement in disabling two nuclear bombs that would have decimated a G8 Summit held in Chicago a little while back. Pat smiled back at Sloan.

"True enough. I'll tell the old man to stay calm and ride it out. Boots are already on the ground."

"Please don't forget to have him get the Joint Chiefs off of my back. Satellites overhead in Europe and the Near East are already being re-tasked."

Paul Spencer was smiling, but clinical in tone.

"No worries. That will be topic number one."

Gene Taggart finished his beer and looked around the circle.

"Well, that should about do it for now. Since this thing is in motion, we can easily do the rest over secure cells. Everyone agree?"

Everyone in the circle nodded in agreement.

"Sounds good. Now, I imagine some of us have places to be."

CHAPTER TWENTY

J ASNA PULLED UP to the garage door of the safe house and flashed her lights. They had been driving around the southern section of The Hague for an hour in an attempt to ensure that they hadn't been followed. It had been hard to act casual and blend into the calm surroundings in a car that was missing windows and was shot full of holes. The entire passenger side of the vehicle was riddled with bullet dents and holes. The windscreen was spiderwebbed halfway across its surface on the passenger side of the car. Both passenger sections of door glass were missing, along with the rear windscreen. The rear passenger side tire was still there, but it was much more rim than tire.

The only two bright sides, if there were any, came in the form of casualties. Somehow, all the gunfire had missed both Jasna and the American woman. And, the red color of the car was close enough to blood red that it didn't announce to the good people of The Hague that Emil had bled all over it after being shot.

Adam Pavlovic looked out the small garage door window and his eyes went wide. The little car looked like it had just driven through the last stand in downtown Baghdad. What the hell had happened since they had left?

The button on the wall was pressed and the garage door rose. Alek Lukic came walking into the garage area whistling some children's song and immediately stopped to draw a long breath at the sight of the car pulling in. Adam hit the button on the wall once more and the overhead door began its methodical descent toward the closed position. Turning around, Adam caught sight of the car's rear and almost gasped. If it was possible for a couple of people with small caliber weapons to dismantle an auto with bullets, it would seem that they were successful. Whoever these two had gotten involved with had all but destroyed the boot and rear markers.

Jasna killed the engine, which appeared to be the one thing still working well, then looked over at Emil. Her expression said, *you're gonna have fun explaining this.* Emil just nodded at his driver and turned to reach for the door handle.

Emil stepped from the car in a controlled manner. He knew that in times of contention, it was the leader who must display the only true voice. Zoran had told him this one night after a long debate about a job in which half wanted to go and half didn't. Zoran had finished the discussion by standing up and telling everyone what was going to happen. It was direct and commanding. Emil thought that a less commanding, but more fatherly tone might work better in this situation.

At some point in the drive south, Emil had ripped off his shirt sleeve and utilized it as a makeshift bandage. The bandage was now saturated with blood, and a small amount was now trickling down his arm. The blood in the soaked cloth was half congealed and gave Emil the image of a poorly put together Halloween zombie.

"It's not as bad as it looks, Adam."

Emil's voice was level and sure. Adam's expression was otherwise.

"That would be true if we were in Syria. But we're in The Hague."

Emil looked at his friend and smiled.

"Valid point."

Alek looked straight down at the floor, trying to hide a smile. It worked only partly. Emil caught sight of Alek and pointed in his direction to refocus some of Adam's energy. Adam caught the image of his younger companion in his peripheral vision and calmed some of his hostility.

"Okay, Emil, what the hell happened to you two?"

Emil sat down in a swivel desk chair and recapped the events of the morning. Parts of the gunfire exchange were blurry, but he gave them the best story that he could put together. Jasna wandered off to the bathroom and collected up enough medical supplies to work on Emil's gunshot wound. It had been evident when he ripped off his shirt in the car that the bullet had passed straight through the meat of his upper arm. It was the best news that they could have hoped for. The wound would heal on its own if kept clean. All Jasna had to do was clean it and dress it.

Jasna came back into the garage to hear the end of Emil's rendition of the gun battle. Bullets were flying in all directions. Tires were screeching as the car fled out of the parking area for the main street. The gunmen chased them on foot, continuously firing as they went. Both Adam and Alek sat transfixed as Emil told them the tale of their escape. Jasna thought that Emil would make a good storyteller. He had a natural ability to draw people in as he talked. He would probably turn into that old man in the village. The one who told the stories all the children wanted to hear again and again. That was if they all made it out of The Hague in one piece.

Emil was just about to the part where they pulled up to the safe house when Jasna walked over and sat the bandages and peroxide on the desk.

"But where did the others come from, Emil?"

Alek's question was on point. It was his tone that made it sound as if he had digressed to a younger person.

"As near as I can tell, they were in the park. If I had to guess, they were also scouting out good scouting positions, the same as us."

"So, you think they have the same plan for us as we do for Zoran?"

Adam's question was more speculation than it was assumption. Emil shuffled in his chair as Jasna dumped peroxide into the bullet wound.

"That's my assumption. That said, I think our original plan is still good. Especially since we know that they are now here for us and are counter-planning. We will definitely need a new observation point."

Adam Pavlovic considered the statement for a moment. He looked over at the car and then back at Jasna and Emil.

"Those are big problems, Emil. The spot we pick wasn't really the best spot, it was the only good spot. And, knowing that someone is counter-planning, in no way tells you anything about how they are counter-planning."

Emil smiled at Jasna and Adam could tell that he was missing something vital.

"Adam, you are quite correct. As for the spotter problem, we can use a rolling spotter. There is enough traffic in the area of the main intersection to insert a car into traffic without any problems. Since the court people have posted all the transfer times, it should make getting a car in the right place to observe things easy. As for the American counter-planning, I think we will be able to figure that out before it becomes a problem. We should know what to expect long before we get there."

The rolling spotter made good sense to both Adam and Alek. Alek had played the part of rolling spotter before. It was actually less suspicious in small towns when compared to having a random auto sitting on a street with a person in it doing the observing.

"All right Emil, I'll bite. How are we going to know what the Americans are going to do?'

Adam could tell that Emil had an ace up his sleeve. Emil smiled at Jasna and thanked her as she finished wrapping his arm with clean white gauze. He stood and nodded his head in the direction of the shot-up auto. The others followed as they all walked to the rear of the auto. Nodding at the shot-out rear window, he listened to the others gasp as they took in the unconscious form of the American doctor sprawled across the rear seat. Emil looked at Jasna, who was trying to conceal an ear-to-ear smile.

"I figured we'd ask her once she wakes up."

"Well, that answers the '*is she still alive*' question." Alek was bent over so that his head was almost inside the car.

Emil looked at Jasna quizzically, and then looked back at Alek. He hadn't really stopped to think about whether she had been injured in the escape.

"I assume she is. She didn't take any fire from her comrades while we were loading her in the car. And Jasna only hit her hard enough to put her down. She should just be unconscious."

The leader of the terrorist cell held a look that said he was unconcerned whether she was alive or dead. Alek Lukic wasn't one hundred percent sure that he liked that. The American woman hadn't done anything to them. And she sure was beautiful lying there as if she were sleeping. She would probably be quite foul when she came around again. He was sure that her comrades would now be out for blood. That just meant more complications.

"It's interesting how they managed to nearly destroy the car, and put one into you, but managed to miss both Jasna and her."

Adam was thinking. He had a far-off look in his eye, like he was reliving some bad business.

"The grace of working against professionals, Adam." Emil was calm and level. Adam agreed with him.

Alek Lukic yanked the rear door of the bullet-riddled car open and leaned in to gather up the American scientist. With a deft hand, he slowly removed her from the car. Reversing out, he stopped in a standing position with her draped across his arms. She was lighter in his arms than he had planned on, and it made him start to wonder. Emil noticed Alek's change in expression and began to ponder.

"Take her in the other room, with the bomb, and tie her to a chair. Don't be afraid to hurt her. We'll find out her condition when she regains consciousness."

Alek nodded to the group leader and turned to be off with their prize. Jasna followed along behind him to help.

Adam had been out picking up supplies the night before. A sturdy length of rope had been one of the items. Alek sat Kristin Hughes softly in a straight-backed metal office chair. He held her up in an unobstructed fashion while Jasna went about binding her. First, her chest was tied to the back of the chair. Next, her arms were secured to the arms of the chair. Finally, her legs were tied to the chair's front legs. Jasna made sure that the ropes were tight and that the knots were out of the doctor's reach. She wasn't going to free herself from this. This American wasn't the first person that Jasna had secured to a chair. The American wouldn't be going anywhere until she was allowed to.

Adam and Emil finally came into the room to inspect Jasna's bondage job. It looked first rate. Emil sat in a chair against the wall opposite her. He looked at the American scientist and then over at the bomb that they had stolen.

"Well, at least she'll be able to say that she found the stolen bomb."

Jasna had to stifle a laugh. Adam gave the terrorist leader a wry smile. Alek was less amused.

"Jasna, grab a bottle of water and a cloth."

Jasna stood to leave the room. Alek looked over at the other two men. Surely they didn't mean to waterboard her? Maybe she would just tell them whatever they wanted to know if they asked?

Adam and Emil sat quietly and waited for Jasna to return. Alek tried as hard as he could to remain neutral. He didn't think Jasna was ever going to return.

The fourth member of the terrorist cell returned to the room with a basin of water and a white wash cloth. She walked over and sat the basin on a table next to the American. She soaked the cloth and rang it out before laying the cloth on the American woman's forehead. Jasna positioned it completely across her forehead and let the cool water temperature penetrate.

"What's the long-term plan here, Emil?" Adam was using his voice-of-reason tone.

Emil scratched his chin and pondered for a second or two.

"Long term? I'm not really sure. I was thinking that we might learn whatever there was to learn about the opposition. After that, we could easily leave her here tomorrow while we free Zoran."

"Then?"

"Well, she went to see Zoran in prison. I don't know, presumably Zoran might like to talk to her again before we leave? Anyway, we certainly can't take her with us back to Bosnia."

"Do you think we'll have that kind of time tomorrow? I mean, to let them converse before we head for the boat?"

"I would say that's completely dependent upon how much resistance the ICC people are able to muster after the hit."

Adam looked at Emil directly. Little about their adventure had gone to plan since they left Bosnia. The heist went flawlessly, otherwise the operation had become a series of bad endings.

"I can't imagine that they're going to take it very well, Emil."

"As near as I can tell, no one has ever attempted to escape from The Hague before. It's hard to say how they'll respond. My bet is that the prison will be slower to respond than the German and the American."

Jasna removed and rewetted the cloth before putting it back on Kristin Hughes' forehead as Alek watched. She put it back into place and shuffled to find a more comfortable sitting position. Alek didn't exactly understand what was going on. He was just hoping that they weren't going to interrogate her. Jasna could tell that Alek was at a loss and decided to help.

"The cool water soaks into her skin. There are a great number of nerve endings across the forehead that communicate with the brain. The temperature change gives the brain something to focus on, and that slowly pulls it back to reality. Unconsciousness can be tricky at times. It can last one second or it can last for hours. What you don't want to do is shake the system back into action sharply. Doing that makes the brain act unpredictably. This is the best way to bring her around without causing further damage."

Alek nodded as she talked. Hearing Jasna say it out loud made good sense to him. Jasna noticed him relax as she talked. He was younger than the rest of them. Maybe he had never had to do this before?

"What did you think we were going to do? Dump water down her throat until she talked?"

Alek looked at her with a child-like expression.

"No."

Kristin Hughes shifted under Jasna's hand and drew in a slow breath. Jasna removed the cloth and tossed it into the basin. The whole room sat quietly for another thirty seconds or so until Kristin pulled herself from the blackness. Slowly opening her eyes, there was a halo of light along the left side of her vision. It matched the pain in her temple. Apparently, she had been whacked from behind. It was probably a pistol butt. The pain in her temple felt like she had been hit with eighteen pistol butts.

She shifted to readjust her position in the chair as her vison came back online. Her body didn't move. The lack of motion caused Kristin Hughes to glance down, taking in the sight of the rope restraints. Tilting her head made it explode in pain. She leveled her head as quickly as she could. It took a second or two for her vision to catch up with her head movements, but finally it cleared. She took in the other people in the room. And then she took in the outline of the green H-912 carrier assembly. She exhaled slowly.

"What the hell?"

The older man in the chair smiled.

"Hello, Doctor Hughes. I apologize for the restraints, but they seem necessary. I promise that we won't gag you, if you don't scream. What do you say we converse about what you might be doing in The Hague?"

CHAPTER TWENTY-ONE

OU STENSON'S F-14 Tomcat taxi ride flew a leisurely 1.5 Mach up the coast of the United States to a refueling point on the rocky shores of Maine. The Tomcat's pilot, a likeable Navy lieutenant named Slippery turned the fighter jet east and pushed the dual General Electric turbofans out to their stops over the open water, launching the fighter jet toward Iceland at a blood-readjusting 2.3 Mach. Lou Stenson sat in the rear radar intercept operator's seat and tried not to sound too stressed during conversation.

Both Lou and Slippery were Navy men, so their standard language was the same. Truth be told, any military man understood another military man. They all just enjoyed complaining about the differences between the branches.

The Tomcat did a hot stop in Iceland to get refueled. The plane had a cruise range of around 1,600 nautical miles, but the velocity that they had been making pushed the airplane down to something around its combat range of 500 nautical miles. The airframe had been unburdened of its missiles before leaving and flew with clean hard points. This helped the flight range. The 600 rounds of 20mm cartridges for the multi-barreled cannon had been left in their trays. This was mostly due to the unloading time the ground crew had to work with.

Lou Stenson and Lieutenant Slippery pounded across the outer reaches of the North Sea at a blistering 2.3 Mach, which was all the Tomcat had in her. They boomed a couple of deep-sea fishing boats before the Royal Air Force came on the air and informed them to back down in the Queen's airspace.

Slippery informed the air traffic controller of their intent to set down at RAF Mildenhall and was given routing and proper airspeeds for travel over middle England. The pilot pulled back on the Tomcat's yoke and lowered her flight speed to something respectable enough for The Crown.

Mildenhall tower was on the air before the Tomcat reached its outer markers and talked the United States Navy pilot straight down onto the main runway. Slippery rolled down the runway's accessway and onto the approach ramp in front of a well-maintained hangar sporting a logo for the 352nd Special Operations Group. The turbofans were still spooling down when the cowl came open and Lou Stenson started to extricate himself.

Lou placed the RIO's helmet, belonging to another affable Navy lieutenant nicknamed Tex, on the seat as he got out. He told Slippery that he would make sure that the flight suit got returned. Slippery told him not to worry and wished him safe travels.

The big ex-SEAL's boots struck the ground and he proceeded without conversation or direction straight to a waiting Lear jet. The nondescript plane turned on the apron and started rolling. The ground crew assigned to the 352nd didn't ask any questions as the transfer took place. They had seen this show in the past and knew what was going on. The head of the ground crew approached the Tomcat, once it was finished spooling down, and asked what he would be needing before he had to be off again.

The captain of the nondescript Lear jet closed the main cabin door as they squared up on the runway. They were unbothered by both the ground crews and the tower. The flight time to Rotterdam was short. Lou Stenson had no more than time enough to go through the gear bag and weapons bag that Gene Taggart had been nice enough to provide. A note on top of the weapons bag stated that all the weapons were clean and disposable in case they needed to be discarded. Lou was happy that Gene was thorough.

The Lear jet descended into Rotterdam The Hague Airport as if it were any other businessperson's transport and rolled all the way to the end of the runway before turning off. The pilot directed the plane over onto an approach ramp and back down the far side of the runway to where the private hangars were located. The nondescript jet was shown into a marked-out section of apron before a nondescript hangar and was given the shutdown signals from the ground crew.

Lou Stenson hoisted up the two bags and made his way to the main cabin door. He thanked the pilots for the flight and asked if they were headed back to England. They responded with an affirmative, so he asked if they could return the Navy flight suit that was rolled up on the seat. The jet captain laughed and said that they would be happy to.

Tossing the gear bag out onto the tarmac, Lou Stenson pushed out of the opening onto a step built into the inside of the door and looked around. It seemed that every airport on the planet looked the same from the step of a jet. Two men stood patiently to one side and waited for the DOE NEST Operations Chief to descend to the ground. He knew one was Robert Dunn. He assumed that the other man was the German, Eric Garver. Where he had talked to the man via video-link, people tended to look slightly different in person. Nevertheless, the look on the man's face told Lou everything he needed to know.

Lou looked past the two men to another hangar. Another private jet had also just landed at the airport. It looked like a Hawker, but he wasn't good with identifying private planes. The logo on the plane's tailfin was what had really caught his eye. The eagle claws sticking straight out and down, as if the bird of prey was readying to arrest a salmon. The script rotating around the eagle claws read Talon Corporation. Lou Stenson rolled the name around his head for a couple seconds. There was something there buried deep down in the memory, but he couldn't pull it out.

He focused on the two men unloading gear bags from the plane's rear cargo hold. The men were not ground crew. From their look, he would think that they were mercenaries. They looked like ex-Special Forces of one variety or another. Maybe internationally schooled, but definitely trained individuals. It was obvious from their stance and movements. Another man, also an operator but more European looking, stuck his head out of the main door. He gave Lou Stenson a quick once-over and moved to the other men to help handle the gear bags.

Lou thought about what Gene Taggart had told him on the phone. He might run into some *mercs* along the way. They would also be here to help. He would need to find out what he could about this Talon Corporation when he checked in with The Group. Ed Crowley and his NSA whiz kids knew something about everything and everyone on the planet.

Dunn and Garver approached as Lou reached down to retrieve the gear bag he had unceremoniously tossed out of the plane.

"Dunn, good to see that you boys are prompt." Lou decided that attempting to start things on a good note would be best. Truthfully, he hadn't really calmed down on the flight over and really wanted to kill someone.

"Mr. Stenson, sorry to have to meet like this. This is Herbert Becke. He's with the German police." Dunn sounded like a businessman.

"Actually, Mr. Stenson and I have been previously introduced." The German's voice was moderate and clouded. Lou guessed that he was trying to mask the fact that his sterling GSG-9 reputation had been tarnished twice in one week.

Lou nodded at Dunn and then focused on Garver.

"Herr Becke, it's good to finally meet you in person. Let's say that we save all of the conversation for someplace better than the airport."

Both men nodded and turned to walk off toward a private parking area. Stenson followed them off the tarmac. A black Mercedes SUV pulled up behind the Talon jet and a dark-skinned man stepped out with confidence. He strode over to the mound of gear and grabbed the top two bags.

"Really Juan? A Mercedes? Do you think we can get any more cliché here?"

Lieutenant "Little John" Baker, an ex-Marine recon scout, shook his head in jest at the third member of their fire team. Juan Sanchez, ex-SEAL and logistical provider for the team, smiled broadly.

"It's comfortable for three. It's just suave enough to blend in with our current operating environment. It will hold all our gear. And, it has Serious/XM."

Thomas Moore, ex-SAS, picked up two bags and followed Juan to the vehicle.

"He's got my vote, based upon radio alone. Remember that job a couple months back? All we had to choose from were those three Bollywood stations."

Little John shook the sound of Bollywood from his mind as quickly as it entered. He wasn't reliving that. He made his way back to the jet's cabin door and informed the plane's pilot that they were bugging out, and they would check-in at two-hour intervals. The pilot shouted an affirmative out the opened door but didn't bother to see them off. The pilot was responsible for the plane, not the people that they happened to be chauffeuring about.

Baker walked back to the rear door of the Mercedes and climbed in behind the driver. Moore had already adjusted the radio to an acceptable rock station and set the volume at a level where they could plan as Sanchez drove.

"Let's hit it."

The black SUV pulled out from behind the plane and headed for the access gate that serviced the private parking area. Baker pulled out a tablet and flipped the cover back. Tapping the screen, a map of the greater Hague area came to life. He looked at the map and thought.

"Okay. First order of business. We need to get established in the traffic camera system and figure out where the kidnapping car escaped to after the gun battle. Just staring at the map, I'm betting that they are holed up somewhere in the south end of the city."

The two men in front nodded as the leader of their three-man fire team spoke. The team had a set hierarchy, and everyone in it had a specific purpose based upon their skillset. The fire team cruising through The Hague was one part of a larger squad-sized unit consisting of three fire teams and some ten individuals. The three different fire teams tended to operate independently as much as they did in a squad configuration.

In the current configuration, the responsibility broke down by skillset. Baker was the team leader, handled commo, heavy weapons overwatch, and spoke German. Thomas Moore was the demolitions man, heavy weapons entry man, and spoke Arabic. Juan Sanchez was the wheel man, de-facto pilot (specifically helicopters), close quarters combat and entry lead, and the logistics man. Sanchez had received cross-training as a combat medic during his regular Navy time. These days, due to his communications responsibilities, Baker was considered the tech head of the team. Of the three, Moore was thought of as the real fighter, which was fine with him.

"First stop is the hub, correct?"

Juan had the SUV out in traffic and headed north toward the seat of the International Criminal Court.

"Affirmative." Little John scanned his map. "We need to figure out where they went to, then we can go smash-and-grab the doctor."

Juan nodded and pulled the SUV out into the passing lane. Several minutes of highway speed and they were pulling down an on-ramp into more congested city streets. The mercenaries made their way along the street at the city speed and instantly blended in with the chic European city traffic.

Contrary to the Hollywood version of reality, where men need to break into heavily fortified federal buildings or secured police facilities and work their way into some protected server room to access computer systems, the reality of a congested European city infrastructural system was decidedly different. A city bureaucracy couldn't run a system of hundreds of CCTV cameras, with dozens of system users, and have it placed in some highly secured facility. Truthfully, a city's metro system was more secure than the CCTV system that monitored it.

In The Hague the individual street camera zones collected and fed information to a central zone collection point. A hub. That hub fed all the collected feed upstream to a bigger hub, which distributed it to different system access points, both public and private. The central collection hub also would archive the feed for playback. When an individual user wanted to see archive data, they would send a digital request back downstream to the hub for a file, and the central switching server went and found whatever they wanted in the terabytes of collected traffic camera data filed into the storage each day.

In this specific case, the central hub that the mercenaries wanted to access was located in a nondescript utility building down in the Voorburg section of the city, sitting quietly down the street from a Domino's Pizza. The building that collected and processed all of the traffic camera data didn't even have a security system of its own. Two standard commercial metal doors with standard door locks were all that kept thieves at bay.

Thomas Moore looked at the commercial lock set and then smiled up at the team leader, who was still trying to extricate himself from the back of the SUV.

"We're sure about no security system?"

"Yup. That's the story."

Baker sounded sure, so Moore popped the lock and let the door break its seal with the jamb. He counted out a thirty count and then nodded. Sanchez killed the engine and climbed out of the SUV to take up an exterior observation position on a nearby street bench.

Baker and Moore disappeared inside the hub and wasted no time finding the section of the server farm that they had come for. Fortunately for Baker, Netherlands Dutch was close enough to his Bavarian German that he could read the signs with little effort.

Baker popped open two server cages and slid a keyboard out of one to access the system controller. The terminal required a password to allow access to the main system control screen, but as was the case in most industrial settings, the password was written on a piece of paper taped to the bottom of the screen. Baker had seen this situation a hundred times. He carried sophisticated code breaking software on the tablet, but seldom needed to utilize it. Cities like The Hague spent large amounts of euros on equipment, yet not nearly as much on personnel. The technicians that serviced and maintained the equipment made life as easy on themselves as possible. As Baker typed the password in to the request box on the screen, he suspected that this password would work at any access point in the city. It felt about right.

A couple of sets of keystrokes and the team made its way into the live camera feed. Baker maneuvered the camera feed through several intersections to get a feel for the way that the computer system navigated. He backed out of the live feed and moved over to the central logic controller. Finding the internal system router, he added a username and password to the list of authorized users in the system. Little John snatched up the tablet and checked the login from a non-connected device. Things booted up nicely on the tablet and he found the tablet-configured interface easier to utilize than the server system. He smiled and reached down to key the mic on his collar.

"Okay boys, we're officially into the system and platformed as an active user. Now it's time to find the archive footage."

Moore nodded over at the team leader as he watched the door and central hallway of the server farm for any unwanted guests. Sanchez, sitting out on a street bench, responded with an affirmative and said that all was quiet outside.

Baker focused on the computer screen and began to sift through the different sections of the city to find the park area where the doctor had been abducted. He knew that the initial break-in was a much easier issue that sifting through all the data to find one red, shot-up car. He emotionally settled in. It would just take time.

In a different section of the city, Kristin Hughes' day wasn't going nearly as well. Since her abduction by the Bosnian terrorists, the status of her condition had been what she would describe as adequate. The headache that had seemed her constant companion after coming to had finally started to recede into the background. She was pretty sure that she had a concussion, at minimum. She had had a concussion once before, when she lived at Fort Gordon. Her father had taken her to the rappelling tower on a Saturday to do exit drills with his group. She had managed to get halfway down the wall before her grip slipped and she plummeted to the ground. The station doctor had called it a closed head injury, but he had written concussion on her medical jacket.

Kristin pushed the thoughts of the rappelling wall from her mind. The fall had come not long before her father had died. She thought that if she made her way out of this situation, she really needed to call her stepdad. She hadn't talked to him in some time. It was overdue.

She was about to close her eyes and focus on making all the bad memories go away when she was joined by her main captor, Emil Savić. He was followed by the man they called Adam. Adam seemed to be the voice of reason in the group. If she had to guess through the fog still in her brain, he was probably the one who was a baker. He just seemed like that type of person.

Emil walked to the metal table stationed adjacent to the chair Kristin was currently secured to and sat a small package on it. He pushed himself up on the tabletop and rubbed his left knee gently. Kristin found the maneuver out of place. Normally, captors portrayed themselves as strong at all times.

"Did you hurt your knee? You seemed to be moving well the last time I was conscious."

Emil Savić smiled at his captive in a zookeeper sort of way.

"No, Miss Hughes. I damaged my knee years ago. I was younger. It was war. I think these types of things just stay with us to remind us of the past. I am usually quite mobile."

Kristin looked at him quizzically. He was a walking contradiction. He was a terrorist and a killer, yet he was quiet and well-spoken. She had no idea how to read the man.

"I feel that we need to return to our earlier conversation, Doctor Hughes. Now that you have had some time to consider your surroundings and the precarious nature of your situation, do you feel like telling us what you are really doing in The Hague?"

And the penny drops, Kristin thought. We're back to interrogation.

"I am here to talk to your leader Zoran and to find the nuclear weapon that your group stole from the German airbase."

"Yes, that is what you had said before. I would like to know how you and your friends planned to retrieve the weapon?"

Emil looked over at the nuclear weapon they were discussing sitting quietly on a different table.

"As I explained before, we really hadn't formulated a master retrieval plan yet. But I'm pretty sure it would involve machine guns and flash-bang grenades."

Emil smiled. Adam smiled too, despite himself. The two exchanged a glance and Emil lowered himself back down onto the floor.

"Doctor Hughes, we both know the types of individuals that both you and I tend to associate with."

Emil turned and began to open the small bundle he had brought in with him. Kristin could see the syringe and the small clear vile of liquid inside the bundle. The sight stopped her cold.

"I tend not to handle things like other men we know. I have no tolerance for men that beat confessions out of other men. And no stomach for those who do it to women."

Emil slid the syringe needle into the rubber vial top and extracted 50 ccs of the liquid.

"That, however, does not mean that I don't need to know things that you know. Information that you seem unwilling to give."

Emil turned and held the syringe out between them. He slowly pushed the plunger up as he tapped the side to release the air bubbles trapped inside the liquid. He sat the syringe down on the table and picked up an alcohol wipe.

"I assure you. I have told you everything that I know about the questions you have asked. We didn't know you were actually in the city until we ran into you on the street. We haven't come up with a plan for the nuke yet, honest."

Emil smiled at Kristin with understanding as he wiped a spot in the break of her elbow. He sat the alcohol pad down and picked up the syringe.

He lined the needle up with a vein and slid it home. She didn't so much as flinch when he stuck her with the needle. Kristin could feel the liquid enter her system and start working its way toward her heart. It was warm and made her feel as if everything would be just fine. She looked at Emil Savić and watched his eyes change from dark brown to speckled green and black. She was sure that her sanity was soon to be leaving.

Emil sat quietly and waited. It took two or three minutes before the serum had completely washed through Kristin's system. He could tell that her resolve was all but gone. It was time to start.

"Doctor Hughes, the serum that you are experiencing is a favorite in my part of the world. It will leave no lasting effect on you, but it will liberate your seemingly secure tongue. Now, why don't you tell me about your friends and about your plan to get the nuclear weapon back?"

Kristin strained against the black, happy, warm grip that was penetrating her brain. She fought to keep calm, even as she felt herself begin to speak.

CHAPTER TWENTY-TWO

THE NORTHERN SUN rose to three men fully engaged in weapons checks and equipment prep. All tables in the central salon of the group's hotel room were laden with rifles, pistols, grenade launchers, binoculars and optics, and electronics of every kind. Eric Garver powered up a small, multi-propeller drone to check its flight readiness. Lou Stenson was reviewing a map of the city streets on a ten-inch tablet computer. Robert Dunn handled the utilitarian work in the group, filling weapon magazines with rounds. He had filled a tabletop with loaded magazines but continued clicking in rounds. It was going to be one of those days where you didn't want to run low on ammunition.

The three men hadn't really exchanged much communication over the hours. Dunn had discussed the situation in the park and the ensuing shootout. Stenson had asked numerous technical questions. From this he had made some assumptions regarding the cell's threat level. Farther along in the night, Stenson and Garver had discussed the initial takedown in Kitzigen. The SEAL was interested in how the terrorist cell operated as a group. What was its strengths? Did the cell show specific operational or tactical strengths? To Garver's surprise, he stayed to operational questions only.

Garver had been waiting for the DOE man to dress them down. It hadn't come. Instead, this new member of their team had stepped off the plane as an active participant in their operation. He wasn't sure how it would all play out, but from what he had seen, he felt comfortable putting his life in the man's hands. Right now, that was what mattered most.

Privately, he was worried about what kind of fury the large ex-SEAL might unleash if Doctor Hughes was found in less-than-satisfactory condition.

A solid knock came to the door and all three men paused. Robert Dunn stood and headed in that direction. He spun a suppressor into the end of his Model 20 Glock while closing the distance. Stopping with his body to one side, so that he wasn't directly behind the door, he rotated over and looked through the door's inspection hole. A man in a crisp white jacket stood before the door with a large metal push cart. The cart had two shelves, both with covered trays. A pleasant smile on the face of the man in the crisp white jacket showed the same features as the man who had delivered every other tray to the suite. It was room service. Dunn relaxed slightly.

The door was opened to the point where Robert Dunn's body could block the view inside. The waiter attempted to enter the room with the cart but was met by several twenty euro notes and Dunn's neutral expression. He released his grip on the cart. Dunn nodded and watched as the waiter moved off down the hallway. Waiting until the waiter was out of sight, Dunn pulled the tray inside and closed the door.

"Food. Glorious food," was the proclamation as Dunn pushed the cart into the middle of the salon.

Stenson looked at the CIA assassin and considered the statement. He was quite hungry. Food would be just the ticket.

All three men took seats at a table devoid of guns, ammo or other equipment. The solid portions of food on the tray was short in its survival. Some of the juice was consumed, but none of the coffee. All three men refrained from the caffeine, deciding not to overcharge their systems with the stimulant.

"So, now that all the required items are out of the way, let's get to the logistics. Is there a spot right on the intersection that we can utilize as an overwatch location?" Stenson was all business and the other two responded in kind.

"There is a multistory parking structure on the south side. It is one building off the intersection, but it should work nicely for observation." Garver had used the parking area on the first day he had driven around the city with Kristin. He had liked it then.

"Good. That will be the drone launch location."

Dunn listened to their new pack leader and wasn't wanting to start a challenge for alpha male status, but he did need to test some ground.

"We do plan on setting up on the intersection to engage the Sons of Sava when they engage the convoy?"

"The Sons of Sava?" Lou Stenson sounded confused.

"That's what they're called back in Bosnia. Zoran's crew, that is."

Garver focused on Stenson as he made a face.

"No. We do not," Stenson said matter-of-factly.

Dunn was obviously confused by the response. Garver didn't seem as shocked. Lou Stenson gave the CIA man a direct look.

"I don't give a damn about Zoran Savić. I don't even give a damn about the nuke right now. This op is strictly a hostage recovery scenario. We are going to get Kristin Hughes back, first and foremost. Is that understood?"

Dunn shifted in his chair.

"I understand Lou. We'll get Kristin back. I just wanted to be clear about our intentions."

Dunn picked up a stray piece of toast and held it up as a defensive weapon. Lou Stenson kept his gaze level and his tone moderate.

"We are going to get Kristin back into safe hands. Then we are going on a manhunt. A no-prisoners type manhunt."

Dunn smiled. Garver sighed. The ex-SEAL turned and took in the GSG-9 man's expression. Garver could tell that his sigh had been misinterpreted.

"Fear not, Mr. Stenson. I will be happy to be involved in the killing when we get to it."

To the south of their conversation, in a different part of the city, Emil Savić sat in the living room area of the safe house and looked at his map. The area around the International Criminal Court provided several ways to attempt an escape. Sadly, there didn't appear to be any good ones. All the escape routes were wide expanses or narrow city streets. There were no moderately sized boulevards in The Hague. If traffic congested, they could have problems.

Adam and Alek had located a construction site several blocks to the west of the strike point. The site held a fleet of dump trucks. It would work fine as the place to get the blocking vehicles.

Emil had already found Jasna a new observation point. They obviously couldn't take the red car out again, so it had been replaced with a mid-sized Mercedes van. The white industrial-looking van appeared the same as a hundred others in the city. It was as anonymous as they could get. Or, anonymous enough for the time they would need it.

Emil could hear the others in the next room and decided to take a break from his map. He didn't know if it was the smell of coffee or the sounds of rounds being loaded into magazines that was drawing him. He decided to go anyway.

Entering the building's former dining room, Emil found Jasna and Alek loading magazines with ammunition. The stack already completed in the middle of the table looked like a grandmother's plate of cookies.

Several submachine guns and automatic pistols were scattered about the room. A pair of two-way radios lay on an end table, along with the military grade communications set they had utilized during the nuke heist. The night vision and the electronics kit were still stowed in a gear bag, not being required for the daylight smash-and-grab job.

Emil smiled at the activity and took an open seat on Alek's side of the table.

"Things in here seem to be going well?"

Jasna nodded a loose nod as she continued to count off rounds into the magazine in her hand.

"We've been through all of the items that we will need. Once we finish this, we should be ready to go."

"That's good. We'll most likely want to start our task earlier than planned. The news said that the traffic was heavier than normal this morning."

The other two nodded in understanding.

"We can pick up dump trucks whenever we want. I have a good place for them to sit where they won't be seen."

Though the youngest of the cell, Aleksander Lukic spoke with certainty.

"Good. That's good, Alek. In that case, you and Adam should be on your way as soon as you are done."

"I only have three or four more magazines. We will leave in twenty minutes or so."

"That sounds excellent."

Emil looked around the room at all the gear. After taking in all the differing stacks of kits, he paused.

"Where is Adam?"

"He went to check on the American woman."

Alek's tone had hardened since his first encounter with Doctor Hughes. He was back to his normal self.

Emil wondered if he had emotionally separated himself from the woman to save himself problems. Emil stood and headed for the hallway that led to the stairs. He ascended the stairs to the second floor and paused at the threshold, a stir of curiosity in his movements. The pause allowed for a brief detection of Adam's interactions with the woman. From the sounds echoing out of the room, Adam had just walked in.

"Doctor Hughes, has your headache subsided?'

There was a pause.

"Yes. It has. I can still feel the impact point on my temple, but the throbbing has passed."

"That is good. Jasna probably swung the pistol a bit too hard. Adrenaline and the situation will make one do that. I'm sure that it wasn't intentional."

There was a second pause.

"My name is Adam."

Emil could hear a splash, the trickling of water into a bowl signifying the ringing out of a cloth. His friend was obviously seeing to her wounds.

"So, Adam, what's your plan for me in all of this?"

"Frankly, I'm not sure that there is a set plan for you in all that is happening now. The start of it was probably just accidental timing. Seeing how we are all here for Zoran Savić. After we have freed him, we will be on our way."

There was a third pause. This time the pause made Emil tense. In the continuation of the pause he headed for the opened door.

"I personally don't care much about Zoran Savić or any of your other agendas. What I am here for is sitting right over there."

Kristin Hughes nodded her head in the direction of the loaded H-912 carrier resting on the table across the room. Emil broke through the door as she was nodding and smiled at the pair. Adam continued along, as if Emil had not entered. Kristin focused on their new participant.

"Good morning, Doctor Hughes." Emil nodded at the bound

American scientist. "Frankly, I'd be quite happy to let you have the bomb and be on your way. Sadly, that would make everything that has happened up unto now pointless. So, the bomb will be returning to Bosnia with us when we leave this place."

"And me?"

"I truly have no ill will toward you, Miss Hughes. I would suspect that my cousin Zoran would like to have a word with you before you go, but otherwise we will just have to wait and see how things play out."

Kristin knew that Zoran Savić was a war criminal capable of committing genocide. Waiting for him to get free once again wouldn't end well. Emil smiled at the doctor and then turned his attention to Adam.

"Alek is almost ready for you to depart."

Adam responded with an affirmative Bosnian expression and stood to his full height. Adam and Emil exited the room, leaving Kristin to consider a way to escape from her captors.

Back up in the Voorburg District, Lieutenant Baker and his two comrades were just exiting the central hub building. The task of finding the red car and then tracking it through the city to wherever it was being stored had taken an exasperatingly long time. The genius IT guys who worked for the city hadn't built in any subdivides into the CCTV feed archive folders. Or, if they had, Baker couldn't figure them out.

As near as Baker could tell, the system simply chunked the feed off into forty-five-minute allotments. Those allotments were archived as bulk data. And the system didn't back up the same way every time. So, every forty-five-minute segment was a new search algorithm. It was massively time consuming. What should have been a one-hour black bag job turned into an all-night, full-system intrusion. The mercenary team had left the city crew a half-eaten pepperoni pizza for their trouble.

Out on the street once again, it was time for a quick assessment of the situation. All three sat in the Mercedes SUV and sipped on espressos that Juan Sanchez rounded up from a corner joint.

"We burned a lot of time thanks to Netherland's IT. So now comes the problem call. Do we set up on the house as planned? Or, do we set up on the strike point, since it's only hours away?"

Moore, the ex-SAS man, looked over at his team leader and shrugged his shoulders.

"We know where the house is located, and we're pretty sure that the strike is a hit-and-run, right? House still feels right."

Little John nodded his head and inhaled about half of his espresso.

"I'm on the house, too, LT. We don't know what's going down after the hit. If they're at the house when we get there, we can save a lot of driving around town."

"I tend to agree with you two. I worry a little bit about what they plan to do with the doctor. If she is just information, then they have no need for her once they're ready to act. If she is something more, they will probably take her along with them."

"Something more," Sanchez questioned, as he crumpled his empty paper coffee cup into a wad.

"Maybe none of them know how to actually use the nuke?"

"Oh, that would be a problem." Moore smiled as he finished his coffee.

"Agreed." Baker looked out the window of the SUV at the passing traffic. "Let's head south to the safe house and see what there is to see."

Sanchez nodded and put the black shiny SUV into drive. Traffic in the Voorburg District was just starting to build toward its normal morning congestion. The three mercenaries in the SUV drifted off down the street without notice.

CHAPTER TWENTY-THREE

L OU STENSON WORKED through a rhythm of sweeping the intersection with binoculars for either the convoy or the terrorists, then checking his watch. The three men had been on station since ten in the morning, the waiting starting to wear on stretched nerves. Dunn sat quietly to one side, the remote controller for the drone in his hands. Garver lay prone on the concrete roof of the parking garage, his eye fixed to the sniper rifle's high-power scope.

What was happening on the rooftop of the garage was not pre-op jitters. The coffee in their various arteries had long since worn off. The three men were experiencing what was known in the trade as operational anticipation - the point where waiting turns to a want of action. All three men understood it and compensated for it in their own way.

Lou checked his government- issued, water-tight, night-illuminated wristwatch. The precision instrument stated that the local time was 12:21p.m. He momentarily wondered if something had happened at the prison to delay the convoy's departure. Or, perhaps, had they taken an alternate route? He was about to state as much out loud when the lead convoy van appeared in the binocular's field of view. The armored van proceeded through the urban traffic followed at marked intervals by two other armored vans, each maintaining the same steady, marked interval. A motorcycle escort was positioned front and rear of the convoy, for a total of five vehicles consuming the area usually accepting of four times as many. Five vehicles that they all were assuming had to be dealt with by the Savić cell members.

"I have them in-scope," Garver said calmly.

"I have them as well," Lou Stenson confirmed a bit more icily.

Robert Dunn began turning on the electronics of the small four-rotor drone that Gene Taggart had so graciously provided. He checked each of the rotors for functionality. Finding them acceptable for the sixth time, he turned on the camera and swung the gimble mount in its various directions. Finally, he cued-up the drone's GPS tracking system. A small red dot appeared on the display screen, just off their own position. He nodded at the unit, as if it was another sentient being, and smiled.

"We're good to go here."

The other two men nodded an affirmative response, not removing their eyes from their individual optics.

Out in traffic, a white Mercedes van flowed off an onramp and fell into line, three vehicles behind the trailing motorcycle. Jasna smiled to herself as she focused her attention on the mounted patrolman. The additional motorcycles had been one of the cell's planned-for occurrences. The Hague authorities had to do something to look in control following the park shootout and the previous notification of impending trouble by the American scientist and her German comrade.

Jasna scanned the road, her eyes absorbing every nuance of the situation. Except for the addition of the motorcycle patrols, all looked as expected. She wasn't sure if this was good or bad, but it was too late to worry about it.

"In position. There appear to be no unmarked vehicles trailing behind the convoy."

"Excellent." Emil sounded equal parts calm and impatient.

"The lead vehicle is passing the Crown Plaza – now."

"Adam and Alek, be ready to go in 4, 3, 2, 1 – GO!"

The lead motorcycle made its turn through a green traffic signal from the road named after Professor B. M. Teldersweg onto Scheveningseweg. The volume of traffic around the convoy gave way to the lead motorcycle opening ample room for all the convoy vehicles to continue on through the intersection. The first armored van entered the intersection and began to make the left-hand turn from one main route to the other when the scene then descended into chaos.

From a small side street off the main intersection, two heavy tractor-trailer dump trucks appeared, pulling straight into the open gap in traffic created by the motorcycle escort. The lead dump truck transited directly into the path of the convoy behind the motorcycle and struck the first armored van broadside. The impact from the collision tossed the heavy van like a toy truck, sending it skidding off of the road on its side. The initial dump truck slammed on its brakes, coming to a stopped position that completely blocked the roadway.

With no time to react to the situation unfolding before him, the driver of the second armored van slammed into the side of the stopped dump truck. The body of the loaded truck rocked up on its outside wheels with the impact, throwing some of its loaded gravel in a wide arc out across the intersection.

The third armored van in the convoy was just beginning to arrest its speed and alter course when the second tractor-trailer dump truck came slicing across the roadway, slamming into it at a considerable speed. The concussion of the two profoundly heavy objects colliding sent the smaller armored van tumbling side over side off the tarmac. Hitting the van with more speed than planned, Adam Pavlovic was thrown all the way to the limits of the seat belt, the big tractor-trailer's front end exploding into a shower of parts. The deceleration of the load caused gravel to cascade out over the cab in an explosive lava flow of stone.

Adam jumped from the cab of the blocker vehicle with purpose, leveling an Uzi 9mm submachine gun at the rider of the trailing motorcycle. Three long bursts of bullets from the weapon shredded the motorcycle and dispatched the rider. Turning, he ran toward the armored van he had pummeled with the big truck. Ejecting the magazine from the Uzi, Adam slid in a second and began pounding rounds into one of the van's side windows. Adam hit the window squarely with controlled bursts of gunfire. As one magazine emptied, another was fed into place and the assault continued. After three complete magazines, the machine gun had punched an orange-sized hole into the spiderwebbed glass. One of the interior guards was attempting to orient himself inside the armored van and utilize the opening for returning fire when Adam shoved a gas grenade into the opening. The interior of the van filled with thick white smoke all but immediately, making the occupants of the van surrender their resistance in seconds.

Finished with his initial task, Adam Pavlovic began running toward the middle van as Aleksander Lukic was finishing up a similar operation on the lead van. Alek, too, turned and ran toward the van wedged under dump truck's bed.

As the two blocking drivers oriented themselves on the prisoner-carrying van, their point man stepped out from his protected position next to a street marker and joined them at the rear of the van. The drivers took up cover firing positions while Emil Savić went about placing a breaching charge on the transport's heavy steel doors. The small C4 poly ceramic blast-focusing cone explosive contained just enough punch to remove the door's locking mechanism without bothering whoever was stuck inside.

Emil positioned the charge directly over the lock and turned his head as the explosive charge did its business. Without wasting time, Emil discarded the explosive's detonator and pulled the door free of its closure. The de facto leader of the terrorist cell stayed protected behind the closed metal door as the prison guard fired a volley of rounds through the opening. Emil angled around the door and fired two rounds into the man's armored vest, throwing him back against the van's interior wall. He fired a third shot to dispatch the guard and turned to look at their captive.

"Zoran, are you okay?"

"I'm fine, Emil. Thank you for coming to get me. I don't imagine that there is much time left, though."

Emil removed the keys from the dead guard's belt and went about freeing his cousin.

On the garage rooftop opposite of the intersection, Lou Stenson watched with cool perspective as the mayhem unfolded.

"They really are better than you would think an underground terrorist cell would be," the big ex-SEAL said in a level tone.

"Agreed," Eric Garver returned, not removing his eye from the rifle scope.

Jasna threaded her way through the improvised traffic blockade created by her dump truck driving cohorts and pulled the white Mercedes van up next to the second armored van. Both Adam and Alek readjusted their cover fire positions to protect the get-away vehicle. Jasna removed an Uzi compact from underneath the driver's seat and set the bolt. With three points of contact accounted for, and the van blocking the fourth, the terrorists had established a solid defensible position.

Zoran Savić stepped from the back of the prison transport van brandishing the dead guard's handgun. He made a quick survey of the scene as he jogged to the get-away van. Emil trailed his cousin a mere foot behind, swinging his weapon from side-to -side.

The three terrorists and their freed leader filed into the van's side door in a precise and controlled manner. The door slammed shut and Jasna dropped the Mercedes into drive.

"Are you ready," Lou Stenson asked, without looking at the other two.

"Yes," came back in unison.

Jasna found it less trouble escaping the traffic catastrophe than she had upon entering it. With the split-lane nature of Professor B. M. Teldersweg autoway, the intersection possessed a wide, clear area around where the ambush had taken place. Jasna made her way around the lead tractor-trailer dump truck, trying not to drive over the gravel debris which had been cast out in the collision, and pointed the van down an open section of street created by the blockade.

"Firing in 3, 2, 1," Eric Garver said in an automated voice.

A quiet mechanical ratcheting sound could be heard as the M300 Intervention Composite sniper rifle from CheyTac Arms discharged a custom-made round. The muzzle break on the twenty-nine-inch fluted barrel had been removed and replaced with a fourteen-inch match grade suppressor, rendering the weapon all but silent.

The round flew some four hundred meters at a descending arc and impacted the Mercedes van's rear plastic molding covering the bumper as intended. Fishhook-like barbs extended from the cylindrical metal round as it impacted the van and secured it fast while the target made its way off into urban traffic.

The 0.408 caliber subsonic, ultra-high frequency, kinetic launch tracking probe was a new instrument in the company's vast array of field options. Eugene Taggart had happily supplied the rounds and the match-grade sniper rifle after talking out the loose plan with Lou while still in Washington.

The tracking round fired like any other conventional round, but once out of the barrel, spins up much like a surface-to-air missile. Designed to enable itself upon impact with the target, it was capable of broadcasting a secure signal for a radius of ten kilometers for approximately twelve hours.

Though the system had never been completely field-tested, it still seemed the best option for the specific mission. Lou had accepted it without rebuttal. The ex-SEAL had utilized non-proven technologies on numerous occasions. In field environments, they usually proved adequate to the task.

Eric Garver broke down the weapon and headed for the BMW parked nearby. Lou Stenson watched the van diminish from the view of his binoculars as Robert Dunn called out directions on the drone's tracking system.

The four-rotor drone, another gift from the CIA storeroom, was sized small enough that it was not particularly conspicuous during flight. The sensor on the drone could follow the tracking round, adding another ten kilometers to the overall effective range of the system. A long-range optical camera mounted on a gimble under the drone kept a physical eye on the suspect vehicle.

Lou climbed into the passenger seat as Eric fired up Dunn's BMW. Garver was the choice for wheelman on the operation, as he was European and didn't have to interpret the European traffic system. Dunn sat in the rear seat and directed them in the direction provided by the drone's on-board tracking system. Several long loops of descending ramps to escape the parking garage and the team was out into traffic, racing off behind the getaway van.

At this point in the getaway plan, two opposing trains of thought were converging to create more chaos than had already been inflicted. First, Lou knew that he had to follow the white Mercedes van if he wanted to find either Kristin Hughes or the nuke. Second, Emil Savić knew that if anyone was going to follow them, they would be following the white van that was seen escaping the ambush. That said, Emil knew that the van had to be ditched. And it needed to be ditched pretty soon. Assuming it would take approximately ten to fifteen minutes for either the ICC security or local police to get some kind of handle on the situation and get in the game, the clock gave them maybe seven more minutes of relative calm.

As the van full of Bosnian terrorists reached the south end of the Zorgvliet, a large green space in the middle of the city, Jasna diverted off the roadway and into a parking area. She made a slow lap around the outside of the Omniversum Playhouse parking block to check for suspicious traffic behind them. All still appearing quiet, she pointed the van toward the parking garage for the Marriot Hotel and stepped on the gas.

"It looks like they pulled into a parking garage south of here," Dunn said calmly.

"They're switching vehicles."

Lou Stenson sounded put-out, but otherwise on task. Garver said nothing while keeping the car at top speed.

Jasna pulled the white Mercedes into an empty parking space next to a slightly used, diesel-powered, blue Volkswagen Caddy Panel van. Though half the size of the Mercedes, the Caddy had no rear windows and concealed the Bosnian terrorists from outside view.

All four men climbed into the Caddy's rear compartment. Jasna climbed behind the wheel and fired up the little diesel engine. She fashioned a large-brimmed hat onto her head, giving her the appearance of a delivery driver, and dropped the van into gear. Exiting the garage, Jasna pointed the blue van southwest on Segbroeklaan and blended in with the rest of the workday traffic.

"Decision time, Lou," Robert Dunn said quietly. "We have two vehicles exiting the garage, and the tracker holding steady inside."

"What type of vehicles?"

"A brown, maybe Renault sedan, headed east, and what looks like a blue Volkswagen delivery type van headed southwest."

Lou paused only but a second, and then went with his gut.

"Let's get on the delivery van."

"Okay. Eric, head south on Segbroeklaan when you get there."

It seemed from reactions that Emil Savić's thoughts about a police response time in the city were spot-on. The group had no more than gone past the hospital on Segbroeklaan when police vehicles of every kind began appearing. Jasna stayed with traffic, blending into the frenzy that was building. Several police vehicles drove by her, not giving her a second glance as they did. All police being on the lookout for a white Mercedes.

The blue Volkswagen drove the entire length of Segbroeklaan staying in the midst of traffic, then proceeded south on Ockenburghstraat through a jumbled, multi-lane intersection. Approximately one kilometer behind the terrorists, and gaining, Eric Garver followed in the BMW. He and his cohorts had also been keeping a keen eye on the growing police presence.

So far, no one had noticed or radioed notification that a drone was flying about the city. Lou wondered how long that good luck was going to last.

Feeling confident about their anonymity, Jasna drove the van down the Escamplaan, headed north, and then pulled onto the first residential street to the left. She slowed and maneuvered her way along several kilometers of local city streets. Growing evermore confident that she was not being followed, or even cared about, she pulled the Caddy west, back onto Karperdaal, and up to the safe house.

"Eric, stop for a moment. They are stopped on the next street."

Eric Garver pulled the BMW into an empty parking space along the street and let the car idle.

"It looks like they're going inside."

"Then this is where the action is. Take a good sweep around the place and then land the drone. We probably aren't going to have a lot of time to assault the building."

Lou Stenson half-racked the slide on his silenced .40 caliber Glock to check for a round, and then steeled himself for the next leg.

CHAPTER TWENTY-FOUR

"**B**OYS, WE HAVE company."

"What kind? SITREP."

Thomas Moore held his position in the shadows of a nearby building and gave a hand signal to Sanchez so that he might hold position. Sanchez, having heard the communication from their team leader stationed in his rooftop sniper's nest across the street, noted his understanding.

"It appears that we have two Americans and a German national assembling to your west, maybe half a dozen buildings farther up the street. It looks like they're also setting up for a breach."

"If the U.S. has a response team, we should let them respond. We can keep our cover intact."

Sanchez was matter-of-fact about it. Everyone in the Talon Corporation understood the stance that was required when operating in a situation that might interface with the United States in any way.

"I tend to agree LT, seems like it's their show."

Moore was a little more on the fence, but happy enough to let someone else get shot during the impending breach.

"I also agree. We hold location. If we can assist, we'll assist. If the other strike force has it all in-hand, we hold fast and exfil after successful completion."

"Roger that," Sanchez responded. Moore nodded in understanding and scanned the street around the building.

Inside the safe house, every one of the terrorists had managed to extricate themselves from the rear compartment of the Caddy and straighten up to original height. Each one of them had taken time to embrace their lost leader before spreading out to find individual observation points about the building. Zoran and Emil stood alone in the kitchen area.

"I'm pleased to see you handled your jail time well, cousin."

"The prisons of the Western world are nicer than my house back home. They really do refer to it as 'The Hauge Hilton' for a reason. I almost wanted to stay longer."

Both men laughed. The idea of Zoran Savić staying at the prison for any longer a period was out of the question.

"The attack on the transportation convoy was excellent, Emil. What is your plan for leaving this place?"

"We will leave by boat. The same way that we came here. There is a man waiting in the marina to ferry us back to Poland. From there we can move south with little worry."

"Can we trust this boat man?"

"The man's name came from the man that brought us here. His name came from the old man at the bakery. I have no reason to believe that he cannot be trusted."

Zoran pondered the whole thing for a moment or two.

"Yes, of course. You are right, Emil. How are we getting to the marina?"

"In the Volkswagen. The marina is due west of here. We will wait until the police have slowed their search, maybe four or five hours, and then drive to the marina. There we will contact the boatman."

"You haven't talked with him yet?"

"I have to contact him now and give him the basic outline of events."

Zoran shook his head in agreement for the second time. His cousin had become quite a good group leader in his absence. Zoran wondered if he had just needed that push into action or if something else was at work.

"That's good, Emil. You have done great work here. I'm thankful that you have come to get me. Did you meet with any resistance?"

"Resistance? No. Until now, The Hague authorities didn't even know we were here. The Americans and the Germans put together some type of group to find the nuclear weapon we stole. We did have a run-in with them."

Emil smiled bashfully. Zoran took that to mean he was holding something back.

"Run-in? What do you mean, run-in?"

"We crossed paths with them while we were scouting your escape. There was a small exchange of gunfire."

"And?"

"And we managed to acquire a source of information which was useful."

Zoran's eyes narrowed like a hawk locking onto a mouse.

"Emil? What source?"

"One female American nuclear scientist, Doctor Kristin Hughes. We questioned her extensively about the whole situation. She and her colleagues are only here for the bomb."

"She came to visit me at the prison."

"Yes, we know. That was why we held onto her. So you could converse again."

"You still have her?"

"Yes," Emil said.

Zoran's brain whirled a bit more with each bit of information released by his cousin.

"She's upstairs, with the bomb. The drugs we gave her made her a bit loopy, but she has been quite cooperative."

"She's upstairs now?"

Emil couldn't tell if the expression of Zoran's face was worry, exasperation, or the smile of the Cheshire Cat. This made Emil worry.

"I would like to talk with her."

"Okay. We have some time for that before we must be leaving this place."

Zoran didn't like the tone in Emil's voice. Emil had sounded as if he was telling Zoran what was going to be happening. That would not do. Now that he was out of prison, he was back in charge. Emil had just been filling in during his absence. That point would need to be straightened out once they were on the boat. Zoran pushed up from where he was leaning against the countertop and straightened his posture.

"Take me to her."

Emil led his cousin up the stairs and into the room which held the bound form of Kristin Hughes on one side and the packaged nuclear weapon on the other. The bomb looked the same as the last time he had seen it. The young doctor was a different matter. She had been securely bound to a metal desk chair with rope and heavy tape. The matted hair and discoloration about her face and temples showed that she hadn't received the best treatment along the way. From the aged yellowing of the bruises, Zoran was betting it had been during the initial encounter.

Kristin looked up at the freed Bosnian war criminal-turned-international terrorist and knew things were about to head downhill. Zoran puffed out his chest and smiled at her.

"Well, Doctor Hughes, it seems that the shoe is on the other foot, isn't it?"

Kristin raised an eyebrow until her temples started to pound. She gave him a wry smile.

"Zoran, I hadn't figured you for the joking type?"

The comment made Zoran's smile grow even broader.

"I'm quite funny at times. Other times, I am not. It is this way with all people, no?"

"I suppose it is, yes."

"As I told you Doctor Hughes, that place would not hold me for long – and I would come find you. Though even I admit that I didn't think it would come about this quickly."

Zoran smiled a smile that made Kristin's blood run cold. She steeled herself and kept her composure solid.

"Yes, you did. And now, here we are."

Her smile caused Zoran Savić to take on a quizzical expression.

"Do you remember what else I told you?"

This made Emil perk up, interested in the exchange of wits. He was impressed with the grit of the American woman.

"Yes," Zoran said thoughtfully. "Something about not being a hero, but a terrorist, and that I would die in prison?"

Kristin nodded her head slowly.

"Yup, that's about right. However, I might have been wrong about the last part."

Zoran Savić roared with laughter. Emil had rarely seen his cousin laugh at anything. His laugh seemed genuine. Zoran appeared to be enjoying the situation.

"You are quite correct, Doctor Hughes. I am not hoping to die in prison. Your future, though, that isn't looking overly bright."

Just then, Adam's voice emanated from a spot down the hall.

"Emil! We have –"

The smallest of noises could be heard as a .50 caliber round punched through the glass window and turned Adam Pavlovic's head into a burst melon. Lt. Baker adjusted his fire and zeroed in on the second observation point visible from his side of the street. A small figure could be seen in the upper floor window of the house, on the far side of the building from where the first person had been. That second person was oriented as to have an overlapping field view and fire from the first person he had engaged.

Baker leveled the barrel of the 82A1 Barret sniper rifle on the small outline and squeezed off a round. The big, fully jacketed .50 caliber BMG round punched a hole through the masonry block just below the window frame and hit what he could now see was obviously a woman in the middle of her gut. Baker squeezed off a second round as the woman began to flail around, silencing her agonizing throws all but immediately. He quickly pivoted the scope down to street level as the American group readied to make their entry.

"Sanchez, move. I took out the two observation points on this side of the house to give them a clean entry. Be prepared to provide backup if it starts to spill out on the street."

"Roger that," Sanchez responded with operational calm.

Lou Stenson and Robert Dunn entered the garage and took up a position behind the shot up get-away car. Dunn looked at the car and shook his head. Lou Stenson crouched and slunk across the garage floor until he reached the inner doorway. A barrage of automatic gunfire came down the stairs to meet him as a greeting. The welcome made Stenson back up into the cover of the garage area.

Aleksander Lukic and Emil Savić had responded to Adam's Pavlovic's call at the same time. Alek made the run right behind Emil to find Adam dead. They had backed out of the room just before Jasna started to scream. Emil ran back to the room where Zoran and Kristin had been conversing. Alek headed back to his position at the back of the house. Halfway along the hallway, Alek had spotted intruders entering the garage and opened fire.

"Zoran, it's time to go. We need to escape this place."

Alek cut loose with another long volley. Kristin smiled at this new descent into chaos.

From somewhere in the building a loud shattering sound could be heard. Emil knew from the sound that someone had just kicked in the rear door of the building.

"Come Zoran, we're going now!"

Emil turned and headed toward the door on the opposite side of the room.

"Hold on, Emil. Not so fast."

Zoran was looking at the American with a strange expression. It wasn't lust or greed or worry. It was more like she was a muse for his thoughts. Kristin didn't like the look any more than Emil did.

Zoran Savić turned and walked to where the O.D. green military transport backpack was resting. He opened up the cover to expose the top of the nuclear device, then reached in to remove a soup can-sized object from an interior pocket. Kristin Hughes' eyes went wide as Zoran extracted the bomb's detonator.

"Zoran, you can't do that! Not here in The Hague!"

Zoran Savić paid no mind to the American's protest, which was quickly drowned out as Aleksander Lukic expended another full magazine of ammunition down the stairwell. This time, two different tones of return fire emanated back up the stairwell. The young auto mechanic bellowed in agony as he was struck by gunfire from both Lou Stenson and Eric Garver.

Aleksander Lukic's body thudded to the hallway floor and an odd moment of silence filled the building. In the back room, Zoran Savić slammed the detonator into the bomb's receiver well and flipped a rubber-coated switch to activate it. He turned the knob on the detonator's top to its maximum and pressed the rubber-covered button to initiate it. A red light appeared on the detonator as the timer began to count down, one digit at a time.

Emil sprayed a magazine's worth of rounds down the hallway to keep the intruders pinned in the stairwell. Zoran pulled his pistol and turned to face Kristin Hughes, who was stilled tied to the chair.

"This should slow down your comrades."

"But, you can't –"

Zoran closed the distance to Kristin before she could finish her sentence and roundhouse punched her in the temple. The strike to her immobilized body instantly knocked her unconscious. Zoran raised a heavy boot and kicked the chair, flipping it on its side with a thud. Turning around, he looked at his cousin.

"Now, we can go."

Emil abandoned his position in the hallway door and headed across the room toward the back. Zoran followed as Emil maneuvered through a couple of small rooms and to a rear door leading to the outside. Opening the door, he descended a flight of metal stairs to a small outside landing.

With Zoran only a step behind, Emil scurried to a small boat tied up along the bank of the canal and hoped in. With a single pull of the starter rope and a cut line from a folding knife, the last two members of the Bosnian terrorist cell raced off down the canal.

"Do we follow the two in the boat?"

"Negative. We stay with the group that's here. Our mission is the girl, not the men."

"Roger that," Moore said, as he returned his gaze to the safe house building.

The American three-man team ascended the stairs and burst into the room that had produced the most gunfire, Stenson in the lead. Seeing his young charge bound and unconscious, Stenson dropped his weapon to the sling position and slid down next to her. A quick assessment of her condition led him to the fact that she was still alive, but otherwise in bad shape.

Dunn proceeded through the room to the open rear door and followed the path through until he was at the top of the exterior stairs. In the distance, a boat motor could be heard, but the two remaining terrorists were nowhere to be seen. With a quick visual 180-degree turn, Dunn doubled back into the building to find the others.

Lou Stenson was cutting Kristin's bindings as fast and efficiently as anyone could without inflicting further damage. He was almost done freeing his unconscious young bomb technician when Dunn reentered the room.

"The terrorists are gone. I'm guessing that they had a boat stashed along the canal."

"I almost have her freed. We need to get her to a hospital fast."

Eric Garver quietly looked down at the falling numbers counter on the MK-54 nuclear warhead and drew an uneasy breath.

"Gentlemen, we have a much larger problem."

CHAPTER TWENTY-FIVE

TENSON, DUNN, AND Garver stood in a circle around the table and stared at the H-912 carrier in disbelief. Protruding from its top, the soup-can-sized detonator of the W-54 nuclear bomb was clearly visible. A red LED segmented display showed a descending number counter. The timer had been initiated at its 5-minute maximum by the two escaping terrorists. The counter was currently at 272 and dropping. Lou Stenson assumed that that readout was in seconds, which would give them nearly five minutes, but he wasn't sure. Stenson thought the counter must have been made by whatever company first made displays for pocket calculators. He hadn't seen anything this old, except in the movies.

"Okay. What do we do now?"

Eric Garver was extremely calm considering the circumstances.

"Kristin's out. She's unconscious and in need of medical attention."

Lou Stenson's voice was resolute, though harboring an amount of concern.

"Well, that looks like it leaves us to handle it. Anybody here good with Cold War nukes?"

Dunn's voice had just the smallest amount of levity to it. It didn't help the situation.

Garver and Dunn both looked up at Stenson quizzically. After all, he was the NEST Operations Chief. This made him the closest thing to a bomb expert in the building. Lou got their gazes and smiled.

"Sorry, boys. I know jack about handling warheads."

Lou Stenson looked down at the timer. The red LED now said 246. Things were surely about to get very bad in The Hague. The three of them would need to come up with a plan quickly or the North Sea population was going to definitely get smaller.

"Do you think they had enough time to boobytrap it in any way?"

Stenson looked at his comrades seriously.

"We kept them engaged, for the most part. I would say that unless it was a planned detonation for here, there are no boobytraps."

Dunn sounded sure.

"I would agree with Mr. Dunn. I think this was a last-ditch effort to slow us down. Unplanned, therefore, no boobytraps."

Garver sounded analytical, which made Stenson calm.

Lou Stenson looked down at the counter again. It read 221. Either it wasn't counting in seconds or the timer was screwed up in some fashion, because he was sure that they had been talking longer than the numbers on the descending display noted. He now seriously hoped that it wasn't an altimeter type device. If the gadget was really designed to read air pressure and the display counter was really just adjusting to sea-level because it had been in a box for decades, they were all definitely going to die.

Lou Stenson reached out and loosened the knot on the rope-pull closure securing the top of the H-912 transport container. The rope was dry from decades of storage and resisted the movement. Lou gently slid the rope backward through the rope loops much the same way that one would slide the cord in a hooded sweatshirt.

Having the top loose, he slowly peeled back the thick canvas cover, starting at the detonator and working his way around to its top. Exposing the top of the W-54 warhead, the cylinder that acted as the device's case was smooth on top. The only openings on the top were the one holding the detonator and one with a series of waterproof wires protruding from it. Lou Stenson visually traced the wires across the top and over to the side of the metal cylinder.

On the side of the H-912 transport container was a square canvas protrusion, approximately the size of a cigar box. Stenson slowly undid the metal snaps that held a nylon closure strap. Releasing the tension on the nylon strap, he pulled back the cover to reveal a second detonator assembly. This second detonator unit, though plugged into the warhead, was not powered on. All three men looked at the second detonator in confusion.

"Why would they use the plug-in one, when the thing comes with a really nice one already attached to it?"

Dunn was calm, and his question was valid.

"I'm betting that they had no idea how to actually use this setup. They simply took it all when they raided the facility, assuming that they would be able to figure out how it worked later. Zoran and his crew probably didn't even know that this assembly is the primary detonator. The secondary detonator was on the shelf, so they took it thinking that they needed it."

"That makes good sense. I would imagine that we might do the same if pressed for time."

Garver still sounded analytical, which made Stenson happy.

Lou Stenson looked down at the counter again. It now read 186. They were running out of time. They needed a reasonable way out of this situation, and fast.

Lou looked up and took in the image of his two comrades. They both seemed completely committed to the task at hand. Committed, yet unable to really help. Then, like lightning on a clear day, it hit him. He didn't need to figure out how to disarm the nuke. He just needed someone to tell him how to disarm it.

Lou rifled through the pockets of his vest until he found his cellphone. He checked the signal. It had five bars. He pressed the encryption key and waited for a tone.

"Are you sure that's a good idea," Eric Garver asked apprehensively.

"The phone signal may set it off. The detonator will set it off. Seems like a justifiable gamble."

Stenson's comment made Garver shrug in resignation. The man had a point.

A number was chosen from the contact list and the green talk button was pushed. The call connected and the phone rang three times before being picked up.

"Chief, what can I do for you? Thought you were out of the country?"

Jim Bonner, the second lead nuclear bomb disposal technician behind Kristin Hughes, sounded jovial and unbothered.

"Jim. You're on speaker with me and two intelligence officers. I have a live and active W-54 warhead. It is wrapped in a H-912 transport container.

The detonator plugged into the top of the warhead has a red LED counter that is descending in its count. It currently says 162. How do I disarm it?"

There was a four click pause count on the other end of the line that seemed to last for the better part of an hour. When Jim Bonner's voice returned to the line, it was all business.

"You said that the detonator is plugged into the top of the warhead. Is it the size of a good-sized soup can?'

"Yes."

"The red-light display, does it look like something from a 1970s pocket calculator?"

"Yes."

"Well, that's no good. The secondary trigger assembly for the W-54 SADM was never the most reliable of devices. It tends to act erratically."

"The timer is dropping, but it seems to take longer than a second for each beat to occur."

"It's been in storage so long that the circuit board has surely degraded. What's the count now?"

"140."

"Okay. You see a rubberized red push button on the top of the detonator, next to the timer counter?"

"Yes."

"That is the activator switch. It should pop back up when we shut it off. And the timer should go dark. However, it probably won't. Do you see a rubber-coated switch on the side of the can?"

"Yes."

"That is the main on-off switch that powers the detonator. DO NOT turn it off. Understand? DO NOT turn it off."

"Yes. Why?"

"The detonator circuitry is already acting erratically. If you shut it off, it will most-likely detonate."

All three men drew in a breath and stared at the detonator counting down.

"Chief, what's the count?"

"119."

"Okay, it's go time. Do you have somewhere you can throw the detonator assembly to let it cook off and blow? It should have the punch about equal to a single stick of C4."

"Yes. Out the back. We can toss it in the canal."

Dunn spoke for the first time since the call started and could feel the dryness in his throat.

"Fine. You get to toss it."

Lou looked at Robert Dunn, who just nodded.

"Is everyone on your end ready, Chief?"

"Yes."

"What's the count?"

"96."

"Chief, grasp the detonator with both hands, making sure not to touch the on-off switch."

"Done."

"When I say go, give yourself a three count and then turn the detonator clockwise. It may have seated. If so, it will need a little nudge to get moving. It should turn about three full rotations before coming free. There is an explosive detonation plunger protruding from the bottom. It's approximately ten-inches long and one-inch around. That's where the detonator's explosive activator is housed. You will need to pull the detonator straight up to free it. Once it's free, get it away from you as fast and as smoothly as possible. There is no telling how the circuitry in the detonator will act to the sudden movement, understand?"

"Yes," Lou said, seemingly shocked at how level his voice was still sounding.

"Good. Now, ready – and go."

The NEST Operations Chief reaffirmed his grip on the detonator. Eric Garver reached out and secured a grip on the H-912 transport carrier to keep it from moving. Lou nodded his head three times and then applied pressure to the detonator. There was the slightest of pauses and the assembly began to turn. Four full rotations and the detonator's threads unseated from the detonator well.

Lou Stenson paused for a beat before ever so gently pulling the soup-can-sized detonator straight up and out of the W-54's housing. As calmly as he could manage, Lou handed the still-live assembly over to Robert Dunn, who turned smoothly and walked to the door at the far end of the room.

Dunn navigated the turn through the first door and then through the second, as he had previously done chasing the terrorist Savić cousins, but with considerably more deliberation. Standing at the top of the small outer landing, he paused for a one count. The canal was an easy underhand pitch out and away from the building, especially at his second-floor angle. The only problem was the location of the expressway directly next to the canal. The expressway wasn't nearly as far away as the safe house was. Oh well, it was only one pound of explosive.

Robert Dunn half-twisted at the waist, and with a smooth underhand motion, swung the live detonator out into the midday air. His movements had the mechanics of a good softball pitch. The live nuclear warhead detonator arched through the air in a smooth and resistance-free path, oriented straight for the canal water. Dunn drew a long breath, which he didn't realize he had been putting off, as he watched the detonator fly free.

The active 1950s nuclear warhead detonator, just as Jim Bonner had so accurately predicted on the phone, turned out to be an unstable creature. Due to the detonator's odd center of gravity, it developed a mild spin as it flew and impacted the canal surface with a slow, two-dimensional rotation. As the 60-plus year-old device came into contact with the resistance of the canal water's surface, the fragile electronics inside gave up their hold on the stored electrical charge and the detonator exploded in a spectacular fashion.

Even though the detonator unit only carried an equivalent of one pound of plastic explosive, the orientation of impact and the flow dynamics of the canal came together to produce a tidal wave of water from the detonation. The liquid excavated by the blast flew in a geometrically perfect arch up and over the nearest two lanes of Lozerlaan, creating mayhem. Vehicles traveling on the expressway instantly skidded this way and that. The sound of numerous collisions could be heard coming from the flood zone created in the expressway. Robert Dunn cringed slightly and turned to go back inside.

Stenson and Garver were finishing the task of making the warhead inert as Dunn reentered the room.

"We may want to get out of here before the police come looking for the terrorist bombers that just created a traffic disaster on the expressway."

The two men working the bomb stopped as he spoke.

"Did the detonator release safely," Jim Bonner asked over the still active phone line.

"Mostly," Dunn replied with a shrug.

"Okay, Chief, that should about do it. The nuke should be safe to transport now."

"Great! We can't thank you enough for the help, Jim. Neither can the residents of The Hague."

"No worries, Chief, it's what we do. Now, three questions."

"Go."

"Where did you manage to dig up a mission-capable, Cold War, man-portable nuclear weapon? Why the hell would anyone want to blow up The Hague? And, why didn't you have Kristin dismantle it? She's supposedly in Europe somewhere."

All three men swiveled their heads over to the unconscious Kristin Hughes, who was lying awkwardly on the floor. The thudding in Lou Stenson's chest reappeared as he took in the image. *No good deed goes unpunished,* rolled through his mind as he looked at her. He started speaking without turning his head to look at the phone.

"Jim, one – I will explain in person. Two – this was a diversion, not a real plan to attack The Hague. Three – because she's currently unavailable. I'll explain it all when I see you in person. Until then, thanks for the help."

"Roger that, Chief," and Jim Bonner terminated the call from his end.

Lou Stenson pulled a folding knife from a pants pocket and snapped the blade into place as he completed the three full strides it took to cross the room. With the deft precision of an artist, Lou sliced through the remaining binding holding Kristin to the metal chair. As the chest restraint was cut, Kristin's unconscious form rolled slowly out and onto the smooth tile floor.

The big ex-SEAL slowly cradled up his charge and stood. With Kristin securely in Lou's possession, all three men exited the room. Lou led the way. Dunn followed him and Garver secured the rear position, deactivated nuclear warhead over his shoulder like a backpack. It had been decided to let Garver handle the nuke, in case they ran afoul of The Hague police. The Hague authorities were familiar with Herr Becke, and that just might help them out.

Lieutenant Baker watched the threesome exit the safe house, the same way that they had entered. The men had both the doctor and the wayward nuke in hand. He rubbed his chin on the end of his closed fist and considered their tasking to be complete.

"Boys, it's looking like job done. Break down and rally at the vehicle."

"Roger that, LT, we're moving," came the unbothered tones of Thomas Moore into his earpiece.

Lieutenant Little John Baker rolled off his prone firing position and began breaking down his own gear.

CHAPTER TWENTY-SIX

ONCE THE IMPROMPTU rescue team had gotten Kristin to the hospital, it had taken Lou Stenson six phone calls and twenty minutes to acquire the two things he desperately wanted. The whole acquisition period had started with a call to Langley, Virginia. That conversation had lasted approximately one minute. The conversation produced a request that was, at absolute best, reluctantly received. The call that followed went from Langley to a non-disclosed location in the Cayman Islands, where it was bounced around the globe a couple times before ending up at a cellphone in another non-disclosed location. This call lasted the same amount of time as the first call had and produced an affirmative response.

A third call, from a non-GPS enabled phone in that non-disclosed location on the global map, went to a satellite phone located in The Hague. The man that answered the satellite phone listened carefully and noted the phone number he was given. This call lasted maybe twice as long as the first two had. The man with the satellite phone dialed the number he had been given and Lou Stenson's cellphone rang. It rang one time.

"Hello. Am I talking to my new overwatch team?"

"Is this line encrypted?"

"Absolutely."

"Then yes you are, Chief Stenson. Lieutenant John Baker, retired. What can I do for you?"

"I would like to utilize your team just a little longer, if that isn't a problem."

"The call I received said to give the man on the phone anything that he wanted, so we're here to handle whatever you need handled."

"I need some personal protection for Doctor Hughes. We're headed out on a manhunt and I want her safe while that happens."

"Consider it done, Chief."

"The Hagaziekenhuis, off Layweg. By the Florence Nightingale Park. Second floor."

"Roger that. Ten minutes."

And the mysterious Lt. Baker severed the connection.

Lou Stenson closed the connection on his phone to kill the encryption. He knew nothing about the men he had just enlisted. Well, except that they were damned good marksmen, apparently quick and accurate with reconnaissance, and were employed by something called the Talon Corporation. Normally, that amount of information would not suffice. Today, his gut was telling him that it was enough. They could have easily been a hindrance, but they definitely had been a help with this solution.

Lou opened a line on the cell and picked a number in his contacts lists. It rang three times before it connected. Not many people had the man's direct line. Fewer people dared to use it.

Paul Spencer, Senior Systems Director for the National Reconnaissance Office, otherwise known as the NRO, was one of those people who did his best work in the shadows. No one on Capitol Hill really knew what he did. They just knew that he was one of those people who you didn't cross. Secretly, he was also a senior member of The Group.

"Lou! Figured I'd be hearing from you pretty soon. How's our girl doing?'

"She'll pull through. We're at the hospital now."

"That's good to hear. Not too banged up then?"

"Unknown at this time. She has a fractured radius, otherwise they're still doing tests. The terrorists also shot her full of something at some point. She's conscious now, and her mood is foul. I think she'll pull through, in the long run."

"That's good to hear. I'll make sure that we get a crew over there to retrieve her and get her home."

"I'd appreciate it if you could make the calls for me."

"Roger that, Chief. No worries. Now, business."

"I need source intel. I assume that you have a bird overhead?"

"Lacrosse Five and Six are both over your head as we speak. The

Pentagon isn't happy about it. I told them to stick it. We've been watching the show in relative real-time since you landed."

"I need to know where the last two members of Zoran's terrorist crew escaped to while we were dealing with the nuke."

"They're currently on a fishing boat headed out into the North Sea. I would say North, toward Denmark, at current trajectory. The vessel's called the Shore Tid."

"Shore Time?"

"I thought the same thing. Guy probably doesn't have any imagination. Anyway, it's your standard forty-five-foot, dirty white, fishing boat. Or, as near as we can tell it is."

"I could really use current grid and speed."

"I can do one better than that. You're going to receive a text link in about two minutes. It's a backdoor into the satellite feed we are streaming over to Ed at the NSA. It should tell you everything that you want to know."

"Thank you, Paul. I greatly appreciate the help."

"No worries. Go kill some bad guys."

"Roger that."

Lou terminated the call and waited for the text message to arrive. Everything in the hospital seemed to be moving along as a hospital should. He looked down the hall to where Robert Dunn was stationed watching the elevator traffic. Who better to spot potential assassins then an assassin? Dunn appeared to be unimpressed by the pedestrian traffic swirling around him. Lou looked down the opposite hallway to where Eric Garver was standing. He was scanning the other two routes onto the floor, a service elevator and the stairs. He, too, seemed unalarmed.

Lou Stenson looked sideways through a large window to where his number one bomb technician, and self-proclaimed ward, lay on an examination table. She looked very unhappy. The look made Lou apprehensive. The doctor in the room was obviously telling her something she didn't like.

Lou was about to step in and see what was happening when Dunn noticeably stiffened. The big ex-SEAL pulled a Glock Model 20 out of his waistband and half-racked the slide to check for a round in the chamber. He had no more than finished the fluid movement when three men appeared from around the corner. All three looked military. Or former military. They all possessed that unmistakable look of mercenaries. Lou recognized two of the men from when they were unloading gear from the Talon jet. He slid the Glock back into his waistband. The largest of the men, and from the way the men moved, the apparent leader, walked straight to Lou Stenson and extended a hand.

"Chief Stenson, Lt. Baker. Good to meet you in person. I've heard a great many things about your exploits in the teams."

Lou Stenson raised a quizzical eyebrow. The man was obviously well-informed.

"Army or Marine?"

"Marine. Recon." The big man turned his shoulders to point to the two men behind him. "Thomas Moore. Formally of the SAS. And, SSgt. Juan Sanchez. Also, formally from the teams."

Lou shot the other ex-SEAL an inspecting look.

"Which?"

"Nine, Chief."

"They've done good work."

The other operator nodded in recognition.

"I appreciate you gentlemen taking over the babysitting. An exfil team is being assembled to pick her up and get her home, but it will be some amount of time before they get over here. I'll make sure that you get looped into the briefing, so all goes smoothly."

The former Marine lieutenant pulled a business card from his pocket and handed it to the NEST Operations Officer. It read: *John Baker, Operational Problem Solving, The Talon Corporation, Cayman Islands.* Lou gave the business phone number a good look and then produced a business card of his own. The other man nodded as he took it.

"We're off."

"Happy hunting, Chief."

The two men shook hands and Lou headed off down the hallway toward Robert Dunn. As he was walking, an incoming text message chimed on his phone. He hit the link on the text and activated Paul Spencer's backdoor. A flash message came up on the screen before the link activated, stating that the text message he was reading did not exist, nor would it exist later.

The message was NSA speak. It was the last piece of what had been the sixth of Lou's phone calls. After the man in Langley was sure that the man in The Hague had made contact with Lou, he had called across the capital to another man. This man was tasked with making evidence of all the calls disappear. Fortunately for Eugene Taggart and everyone else concerned, Ed Crowley and his cyber-spooks at the NSA were experts in doing that very thing. Three young people sitting in a windowless subbasement room quietly dissolved all traces of the multi-continental exchange. It had taken less time to make it go away than it had for it all to unfold. Lou read the disclaimer note and smiled, happy that Ed was on his side.

Eric Garver appeared beside the other two men as the elevator door opened. Lou Stenson punched a button on his phone as he stepped inside the elevator and a small white fishing boat appeared on the screen, chopping through the waves of the North Sea. He held it up so that the other two men could see it. Both the boat and its ten-digit satellite grid were evident in the display.

"That's them," Lou said, looking at Garver. "Can you get us a chopper?"

"Yes."

The elevator descended to the ground floor. A small black dot appeared on the phone screen coming out of the boat's rear cabin door. Lou didn't know if it was Zoran or Emil, but he was sure that it was a person.

In reality, the emerging figure was Zoran Savić. He had stepped outside to take in the fresh air of the North Sea. His escape to freedom on the fishing boat had not gone nearly as well as Emil had envisioned. Unlike its planning, its enactment had been a fiasco.

The two men managed to make it out of the safe house well enough, leaving the remainder of their dead team behind. Emil had staged a small boat in the canal as a last resort, and a last resort it had turned out to be. Zoran and Emil had no more than fled the gun battle, after activating the nuclear bomb, and realized that getting away by car had become out of the question.

Where the activation of the bomb had caused Emil to panic, to Zoran it seemed a simple enough affair. He honestly didn't believe that the nuclear bomb would really explode. He thought that the Americans would disarm it, as opposed to chasing after them. This was the only part that seemed to happen correctly.

Emil pointed the small boat west and headed down the canal. The Hague had waterways everywhere. Little canals bisected every part of the city. It should have been an easy affair to just continue west along the canals until one of them daylighted out in the sea or by the marina. In the hurry of a gun battle, the plan made good sense. In reality, the waterways of the city were not a single connected canal system. They were a great many small individual canals that didn't actually connect. This meant that the canal the two terrorists were escaping down really went nowhere – at least nowhere they needed to go.

Emil piloted the small boat down the side of Lozerlaan and then turned north. The canal ran straight to a four-way intersection that led back into the area of the safe house, where it promptly stopped.

Not knowing what to do, Emil ran the small boat up onto the edge of a landing area and told Zoran to get out. The normal leader of the group didn't like the tone of being told to do things, but he jumped out anyway. Emil followed and they scurried up the concrete steps to the street side.

Next came a dash through the intersection traffic to a small shop on the opposite side. The shop sat in a circular drive and had parking in front. The windows were smashed out of a grey Ford hatchback that Emil hotwired while Zoran scared people away with a gun and a menacing look.

Car finally running, the two men headed out toward the marina once again. Emil swung the car east toward a set of McDonald's arches visible on Escamplaan, as that was the only route he had driven. The maneuver put the two terrorists and their stolen Ford back on Lozerlaan just as a wall of water from the exploding detonator turned flowing traffic into an impromptu submarine race. Several cars wrecked directly in front of them as Emil swerved first right and then left in an attempt to avoid the melee. The wall of water was just starting to clear as Emil was forced to slide the Ford sideways between two large trucks before stuffing it into a metal guardrail. The impact slammed Zoran against the passenger door and made him curse loudly.

Emil extricated the stolen car as the police began arriving in the area. Stomping on the gas, the Ford swerved through the stopped traffic and escaped into a free roadway beyond the scene. A police car in the midst of the chaos noticed the fleeing Ford and radioed that the car must have been the cause of all the mayhem.

197

Emil had pushed the stolen car almost all the way to the street's intersection with Laan van Meerdervoort, which headed north once more, when they found themselves in a highspeed chase with the police. Seeing the North Sea in the distance, Emil cursed his luck and headed north.

What happened next was a car chase that flowed through a countless number of small city streets. Several police cars were damaged and two were ruined. The stolen Ford hatchback was beaten in at every corner, and two more windows had been smashed out, as the car had been slammed into various objects. To Emil's complete surprise, the car never stopped running once during the whole event. It was definitely louder than when they had started, and the interior was completely soaked down from the tidal wave, but it was still running.

Emil and Zoran abandoned the battered car in the parking area of the Harbor Club on the south side of the marina and began a foot escape toward a waiting man on a boat. Sadly, as with everything else that had happened during the escape, this part didn't go well either. The fishing boat captain decided that the two Bosnian terrorists were becoming way more trouble than he wanted, and he started putting to sea without them. When they arrived, Emil and Zoran found their designated boat slip empty.

Cursing his continuing bad fortune, Emil started looking for the next viable option. He found two boat slips farther down the dock. His next option turned out to be a white fishing boat named Shore Tid.

Emil read the vessel's name and shrugged. Right now, transport was transport. Emil boarded the boat with Zoran on his heels and made his way to the main cabin. Fortunately for the terrorists, the keys were in the ignition, so it was a start it up and go situation. Zoran cleared the lines as Emil guided the boat out and away from its slip. Following the buoys, as the previous boat captain had explained to him while they were making their way to The Hague, Emil maneuvered the craft out and into open water.

Once free of the marina, Emil turned the boat north and put on some speed. If things in the marina went unnoticed for just a little time, they would be all but disappeared. Zoran found cause for disdain in Emil's optimism and went out on the rear deck to get some air. Emil continued to guide the boat north on good seas.

CHAPTER TWENTY-SEVEN

I T TOOK THE better part of two hours before a broad outline of the WS-61 Commando helicopter could be seen in the distance. The variant version of the S-61 Sea King was borrowed from a German Navy ship cruising around the lower end of the North Sea.

Lou Stenson was impressed with Eric Garver's ability to mobilize equipment and to make things happen. He wasn't sure that he could do any better, even inside the United States. Maybe he needed to rethink his stance regarding the GSG-9 man.

The Commando came in for a low pass over the hospital's helipad and banked hard for a return trip. Seeing all things to his liking, the pilot of the Commando throttled down the twin Rolls Royce turboshafts and settled the bird down in the middle of the pad's large H symbol. The five sixty-two-foot rotors threw wash out in a constant wave while the three men entered the open transport door. The rotor wash warmed Lou Stenson's blood. It signified combat, and combat was good.

Robert Dunn's second foot was no more than lifting off the surface of the rooftop helipad when the pilot had all three of the SW-61 Commando's tires back in the air. Not being a natural military man, Robert Dunn was more taken aback by the rapid exit than the others in the craft.

The pilot rose to an elevation some 1,000 feet over the top of the city's buildings, so as not to draw undue attention, and pointed the craft back out to sea. The pilot spoke something to Garver in German and waited for a response. Garver turned to the big ex-SEAL, who was checking the mag in a Heckler and Koch MP5SD6 submachine gun. The weapon's buttstock was collapsed against the receiver, and the standard sound suppressor was attached.

"Mr. Stenson, could I borrow your phone for a moment?"

Lou nodded and handed over the fully encrypted special edition iPhone to Garver, then went back to his weapons preparations. A flat German paramilitary blade and a Glock Model 19 9x19 sat on the bench from where he had picked up the submachine gun.

Eric Garver hit the function key and the phone's screen illuminated with the active satellite coverage of the white fishing boat. The boat cut a smooth line through the water and moved in an unbothered fashion. Obviously, the Savić cousins believed that they had eluded capture. Little did they know that the game was still quite alive and happening.

The pilot of the Commando punched the scrolling ten-digit GPS numbers into his navigational computer and muttered something to his copilot. Both men looked at each other and shrugged. The pilot of the German helicopter banked the machine over on its right side and adjusted its trajectory to due north. The big Rolls Royce engines ramped up and the helicopter was off over the Netherland's countryside.

Eric Garver leaned back into the crew compartment and settled back into his nylon-strapped jump seat. He handed the phone back and looked to both of his comrades.

"The helicopter maxes out at about 129 miles per hour in clean air. With the lead that the boat has on us, we are going to take a parabolic trajectory overland to cut out the distance. We should make contact with them right around the Netherlands-German border."

Both men nodded. Lou was rotating the flat German blade around in his hand. He seemed as calm as any man ever had been. His calm made Garver somewhat nervous. He had never worked with U.S. Navy SEALs before, but was well aware of their untarnished reputation in black operations. Looking at the NEST Chief of Operations, he could understand how the teams had received such a reputation. Robert Dunn, U. S. Government CIA assassin, wasn't as calm as Stenson, but also wasn't in the least concerned outwardly about what was soon to transpire. For a hastily assembled fire team, the three men were about as good a choice as anyone might hope for.

"Is it cool that we are just blasting over Holland in a German military helicopter? I mean, you guys have treaties in place for such events?"

Robert Dunn's voice was as mellow as one should be able to modulate. The question, however, was legitimate.

"Actually, the pilot was ordered not to stay in Netherland's airspace one minute longer than necessary. I'm going to need to do some damage control later, as you Americans say."

Lou Stenson looked up and smiled but didn't stop what he was doing.

"Well, as long as we don't get shot down."

"Exactly."

Everyone in the helicopter quieted and went about their individual tasks. The helicopter's flight crew conversed at random intervals in their native language. Otherwise, it was just the groan of the engines offset by the whop of the rotor blades thundering through the atmosphere. No one in the crew section looked out the windows, they just sat quietly. All their individual gear had been triple checked and attached to their persons. There wasn't much to do now but contemplate the intercept.

Robert Dunn reached into his pocket and pulled out his cellphone. Fumbling around on the various screens with his thumb, he pressed a virtual key and smiled. Replacing the phone in his pocket, he looked up at the quizzical faces in the craft. Even the flight crew was curious about the maneuver.

"I was checking to see if I had locked my car at the hospital. I couldn't remember if I had or not, so I figured that I'd check. That type of stuff drives me crazy."

"Checked on your car?" Eric Garver sounded irritated.

"Yup. It's that BMW car service. The European version of On-Star. It works everywhere."

Lou Stenson looked up at Dunn and shook his head. He had seen it a hundred times before. Guys listening to music, doing crossword puzzles, or cutting x shapes into the heads of their bullets. Anything to make the time pass. It was the way of such men to desire action over waiting.

A red light flashed in the crew compartment and Eric Garver stuck his head back up into the flight control cabin to speak with the pilots. A couple of sentences were exchanged in German between the men. Dunn picked up most of it. Lou Stenson's German was basically junk at this point in his life, so he waited for the translation. Garver returned to his seated position and retrieved his own submachine gun.

"They have the boat on their radar screen."

The other two nodded and picked up weapons. The pilot lined up the fishing boat on the radar so that the helicopter would approach from the boat's stern. The approach gave the helicopter the limited amount of stealth which might be achieved when closing on an objective over open water. It also allowed for maximum maneuverability. It was the standard tactic for engaging a moving vessel.

The SW-61 Commando's crew chief rolled a large black canvas bag to the crew door, retrieving the end of a thick black rope from the bag. He attached the rope to a mount on the top of the door frame. The crew chief turned and looked at the fire team.

The red light in the crew compartment began to flash. The crew chief placed his hand on the side of his communications headset and listened. The man spoke a few words into the headset's microphone and then gave the members of the fire team a sign that signified three minutes until intercept. All three men nodded. The crew chief pointed at the fast rope bag and then toward his backside. This signified that they would be fast roping onto the boat's open stern area. Once again, all three men nodded an affirmative. They were ready. It was time for combat. It was time for a little justice.

A green light flashed in the crew compartment, replacing the red light. The crew chief pushed the sliding door open to its stops and kicked the big black canvas bag out of the opening. Lou Stenson was moving by the crew chief, submachine gun out in the combat position, as the crew chief looked back to signal the go-ahead to the men.

During the boat's travel up the Netherland's coastline, Zoran had found time to calm himself from the earlier incident of being ordered about by his cousin. He realized that Emil was doing exactly what Emil needed to do to get the job done. The same things he would have done if the circumstances were reversed.

The weight of all the deaths had pressed down on them both. Friends and family who they had stood shoulder-to-shoulder with on countless occasions were now gone. Grief did funny things to people, and the two on the boat had enough grief for a whole community.

As Zoran Savić stood on the rear deck of the fishing boat, he came to realize that the whole quest for the nuclear bomb had been folly. Not only did they not have the nuke, but they had lost almost every member of the terrorist cell in the last days. The last two members of the Bosnian group were both internationally recognized criminals now. Every possible thing that could go wrong on their mission had gone wrong. Every chance they had taken had been for nothing. And now, even if they could get out of the North Sea undetected, they still had to travel across half of Eastern Europe without getting recognized. Things were really starting to look bleak.

Zoran collected what little bit of pride he possessed and put it away. He looked out over the black water and sighed, and then turned toward the cabin door. He could see Emil inside the cabin driving the fishing boat. He needed to stabilize things with his cousin. Zoran made his way back inside the cabin of the fishing boat and closed the door to stop the sound of the breeze created by the boat's motion.

The two men had been conversing for the better part of a half-an-hour when the large black canvas rope bag from the helicopter slammed down on the open rear deck of the fishing boat. Zoran Savić reacted immediately, pulling a compact 9mm pistol from his pocket and turning for the door. With the determination of a seasoned soldier, Zoran pulled the door open in a single swift move, ready to shoot anyone standing on the other side. Instead of engaging any potential enemies on the rear deck, Zoran's outline in the door was greeted by four silenced rounds. Zoran Savić gasped as two rounds shredded his left knee and one round pierced his forearm just above the gun hand, throwing his pistol in a wide arc back into the boat's cabin. The fourth round punched a through-and-through into Zoran's upper torso, somehow missing anything vital.

Lou Stenson kept the MP5SD6 trained on the target as Zoran collapsed to the deck in a howl of pain. Refocusing on the scene, Stenson didn't wait for the others to react, but sent a three-round burst into the Emil Savić's torso as the boat driver turned to see what was happening. Emil dropped to the deck straight-away, a mass quantity of blood pouring out of his chest.

Lou Stenson lowered the barrel of his weapon fifteen degrees as the other two members of his fire team entered the boat's cabin. Dunn went through to the inner cabin door as Garver covered him. The two made entry into the boat's inner cabin area and checked for resistance. Lou

Stenson leaned down to inspect Emil's corpse before turning his complete attention to the still-alive Zoran Savić.

Zoran realized that, even in his current state, he had an opportunity. One didn't survive as long as Zoran Savić had in a war-torn country without seeing survival opportunities when they came along.

As the gunman bent down to inspect his cousin for an obviously non-existent pulse, Zoran summoned up all his remaining strength and moved. Rolling forward, he rotated up onto his good leg. Grasping the door frame with his good hand, he spit out a mouthful of blood and pushed off with all the strength he had remaining. The Bosnian war criminal made two full hops on his good leg before falling onto the boat's side rail. Zoran Savić pivoted at the waist and fell oblong into the North Sea as his motions registered in Lou Stenson's peripheral vision.

Lou pushed off and was halfway to the cabin door before he managed to get his feet under him. Two more bounding steps and he was at the side rail. He looked over the bloody side rail, gun barrel first, at blank water passing by the boat's hull. Somehow, there was no body in the water. The Bosnian terrorist had momentarily disappeared. Lou Stenson cursed loud enough for everyone alive on the fishing boat to hear.

Dunn and Garver joined Stenson on the rear deck and looked down at the bloody side rail.

"Ship's empty Lou, just the two tangos."

Dunn sounded calm and sure.

"Where's Zoran's body?" Garver asked in a calm but seemingly edgy tone. The tone reinforced Garver's need for closure.

"He escaped and evaded. He mustered up enough willpower to pull himself up and over the side while I was checking on the other guy."

"But where is the body?" Dunn's voice had changed to quizzical.

"That is a very good question. Apparently, I didn't hit him as hard as I thought I had."

"How hard did you hit him?" Garver's voice had become quizzical as well.

"Two in the knee, one in the gun hand, and one in the upper torso."

"Hell, that would put me down for a minute or two."

Both men turned to look at Robert Dunn, who simply shrugged his shoulders.

"So, now what?"

"Well, if your target goes to ground, you remove his cover."

Both men nodded at Lou as he spoke. Garver signaled the helicopter and all three men returned to their waiting ride. The crew chief retrieved the down rope and closed the door. Lou Stenson looked in at the pilot and made a circular hand signal that could not be mistaken. The pilot nodded and banked the helicopter over to head out.

The pilot slowly circled the boat in an ever-widening arc, until they were out a good half-mile in distance. At a good standoff distance, weapons went hot and a live Mark 44 torpedo hit the water. The screw wake could be easily followed by everyone onboard the helicopter as the torpedo headed straight in at the fishing boat. A bright flash and the shredding boat could be seen in the windscreen just before the concussion of the explosion washed over the helicopter. Everyone watched as the stolen fishing boat and its lone corpse were consumed by the North Sea.

Lou Stenson leaned back in his nylon- webbed seat; his eyes still fixed on the point in the ocean that he had last seen Zoran Savić.

"Now, we wait and see what surfaces."

"No, we can't," Eric Garver said pointedly.

Lou looked down at the pilot's instrument control panel and took in the flashing reserve light for the helicopter's fuel supply.

"The helicopter only has 1,230 kilometers of range, Mr. Stenson. We need to get back over land before we run out of fuel."

Lou nodded and swore to himself as the helicopter pulled off station and headed for land. Zoran Savić had to be dead, but Lou Stenson wasn't stopping without a body to prove it. They weren't dead until there was a body.

CHAPTER TWENTY-EIGHT

I T TOOK TIME for Zoran Savić's vision to adjust to the salt water, pain, and blood loss. He had been floating for an unknown amount of time, but was sure that he was still alive. It was the pain that reassured him. The pain told him he was living.

The torpedo dropped by the attack helicopter had struck the fishing boat just below the waterline. For reasons known only to scientists, the explosive geometry of the warhead's detonation had a two-fold effect on the fishing boat. The vessel above the waterline was vaporized in a cataclysmic surge of fire and flame. The lower half of the boat's keel, full width of the beam, responded to the energy much more like a pressure plate on a shape charge, except the boat's bottom didn't invert like a pressure plate but was simply pushed straight down into the sea water. The pressure envelope produced by the solid object pushing through the water column also pulled Zoran Savić's body deep into the ocean depths.

Zoran grew up in a small town nestled in the mountains of Bosnia. He knew nothing about ocean currents or prevailing winds, nor did he understand cold water shutdown of bodily systems and the effects of such biological processes. He vaguely understood that his body was going hypothermic from the water. He had seen numerous people die from exposure during the mountain winters, but that was snow, not water.

Zoran had enough functioning brain power to understand that the cold water was slowing his blood loss. That was a short-lived gift. He needed to get out of the water before he either passed out or bled out.

After he resurfaced, he concentrated on establishing where in the ocean he had ended up. At first, it all just looked like a blue expanse. It was endless water around him on all sides. But slowly, as he adjusted his distorted vision produced by the saltwater in his eyes, the outline of a shore could be viewed. The building outlines and grey-black shore edge on the blue horizon told his sluggish mind that he had been blown toward shore. Being blown toward shore was good.

Zoran began to kick and paddle with his working limbs and slowly pull himself further toward shore. The process of his beaching was agonizingly slow and painful. The activation of good muscles propelled torn and blood-soaked muscles to involuntarily movement. The pain it produced was searing and made Zoran kick and paddle that much harder.

An undetermined amount of time passed this way before a vague outline turned into individual buildings and landmarks. It was a small fishing town, or maybe a harbor town of some type. He didn't know what country it was in, but he assumed that it was still the Netherlands. After all, that was where they had been when the attack had taken place.

Zoran kicked and paddled. He could feel the cold setting in for its final assault on his body. His limbs were getting progressively harder and harder to move. Once creating noise, the chattering of his teeth had stopped. He was sure that he would drown before reaching land, but he drove himself on.

What Zoran didn't understand about the ocean was a thing called thermodynamics. Zoran's body had been shocked by the cold at the ocean's depths, and then continued to be assaulted by cold as he made his way through the open water. But as he had pulled himself closer to land, the depth of the water had become shallower and incrementally warmer. As he swam, the warmer water was working to counteract the damage from the cold. If he had of been in a sound mental state, he would have realized that the water he was swimming through was as warm as bathwater.

Nevertheless, Zoran's nerve and sheer will kept him moving on. He came to ground on an area of beach where the villagers came to play and swim. Putting foot to ground, he pushed forward until he could stand on his one good leg and catch his breath. The area around this open section of beach was quiet in the afternoon sun. It didn't seem as if anyone was out enjoying the day. This made Zoran Savić both extremely happy and mildly concerned. The remnants of cold were still rattling his senses, so he didn't stop to question his good fortune. He was going to accept this window of opportunity while it lasted.

Zoran pulled himself from the surf and laid his beaten body down on the rocky shoreline. Drawing all the energy that he could muster, he pulled himself up onto his good leg. Every muscle in it ached from the continuous swimming, but he did his best to push the pain from his mind. He began to hop, one-foot length at a time, across the rocky shore. He fell down several times but pulled himself back up and continued. On the opposite side of the shore, a tree line separated the shore from a line of buildings. Zoran leaned against a tree and viewed the quiet street. He could hear industrial noises coming from farther inland, but the surrounding area was quiet. Several of the buildings looked unoccupied, including the one directly across the street. They were a row of similar sized two-story buildings, presumably with storefronts on the ground floors and living areas above. That was the way in small European towns. Zoran observed the building directly across the street until he felt sure that it was empty. Once sure, he started hopping again. The effects of warm water and bright sunlight made hopping across the street easier than going up the beach had been.

Zoran leaned against the side of the building, doing his best to look natural. His sore muscles and injuries were making it difficult. It seemed that there was an alley running back around the building. He guessed that it went to a rear entry. That seemed the preferred entry point for the wounded terrorist.

Zoran drew a deep breath and continued on. The building was deeper than it had appeared from the street and it took him a considerable amount of time to reach the rear door. Fortunately for his many wounds, there was only a small rise of steps between Zoran and the rear doorway.

Enough life had returned to Zoran Savić's wounded body by the time he had made it to the landing that his wounds finally began leaking blood. As Zoran leaned against the building to catch his breath, blood soaked through his tattered clothing and left a large stain on the side of the building. He didn't care. He needed to get somewhere he could stop. He needed to assess his wounds. First, he needed to get inside so he could sit.

Zoran only worked the rear door's knob for a moment before it gave way. The Bosnian terrorist hopped his way inside, each hop now leaving a blood trail on the floor. Once inside, he closed the door and collapsed.

To the south of Zoran Savić's position, Lou Stenson paced the tarmac of the Emden airport. The small airfield outside the ring road of Emden City was the closest thing the helicopter pilot could manage before the SW-61 Commando finally ran out of fuel. The fact that Emden was across the border in Germany made Eric Garver's life considerably easier. The GSG-9 commando only had to request assistance and flash his German Federal Police badge, and men came running from all directions. It was only minutes before the airfield's fuel truck came barreling up to assist the flight crew.

Robert Dunn passed his time by sitting in the shade of the terminal building and conversing with a young local woman. Eric Garver interacted among the military flight crew and the airfield personnel. He seemed to be more about staving off local political problems than explaining anything to anyone. No one dared question the federal police credentials, and all requests were granted.

Lou Stenson was left to pace the area around the helo and contemplate the future. The original mission had come off as expected. The two Bosnians had been gunned down and their escape craft had been blown up and sent to the bottom of the ocean. Still, something had gone wrong. Something was off and it just felt wrong. He was sure that it all came down to Zoran's missing body. Emil had died where he stood, but Zoran had managed enough fortitude to push himself over the side. Still, he couldn't have survived the explosion or the North Sea's cold waters. He had to be fish food. Still. SEALs didn't disengage until they had confirmation of the finished op.

Lou was about thirty meters upwind of the hustle and bustle around the Commando when his phone began to vibrate in his pocket. He extracted the phone and looked at the display screen. The head shot of a grumpy-looking Ed Crowley filled the display. Lou thought back to Pat Sommers' complete fleecing of the NSA Deputy Director, which had caused the look during a card game. Lou had snapped the picture before Ed could change his expression. He smiled at the phone screen and pushed the call button.

"Ed, what's up?"

"Have you been monitoring your satellite uplink?"

"Not in the last twenty minutes or so, why?"

Lou Stenson could feel his pulse slowing and his brain clearing as he spoke. They weren't finished yet. It was time to get back to work.

"Paul kept Lacrosse 5 locked down on your A.O, even after you guys peeled off."

"We had to exfil. The helo was bingo on fuel. There was no way to stay on-station."

"From the directness of the outgoing flight path, I figured as much. It really would have been better if you guys could have hung in just a little longer, but it's understandable."

"Give it to me straight, Ed."

"The fellow that flipped over the side –"

"Zoran Savić."

"Zoran Savić survived the gunfire and the torpedo strike. He must be one strong- willed son of a bitch."

"It would seem that way. Where is he now?"

"He resurfaced about a full minute after the explosion on the opposite side of the vessel from where he went in. After about a minute of treading water, he started for shore at an awfully slow pace."

"Did he make land?"

"Affirmative, Lou. He hit land on a rocky patch of shoreline, approximately in the area of Flüthorn. It's the shore side of Norden, Germany. Almost dead north of your current location."

"You sure?"

"Affirmative. He came ashore. He collected himself and hopped across a rocky stretch of beach to a treelined residential street. He must have injured his leg in the explosion."

"I kneecapped him on the boat. I should have done both knees," Lou let out in a cold, matter-of-fact way.

Ed just swallowed.

"Well, hopping boy continued on to a vacant looking building across the street. He went around the back and let himself in. He's there as of right now."

"You have good feed?"

"Lacrosse 5 is stationary over the situation and will stay there until the task is complete. We're not going to let you go at it blind, Lou."

"Thanks, Ed. Thank Paul for me as well."

"He knows."

Lou's mind was already thinking about door kicking. They needed to get moving. He looked over at the helo. The fuel truck was just pulling away, so they could leave as soon as they wanted.

"Ed, could you send me the footage of Zoran coming ashore and going into the building?"

"It's already in the email. And your live feed link should still be active."

"Thank you. I owe you guys."

"No worries, Lou."

Lou Stenson terminated the call and began running toward Eric Garver and the helicopter crew. The instant action brought Robert Dunn to his feet and he headed in the same direction. Both men arrived at the Commando within a second of each other.

Lou handed his phone to Garver and began a quick recap of his phone call, as Garver and the flight crew watched the video of the injured Zoran Savić emerging from the water. Lou spoke calmly and clearly, but at an informative rate. Everyone in the group took in and processed the information and potential tasking at combat speed. The flight crew broke away from the fire team and began warming up the Commando's big Rolls Royce engines.

"It's German soil. Does this need to turn into a GSG-9 operation?"

The big ex-SEAL didn't want to put his new comrade in a problematic situation with his leadership. Lou had done such on occasion and it never ended well.

"I don't think that's necessary. As long as the government has a representative present, that is what's important. I can give you temporary authority to operate inside our borders. Besides, it would take time to assemble my team. Time that I would rather not spend."

"Back to the hunt then," Dunn said, turning toward the Commando's crew door.

The three men piled back into the attack helicopter and Lou Stenson handed over his phone to the copilot. The pilot pulled up on the sticks and sent the big machine back into the air.

CHAPTER TWENTY-NINE

HE BIG SW-61 Sea King Commando pounded through the air with the Germany countryside hurdling along a mere thousand feet below. Stenson, Dunn, and Garver sat in their seats with none of the pre-assault apprehension they had needed to dispel before the first engagement. This time they were ready at the jump. This time they were hunters. They specialized in the hunting of men, and the man they were headed to find wouldn't survive this encounter. This time he would be a dead man.

This action was wholly necessary. All three men knew it. Too many people had already been hurt or killed by the reckless action of this terrorist and his compatriots. They had almost reduced The Hague to ash. A reckoning was required. Penance must be extracted.

Lou looked over at his German counterpart for a moment. The man looked sure and ready. Still, there was something behind the man's eyes that unsettled him. It took a moment for the ex-SEAL to place the expression, but when he did, he understood. The look dwelling inside Eric Garver was one of compensation. Not the monetary or legal kind used in a civilized land, but the biblical equalization of a blood debt kind. The one that underlies the law of the jungle. The law of the jungle stated that when you were wronged you got to seek retribution.

Lou Stenson had already cut out his pound of flesh. His wounded comrade was still alive, so the kneecapping and torso shot he inflicted had emotionally cleared his slate. Eric Garver had lost men to the Bosnian terrorist. The war criminal rolling over the side of the fishing boat to cheat death had denied the German his chance at clearing his own slate. *That debt needed settling*, Lou thought.

"All right Lou, what's the plan?"

Robert Dunn was just releasing the bolt on his MP5 submachine gun after checking that the chamber still held a live round. Lou looked over at Eric Garver, who was sitting stoically.

"Any thoughts, Eric?"

The German commando smiled at the sound of his real first name. It had been the first time that the big American had used it. It was a sign of building trust.

"Well, Zoran has apparently holed up in a building. I say that we go in and get him."

He smiled at the other two before continuing.

"It's probably best if we do a two-faced attack. Two-pronged, I believe you call it. Hit the front door and draw attention, and then hit the rear door where he went in with the second half of the assault. He probably didn't go far from the door once he got inside."

"That sounds good to me," Dunn said casually. "I'll take the front door. Solo assault entry is pretty much my standard thing. You two can have the guns blazing breach and enter."

The other two men nodded at the CIA assassin. For all his displaced abilities and strange quirks, Lou was more-and-more considering the CIA man to be quite a competent field agent. He needed to pass that along to Gene Taggart when he got back to the capital. He was too aware that field agents often didn't get due credit for handling the complicated situations they were placed in. He had been in that position many times while on active duty. A little backdoor reassurance was the least that he could do for his bomb technician's bodyguard.

The red light came on in the crew compartment and Eric Garver stuck his head up in the pilot's area. When he extracted it again, he wore a semi-sure expression, which was about as good as things got in the trade.

"South, along the coast road from Flüthorn, is a campground. The Nordsea-Camp Noddeich. It's the best place to sit down without being in hearing range of our target. A local police car will meet us there and transport us to our strike point. The polizei man will stay and block traffic on the street for us, just in case."

213

"Sounds good. How far is the campground from the house?"

Lou Stenson was doing the logistics in his head. He could tell that Dunn was doing the same.

"Maybe four kilometers. Not much more than that. It's a direct route from one point to another."

"That sounds good to me. I've had a lot of worse entrances than a polizei escort."

Dunn was attempting to lighten the mood in the crew cabin. He was successful, though neither of his comrades would admit it. The helicopter crew chief gave the CIA man a sideways glance and tried not to smile.

The green light replaced the red light and the crew chief snapped back to the task at hand. The three men in the assault team collected their weapons and readied themselves for touchdown at the campsite. The crew chief leaned over and spoke in Garver's ear. The GSG-9 man told the other two that the helicopter was going to stand by at the campsite and exfil them when the situation was resolved. Both of his American counterparts said nothing, just nodding in understanding.

The two Rolls Royce turboshafts powering the helicopter ramped up, flaring the five main rotor blades and stalling the machine's descent. The pilot expertly adjusted the attitude of the machine and sat the wheels down on the grassy lawn without so much as a bump. The rotor blades began winding down to idle as the crew chief slid the compartment door open to its stops.

The polizei patrolman that was to be their escort had been directed to the campsite from his patrol area in the southern end of Flüthorn without much information about what was to happen when he got there. All being quiet, he had gone without protest. The desk officer had said something about the federal police arriving in a helicopter and needing a ride to somewhere in town. They were picking up a suspect individual of some type. The idea of transporting federal police agents seemed a much better use of his time than just traveling the same old streets in a small town where nothing much ever happened. He figured whoever the federal police were coming to apprehend was not a local man. Nothing criminal happened in Flüthorn. It wasn't that sort of town.

The local polizei man got excited as the German Navy helicopter came in low over the campground and sat down in front of him. He was still leaning against the side of his patrol car when the helicopter door slid open and three black-clad commandos jumped out. The heavily armed men were completely covered in black tactical uniforms. They even had black balaclavas covering all but their eyes. They were literally bristling with weapons, with each man having a Heckler and Koch submachine gun slung across his front. The boots of the three men hit the ground almost together and they were headed in unison toward his patrol car.

The polizei man's heart rate shot up to its maximum. He had been expecting a couple of men in ill-fitting government suits who did all things out of self-interest. Men who made local jurisdictions do all the work, while they collected all the credit. He was not expecting commandos with submachine guns.

The lead man pulled to a stop directly in front of him. The other two men continued to the rear of the patrol car, where they climbed into the back seats and closed the doors.

Eric Garver handed the man a slip of paper with the building's street address on it. The local man looked at the slip of paper.

"Do you know where that is?"

The polizei man looked at the blacked-out commando. He spoke natural German. It was the central district style of the language. He must have come from Frankfurt.

"Yes. I know where this is," the polizei man responded a bit hesitantly.

"Good. Take us to the end of the street that the building is on. Once there, you are to block the street to traffic until I tell you to open it back up again. Understand?"

"Yes, sir."

"Good. Let's go."

The commando walked around to the passenger seat and climbed inside as the others had done. The polizei man almost ran to the driver's door, even though he was only about a foot from it.

All three of the black-clad men sat bolt upright in their seats and looked in all directions as the car moved. None of them spoke. The lead man, sitting in the front passenger seat, repeatedly tapped his trigger finger on the receiver of the submachine gun. The tapping sound sent electric shocks up the polizei man's spine. He had never encountered such men before. They were the type that didn't ask for permission or check for jurisdiction. They were the type who went where they wanted and did as they chose.

The driver maneuvered the patrol car out onto the main road and headed toward the water. At a tee intersection with the local main route he turned right and headed north. The car pounded up the sunbaked asphalt, the reverberations rebounding up through the patrol car's worn shock absorbers. None of the commandos reacted to the road vibrations, which made the polizei man even more nervous than he already was.

At a point where the roadway turned and headed inland, the polizei man applied the brakes and turned the patrol car left on to an adjacent street. A small hotel, or at least the sign for one hooked to a different building, streaked by on the righthand side. One of the commandos, a large and imposing man, looked at the screen of a smartphone. Two small dots could be seen on the phone screen. A red stationary dot and a moving green dot that seemed to be closing in on the other. The driver couldn't help himself as he snuck curious looks in the rearview mirror at the man when it was safe.

The driver brought his police car to a sudden and sound stop at the intersection of the road's first main cross street. A tee intersection, with a street named Fledderweg going off to the right. The driver turned the car sideways so that it blocked the entire intersection. He put the car into park, pointed up the street to a building on the right side, and then looked over at the commando sitting next to him.

"That building. The third one in, is the building that you are looking for. Up past it, some three buildings, is another intersection. That street runs inland for a block or so, and then turns in this direction and runs behind the building you are looking for."

"Is it accessible?"

"No, sir. There is a large fence and some other obstacles that separate the street from the storefront buildings on the main street."

"Excellent. Stay here and block the traffic. We'll call for you when we need you."

Their driver was attempting to respond as all three men climbed from the car and jogged off in a tactical formation, staying tight to the building edges. He knew that no one at his station was ever going to believe the story he would tell, if he was allowed to tell it.

Eric Graver paused at the edge of the building adjacent to the one they wanted and gave the men behind him a hand signal to stop. He sliced a pointed hand toward the front door and then at Robert Dunn. Dunn nodded. He then arched his open hand to an entrance alleyway that separated the two buildings and pointed down the alley toward the rear. Lou Stenson nodded. With a beat of quiet between movements, all three men moved off with purpose.

Eric Garver led Lou Stenson down the alleyway in the standard two-man approach with such calm that it reinforced Stenson's increasingly deep trust in the man's abilities. The two moved as a well-oiled unit, independent of the fact they had never actually operated together. Some tactical teams trained for years to reach this level of understanding. They just worked well together right off the bat.

Garver paused at the building edge and Stenson continued, rotating his position cover as he moved to an area just off the rear landing's edge. He nodded to his counterpart. Garver came around the corner and ascended the steps without making so much as a single sound. He took up a cover position on the hinge side of the heavy exterior door and nodded that he was set. Stenson made the landing in a large single step that also made no noise. He took the entry position on the lock side of the door and nodded that he was ready to act. Stenson pulled a dead blow hammer from an attachment point on his vest and baseball gripped the cutoff handle. Garver nodded and both men were ready to go.

At the front door, Robert Dunn was working with the speed of a man that didn't want to be noticed, which was an accurate assessment of his actions. The CIA assassin was a natural at the art of breaking and entering. The shop building door he was given this day had put up all but no resistance to his lock-picking skills. Dunn inserted a long screwdriver-looking object into the door's lock opening, gave the handle a good squeeze to set the mechanism, and then added a firm but soft twist. The tool, known as a "bump" in the burglary world, worked like a chainsaw on tumbler lock sets. The tool was extracted from the keyhole and the doorknob twisted easily, now as unlocked as any door opened with a key.

Dunn stuck the bump back into its holder on the tactical vest and removed a 9mm pistol from its holster. A sound suppressor was removed from a pocket on the vest and screwed onto the barrel in a counterclockwise direction. The suppressed handgun was a more natural weapon for Dunn, and he worked better with it in closed confines like those probably existing inside the storefront. Pushing the door open gently, Dunn slunk inside and closed the door behind him, making only a moderate amount of noise. He could have made no sound at all, but that wasn't his part of the plan. Instead, he made the same amount of noise as your standard policeman would have made. Straight away, the noise had the desired effect.

In a backroom, having just finished patching up his wounds, Zoran Savić heard the front door close. He may have been wounded and in some amount of shock, but he was not even remotely without his wits. The Bosnian terrorist picked up his waterlogged 9mm pistol and turned his attention in the direction of the noise. He had actually planned on checking his handgun after seeing to his wounds, but that was now irrelevant.

A footstep or two could be heard by Zoran coming from the front room. To Zoran, it sounded as if the policeman was looking at the different doors and rooms. Zoran Savić took a few loud steps on his bandaged knee and bit his lip in pain. The wrap he applied was holding his knee together, but it was doing nothing for either its mobility or the pain. Those things would need to wait until after he dispatched the would-be policeman.

With the sound of his fourth loud footstep pinpointing Zoran's exact location inside the room, Eric Garver held up a hand. There were first two fingers, and then one finger, and then Lou Stenson let go of his windup and allowed the dead blow hammer to shatter the lock of the rear door. The latch and bolt assembly exploded inward as the door swung backward in a quick arc. Eric Garver entered the opening made by Stenson's entry work, taking in the layout of the interior space. Lou Stenson dropped the hammer and raised his submachine gun in one fluid motion, entering two steps behind the point man.

The explosion of the rear door took Zoran Savić completely by surprise, just as planned. He was only a quarter turned at the waist back toward the rear door when Eric Garver came into direct fire orientation. Without hesitation, Garver squeezed off a three-round burst from his suppressed MP5. All three rounds slammed into Zoran Savić's shoulder, just to the side of the one's Lou Stenson had put in him. The three rounds held a tight grouping of a quarter in size. Their exit hole was significantly larger.

The simultaneous concussion of the three rounds almost flipped Zoran over backwards as he crashed to the ground. The waterlogged pistol he had been brandishing went skittering across the worn floor and stopped in the corner of the room. The two rear entry men drew down on the Bosnian as their third member came in from the front room, his suppressed pistol leading the way. He looked at his two comrades and then down at the terrorist writhing on the floor. He nodded and leveled his pistol on the Bosnian.

"Hold up," Lou Stenson said in a calm, yet commanding tone. Dunn paused and looked at the big ex-SEAL.

"This one belongs to our friend here. He's in need of some closure. For his comrades."

Dunn nodded his best nonchalant masked approval and began unscrewing the suppressor from his handgun. Lou Stenson looked at their German comrade and nodded. He didn't need to see the smile on the man's face; he could see it in his eyes.

Eric Garver flexed the grip on his submachine gun's handholds and suppressed the trigger. Zoran Savić was spitting curse words in his native tongue as three rounds, and then three more rounds, punched a gapping void into his forehead. The smallest bit of powder smoke rolled from the suppressor's end as the GSG-9 Lieutenant let the submachine gun drop to its slung position. Lou Stenson pulled a military issue body bag from a large rear access pouch on his vest and enlisted Dunn to assist him in bagging up the dead Bosnian.

The local polizei man was standing in the middle of the intersection attempting to look authoritative when the three black-masked men came jogging back toward him in unison. The look of a body bag slung over the tallest man's shoulder almost made him go into fits. The tall man was jogging at a moderate stride, as if whatever was over his shoulder weighed nothing at all. All three men came into the intersection and stopped in front of the polizei man. The lead man spoke.

"Open the trunk."

The local polizei patrolman stood there in shock.

"Open the trunk. Now."

The polizei man jumped in realization of the command and headed for the car's rear compartment. The tall man unceremoniously tossed the full body bag into the space as the other two climbed into the passenger compartment. He climbed into the back seat, as he had done on the way into town, and closed the door. The lead man rotated his head over toward their shocked driver.

"Helicopter."

The car sped off with a jerk. No one spoke on the return trip, just as they had not spoken on the way into town. Over the icy chill, the polizei man could sense satisfaction emanating from all three men. He didn't ask any questions.

CHAPTER THIRTY

K RISTIN HUGHES SAT sideways in the passenger seat of Robert Dunn's BMW with her feet resting on the taxiway ramp of the private hangar the CIA used when in The Hague. She was doing her level best to keep a pleasant look on her face, but the throbbing pain from her broken arm was making that a trying process. The arm was trussed up in a nylon sling and secured at a ninety-degree angle across her chest. The utilitarian arm strap in no way matched her OJ Gülsen dress.

The doctors at the hospital, the members of her shadowy security team, and her boss all tried to get her to take pain medication. She had abstained because the pills made her mind goofy. The lucidity of it reminded her of the stuff Emil had pumped into her, and she wasn't having any more of that. The hairline crack in her skull that the pain meds would have helped with wasn't bothering her nearly as much as the arm was. Well, that was as long as she didn't move her head too fast. If she did, the instantaneous pounding it produced was blinding.

The doctors providing her care had been opposed to releasing her from the hospital with her head wound in such a state. They wanted to keep her for observation, to make sure that nothing abnormal happened while it was healing. They had been overridden by the United States government. Her handlers wanted her back where she belonged. They didn't know if the drug cocktail given to her by the Bosnians caused her to say something compromising. If it had, they wanted to get her out of the country before anybody came asking more questions. Since Kristin's brain showed no signs of trauma during any point of the hospitalization process, the CIA doctors reviewing her records from America concluded it was a one-off head injury. Right afterward, they told the doctors in the Netherlands to let her go.

It had taken all the time she was in the Dutch care facility to flush Emil's chemical concoction from her system. It seemed that the only way they had to really remove it was to wash it out, so she drank water and peed. Once done, she drank more water and peed again. When she was tired of the water, the doctors gave her saline IVs to keep the flushing moving along. And it continued ad infinitum until her release. Kristin was sure the whole affair was going to end up giving her a urinary tract infection. So far, she had somehow managed to avoid that little bit of added insult.

The doctors attempted to explain to the collection of hard-looking men before them that she couldn't fly in a commercial airline. Her head injury couldn't take the change in pressure. Once again, the U.S. government officials waved a dismissive hand and told them to find her clothes.

Kristin had slunk her way, as femininely and painlessly as possible, into the provocatively cut summer dress, and then plopped herself into the institutional wheelchair, which was the vehicle of choice for her hospital escape. With the way the dress clung to her curves, she assumed that it was selected by Robert Dunn. So be it, he had good taste. Once situated, she was rolled out the hospital door by her boss and a selection of well-armed mercenaries to a waiting BMW inhabited by a CIA assassin and a German commando. She had a strange life.

Eric Garver and Robert Dunn were leaning against the side of the car, wearing approving expressions, as she burst out onto the sunshine-covered sidewalk. Well, Eric's look was approving. Robert's was a bit too approving. Kristin smiled at her CIA sidekick.

"Bob, I knew you bought the dress when I tried it on."

"It suits you, being summertime and all."

Kristin started to laugh, but then winced from the pain. No more jokes were made. The group of armed men loaded up their charge and headed for the airport.

The Talon Corporation jet sat quietly on the hangar ramp next to a nondescript white executive jet. The Talon plane and flight crew were the same as when the two groups of men had originally arrived in the country, and were on their way back to their original mission in Spain that they had pulled out of at the request of the CIA. The CIA jet was new. The one Lou Stenson had arrived on had been switched out for something more purpose-built. The CIA had several such *exfil and critical care* birds stationed around the globe. They could be pressurized to sea level and contained a full medical suite. The plane had also been quickly appropriated by The Group for their favorite non-company asset.

Currently, that specific non-company asset sat on the apron of the private jetway taking in the odd assemblage of characters that she had made come together. The men from the mysterious Talon Corporation seemed to be quite nice, for the military mercenary sort. Their big lieutenant in charge of the contractors had given her a business card. He said that if she ever found herself in deep water again, just give him a call. Or, if she ever wanted to have dinner. Kristin had given him a card of her own, tapping her fingernail on the Las Vegas address, and thanked him for all of the team's help. The contractors finished loading their gear and were readying to leave.

Robert Dunn, her very own CIA assassin, broke away from the group of men and came over to where she was sitting.

"Time to put you on a plane, Missy."

Kristin sighed at the thought of more pain. "Fine."

Dunn smiled and gently helped her to her feet.

"Just so you know, the nuke has been safely returned to the inventory. The private reserve, as they refer to it, is going to be moved now that Büchel has been compromised. The armament group is going with them. It's being called a troop realignment or some such thing. Garver has talked with his people and given them a full rundown on the situation. Well, minus a half-dozen real names and a couple of specific events. Everything is good on his front. The Germans are fine with it all."

Kristin mumbled in the affirmative and thought for a moment.

"What about on the Bosnian front?"

"An old man told me not to worry. No one is going to bother that the Sons of Sava are all missing."

"That's nice."

Kristin stretched and moved in her arm restraint to get in a more comfortable position. The movement made her wince. Dunn's expression turned somewhat dour.

"Kristin —"

She looked at him. He was battling an odd expression.

"Spit it out, Bob. While no one can hear you."

Nowadays, she only called him Bob when she wanted to annoy him. She knew that he hated the name.

"Back in the park. I should have been more — attentive to what was going on."

Kristin instantly knew where the conversation was headed. The thought of it made her uneasy. She had known several CIA wet work men over the years. None of them had ever apologized for inaction. She didn't even know that they were capable of it.

"Robert, you were there when it counted. That's the important part for me."

"Just know that it won't happen a second time."

Kristin patted Robert on the arm and stepped off toward the group. He followed at her side. Kristin stopped by her boss and patted him on the arm as well. Lou looked down at her with a fatherly expression and smiled back. Then, as quickly as it had come, it was gone, replaced by the chiseled expression of a career soldier.

There were several lewd jokes and several indecent comments at her expense. Everyone but Kristin laughed. The men from the Talon Corporation excused themselves and climbed onto their waiting plane. As their jet rolled off, Kristin looked around at the remaining group.

"Not that I'm complaining, they are a good bunch to have around in a pinch. But does anybody know anything about our new friends from the Talon Corporation?"

All three men shrugged in unison. This told Kristin that the answer was yes, they just weren't telling.

"Fine. Be like that."

All three men smiled. She turned to face Eric Garver.

"Is everything good with you and your bosses? I kind of drug you off into a completely different affair."

Eric Garver had returned to the stoic German government operative look he had worn so well when they had first met.

"We managed to retrieve the nuclear device and return it. They really didn't need to know the specifics of how that happened."

"I like your style, Keith Nash."

All three men looked at her with varying odd expressions. Once again, she realized that no one understood her sense of humor or her movie references.

"It's a line from the movie *Paul*."

Garver made the vaguest of moderate expressions.

"Then I shall have to watch it."

Robert Dunn looked over at the GSG-9 commando.

"Well, what do you say? We probably should be going."

Eric Garver nodded to the affirmative.

"Mr. Dunn has offered to give me a ride back to Frankfurt."

"Yes, and Herr Garver had requested that I let him know when I'm rummaging around in his country, just in case."

The CIA assassin tilted his head toward his NEST field counterpart and winked a conspiratorial eye.

"Not entirely sure that's going to happen."

Kristin laughed and winched. She couldn't help herself. The two men embraced her cautiously and headed for the car. They had made it about two or three steps when Kristin decided to chance fate.

"Herr Becke."

Eric Garver stopped and turned to face her.

"If I decided to rummage around your country, do you think I might be able to find a tour guide?"

Garver held his naturally stoic demeaner for a second or two, just to make her sweat, and then smiled genuinely.

"Whenever you decide to visit, Miss Hughes, just let me know. I'll send a plane to pick you up."

Kristin's heart stopped for one or two beats. She knew that she would be vacationing in Germany very soon. The men climbed into the car and it pulled off the apron toward the entrance gate. Lou Stenson motioned toward the plane. Kristin nodded slowly and started for the stairs. The CIA flight crew stood by silently as the two passengers boarded the plane and settled into the main cabin. Lou said a few words to the flight crew's head nurse, and the crew disappeared into the rear of the plane.

Once they were completely alone and enough engine noise was being produced, Lou Stenson reached out and pushed a button on the wall panel adjacent to his seat. A pair of flat screen monitors rotated out of the ceiling and flickered to life. The two monitors divided into an equal number of sections. Each section of screen illuminated with a group member. CIA, NSA, FBI, NRO, Secret Service, and Justice all came to life, one by one. The square designated as NEST stayed greyed-out because Lou was already on the plane's viewer. Each of the men on the screens smiled broadly at the image of Kristin Hughes sitting in the oversized seat.

The CIA DCI Eugene Taggart, the mysterious man from Langley, was the first to speak.

"How do you feel, kid?"

"I'm okay Uncle Gene. Broken arm, hairline skull fracture and a severely bruised ego. Otherwise, I'm tip top."

Gene Taggart wasn't Kristin's real uncle, but it made him happy when she called him that. She called all the older members uncle. It was her personal way of showing respect for the position.

"My sweet girl, we give you assets precisely so you don't end up like this. I'm glad to hear that you're on the mend."

All of the other men on the monitors nodded in agreement, and then added in their own thanks that she was headed home.

"Kristin, all of the issues surrounding your primary mission have been tied off. The op is over, with a satisfactory result. You do fine work."

Bob Sloan, the Director of Operations at the FBI, was another one of the men she called uncle.

"That's nice to hear, Uncle Bob. Has anyone given any thought toward my comments regarding the men at Büchel Airbase?"

"Nothing detrimental will end up falling at their feet. The old man promised."

Pat Sommers, Secret Service head of personal security for the President of the United States of America, was referring to his boss.

"Thank you, Pat."

Kristin looked at each one of the faces on the two screens and smiled warmly. They really did care, even if they did send her out into the black spaces to handle things that would make normal people cave.

"I heard something about I owed Doctor Paul compensation for the unsolicited manhunt satellite coverage?"

Paul Spencer, the Senior Systems Director for the National

Reconnaissance Office, and possibly the second most truly powerful man in the country behind Ed Crowley, started laughing.

"Looking after your interests is what I do, Doctor Hughes."

"You mean helping my boss and the GSG exact a little well-placed vengeance, don't you?"

Paul Spencer's expression was enigmatic, at best.

"Where did you hear that? Lou telling you stories again?"

Kristin slid a business card out of the neckline of her sundress and rotated it in her fingers so that all the men could see the Eagle's Talons embossed in its middle. Lou Stenson looked at the card as if it were a weapon and wondered which one of the men had given it to her.

"No, sir. I got the intel from a very nice mercenary that works for the Talon Corporation. Would anybody here happen to know anything about them?"

Paul Spencer brandished an expression that said no outside entity could access the feed from his orbital assets. Several others had blank expressions, like they had never heard the name. Gene Taggart's expression was flat neutral, which was bad. Ed Crowley, NSA representative, and the first man asked to join the group by the president, was a little slower masking his understanding with a blank expression. That one slip was all Kristin had been looking for.

Kristin was now sure that the mercenaries had been summoned to her defense. Most likely it had been by the stone-faced Eugene Taggart. The CIA was a clandestine operation after all.

"Kristin, we know nothing about this group of men. Do you understand that?"

Taggart's voice was more hard-edged than Kristin had ever heard it, and completely unforgiving.

"Yes, sir. I understand."

"That's good. Now, burn that card."

"Yes, sir."

With that exchange, the conversation wrapped itself up. The faces dropped off screen one-by-one until Kristin Hughes and Lou Stenson sat quietly alone in the cabin.

"I think the skull fracture has rattled your brain, girl."

Lou Stenson; her boss, her impromptu dad, and one of her personal rescuers, looked equally proud and put-out.

"Yup. Not my best move."

Lou slid his hand into his pocket and removed a Zippo lighter. The silver face of the lighter was emblazoned with an insignia of some sort, an object with a knife through its middle. She assumed it was Navy. Lou held out the lighter to her. Kristin twirled the business card in her fingers a couple times and then returned it to its hiding place inside the neckline of her sundress.

"I'll get to that – eventually."

Lou pocketed the lighter and thought about the similar business card that he also possessed. Kristin turned and looked out the window by her seat. The deep blue of the sea below them was comforting to her. She needed to rest. She needed to recover. Then, she needed to take Herr Becke up on his promise of a plane ride.

"Lou, is there anything pressing waiting at Nellis when we get back?"

She turned back to look at her boss. The big ex-SEAL smiled nonchalantly at his number one nuclear weapons technician, and part-time spy.

"Nope. All quiet."

"That's nice."

Kristin smiled and looked back toward the sea.

"Cause, I really need a couple days off."

The deep blue passed by under the plane as Kristin closed her eyes. It had been a long strange journey since she was pulled out of India. But that was the way her life was. And, it was good. Mostly.